TAKEN FLIGHT

for Linda

IAIN CHARLES

"You haven't seen a tree until you've seen its shadow from the sky"

– Amelia Earhart

ISBN: 9781687354761

First published 2019
5th edition Jul 2021 print revisions

5 7 9 10 8 6

Now also available as audiobook through major distributors

The events and characters depicted in this book are entirely fictional. Any resemblance to any events or any person living or dead is purely coincidental. Blue Yonder Airways is an entirely made up organization and any resemblance to any existing airline is purely coincidental

Prologue

The boy was only 12 years old the last time the volcano had erupted. Without warning it just happened. Sudden, seismic, and brutal, a huge gas cloud vomiting molten rocks two miles high.

He saw it coming. His first thought – *save yourself.* With adolescent agility he scampered up a tree. His body trembled as shock waves of energy engulfed him. There was flying debris all around. His ears popped. The ground shook and the air temperature shot up as surely as if nature had ignited a blow torch. It took away his breath. And his parents.

It was still early when he had crept outside, leaving his father and mother sleeping in their tent on the ground below. Now their flimsy nylon cocoon melted instantly under the debris. Unwarned, their bodies suffocated in scalding ash.

Beneath his tree, a landscape of devastation. The volcano had left his family split by two fates.

The boy, a survivor. His parents the unlucky ones.

Chapter 1

London time: Wednesday 15:15

Andrew Barnes was no stranger to sleeping like a log. Usually jetlag. Occasionally alcohol. Drugs, never. But this was his favourite. Nightshift.

It was always bliss to come home, as he had done that morning, to a big breakfast and then quickly tumble into bed at a time when everyone else was scurrying off to their day jobs. It felt so deliciously right to be doing it wrong. He never had any trouble in immediately drifting off to sleep after a long night's work just a few miles away in the Blue Yonder Airways office at Heathrow.

He awoke abruptly to the sound of his ringing phone. The ring-tone, like an old-fashioned landline from a 1970s movie, shot a bolt across his synapses. Urgent and harsh.

He grabbed the device from his bedside table.

"Hello?"

There was a short silence before an automated voice message kicked in.

"*This is not a test. Repeat, this is not a test.*"

Another short silence. He took a breath, readying himself. He had been here before. Two months ago was the last one. He sat upright. He knew what was coming. But he did not know what was coming.

"*Blue Yonder flight 010 that left Singapore at 19:55 local time yesterday evening and bound for Brisbane Australia has lost all contact with air traffic control for the past 60 minutes. At this time as a precaution we are activating OCC. Please attend urgently. This is not a test.*"

Even before the message had finished the adrenalin kicked in. His shirt and socks were on before his brain fully caught up with what he had just heard. OCC was the Operations Crisis Centre, the command area which existed to deal with all serious threats to his employer's unblemished safety record. As a key member of the support team it was imperative for him to move fast and get back to the office.

Immediately he called for a taxi. In less than three minutes he had added a few things to his 'grab bag.' In another two he was downstairs, standing outside his front door waiting anxiously. For the first time he looked at his watch. It was just after 3:30 pm here in Ealing. He mentally added eight hours. 11:30pm in Singapore.

He must have had more sleep than he thought. But he still felt tired. The cab came quickly and was soon weaving its way westwards.

"Off somewhere nice?" asked the driver, noticing the bag.

"Not really, just another day in the office." He did not feel like chatting. Most cab drivers would get the hint. "The bag is just my work stuff."

As a member of the OCC team he always kept a minimum of clothes and toiletries packed. It was mandatory. His role as Investigation Liaison Lead meant that in the event of an accident he might actually be required to fly off to attend the scene. In such circumstances there would be no time to return home for a leisurely pack.

The cab driver took the hint and the rest of the journey passed in silence as they reached the M4 and sped out of town against the steady stream of inbound traffic.

* * *

Andrew knew from experience the odds were that in a couple of hours the whole thing would blow over and he would be heading back to his now cold bed. In his own tally at the OCC false alarms had so far outnumbered real incidents by five to zero. His role in the airline's revenue management department depended on numbers and probability. 'You can't always predict the future based on what happened in the past,' he used to tease his colleagues when he had a hunch to bet against the computer forecasts of flight bookings. He desperately hoped now that his homily was untrue.

Five to zero, statistically reassuring. But logically he knew that flipping a coin five times landing heads had no bearing on the sixth toss. *Each safely resolved callout was surely one closer to…..* No, it didn't bear thinking about. But his brain wasn't listening. He was already thinking the unthinkable.

Please, God, not this one.

He tried to console himself by remembering that the most recent event had turned out to be a bomb hoax call from a late arriving passenger. Someone who stupidly thought he could delay the aircraft departure until he reached the airport. Using his own mobile phone had not been the smartest of ideas.

In less than 20 minutes the cab had reached the Blue Yonder head office. He eschewed the elevator and bounded up the four flights of stairs to the top floor OCC room clutching his grab bag and breathing heavily. Outside the locked OCC door he was confronted by a diminutive, serious faced security guard.

"ID please."

Andrew pulled out his lanyard from beneath his sweater and showed the grainy picture of his younger self. The guard eyed it scrupulously and then checked off the employee number on the badge against the printed list he was holding.

"OK, in you go. Glad you are legit. The last one five minutes ago was a journalist. I sent him packing. A scruffy little bugger so he was. These bastards don't take long when they smell blood."

The guard unlocked the door and Andrew stepped into the hushed atmosphere beyond. There were already a dozen occupants with just a few remaining vacant chairs. He was relieved to see his colleague, Dave, already in the command position at one end of the table. In addition to his regular job Dave doubled up as one of the three OCC duty managers whose role was to direct any incident response, making whatever decisions necessary, subject only to the over-ride of the CEO. With a phone in one hand and the other on his keyboard, Dave had the whole room on his radar. He looked over in Andrew's direction.

"Hi there, take your seat. It's still not clear what has happened. We have only been in here for a few minutes and so far, the only thing we know is that we know nothing."

"Nothing?"

"ATC lost contact about 120 minutes after take-off from Singapore. Jakarta, Indonesia signed them off and since then no one else has picked up."

Beyond all others the airline industry was awash with jargon. ATC being Air Traffic Control was one of the terms universally understood by those gathered.

"So, what was the last exchange?" Andrew felt confident asking the question that Dave had probably already answered to each new entrant to the room. In OCC no one was made to feel stupid.

"There was no indication of any trouble when Jakarta handed off. Nothing untoward. The last thing they said was simple really – 'Goodnight, Blue Yonder.'"

Chapter 2

Singapore time: Wednesday 17:30

Captain Simon Porter rolled over in bed in his corner suite of the Fairmont Hotel, Singapore. The light was fading. Across the street from where he lay and several floors below he could see the tiled roof of Raffles Hotel. Soon the tourists, mainly Australians and Americans, would be trickling in for their over-priced Singapore Slings unaware that where they were sitting was not the original, but a clever extension of the older property that had so captured the imagination of British Empire lovers.

He removed his arm from underneath the body of the woman beside him and squinted at his dual-faced watch. One of the dials told him that here it was already 5:30pm. It was one of the delights of his occupation to be able to sleep during the afternoon. And even more of a delight on this occasion, after having spent two glorious off-duty days with one of the most attractive cabin crew he had ever managed to bed. This one was different. Very different from the bubble-heads, the promotion seekers or the good-time girls. And she certainly was not just one of those who hankered after becoming a Captain's wife as soon as possible and settling down to raise kids, living precariously ever after, waiting for the inevitable day when the next younger model took her place.

Julie was different. She had captivated him from the start. Intelligent and self-assured enough to know exactly what she was getting in to. It had been six months since they had first both flown together. .

"It might be better if on this trip you keep your joystick on the flight deck," was her reply when he had flirted with her in the crew hotel bar on the first night. She had a sense of humour too. He liked that. But the next day he did persuade her to accompany him sightseeing. It was her first time in New York which had given him the chance to play the man of the world act and take her several places that were not in any of the guidebooks.

"Thanks for a great day," she said over dinner. From then on he would remember that second night as their first.

In the intervening months they had inveigled four more trips together. More than enough to make up his mind. Things with the current Mrs. Porter had not been right for some time. He had even begun to wonder if she had someone else, a thought that more excited than bothered him. Still he had been careful to avoid any evidence of his behaviour. On this trip he had even lied about where he was bound. Captains' wives were adept at forging informal links with the Crew Scheduling department in order to keep tabs on who was flying where and with whom.

He watched as she snuffled and turned. He struggled to think of anything he would not do just to be able to spend the rest of his life with this woman. It was an empty list.

Five more minutes and it would be time to rouse her and ready themselves for the onward leg of the trip, taking command of flight 10 to Brisbane. Hopefully they could do the same thing again in Australia followed by a repeat performance here in Singapore on the way home.

As the final minutes went by Simon realised Julie had moved into that state she called 'asleep but not asleep' as he heard her murmur "Is it time yet?"

"Sadly, yes."

One last cuddle and they rose in unison. Simon took his uniform trousers and newly laundered shirt from the closet while Julie rummaged in her trolley bag en route to the bathroom. As she grabbed a make-up bag a package fell out onto the floor.

As he heard it drop Simon noticed it was neatly wrapped in newspaper. "What you got there? Good old English fish and chips?"

She smiled. "Nope. Singaporeans are economical people. They don't waste money on plastic bags. I was at one of the digital malls yesterday and I saw this perfect gift for my 10-year-old twin nephews. They love playing at spies creeping around their house and garden whispering to each other on their mobiles but that uses up all their phone credit. These are short range walkie talkies. They'll love 'em. They can chatter away until the cows come home, or at least until they need to replace the batteries."

"I didn't know you had nephews."

"There is a lot you don't know about me."

"In that case I better stick around and find out more." He gave a playful smack to her naked behind as she headed towards the bathroom leaving the door ajar.

"I do know you have been taking flying lessons," he called through after her.

"Yes, watch out or I'll have your job one day."

It was yet another thing that Simon found attractive about her although he was not quite sure how he felt about a woman who might one day become his second wife also sharing his occupation with its attendant respected status. It was something he might have to adjust to.

"Are you going to be much longer in there, Amelia Earhart?" Simon's voice cut through the hissing of the shower spray, the use of her pet name underlining their closeness. "Remember we have got a plane to catch." A well-worn joke but still mildly amusing.

"You could always come and join me."

Simon needed no further encouragement.

Chapter 3

London time:Wednesday 15:45

"We will have an action update in 5 minutes," announced Dave, "In the meantime anyone that wants coffee or to nip out for a smoke had better do it now. We could be here for some time."

About half the room emptied. Those who were left either indulged in hushed chat or sat grimly silent.

Andrew knew the possibilities. Either this would turn out to be the calm before the storm or alternatively the unnecessary holding of breath, like watching a skilled trapeze artist at the circus. The trouble lay in not knowing which this was to be. That last time when the bomb hoax had resolved to be just that, a hoax, he had felt guiltily disappointed. All psyched up, ready for action and then somehow deflated. It was perverse, and he hated himself for it. But this time he was desperately willing everything to come right. After all it was not unknown for an aircraft to lose contact with ATC for an hour. But two hours? It was already well past that.

He settled into his allocated seat and logged on to the desktop in front of him. While it was whirring through the inevitable start-up routines he reacquainted himself with his surroundings.

The OCC was a room like no other. A hallowed space kept ready at all times 'just in case'. For months or even years on end nothing happened here. No one entered except for the cleaners and quarterly technical checks and servicing. Otherwise the door was locked shut.

Few employees, other than those trained up as responders had ever been inside and most of the workforce were completely unaware of its existence. It was especially not mentioned to the new hires on their induction training. That was certainly not the time to dampen their enthusiasm by reminding them that they were entering an industry that occasionally injured and killed its customers. Much later on, those who showed the right attitude would be quietly approached and asked if they were willing to join the team. Skills were less important than the potential to keep calm in a crisis. Under strain team members had to be able to respond quickly to serious events by making decisions that blended empathy with practicality.

Andrew was pleased to have been chosen for the team. In the harsh commercial world he knew it was a luxury to have such a large space held empty pretty much the whole time. The accountants hated it. They periodically suggested it could double as a conference room or a training classroom.

But Tom Nichols, the Blue Yonder CEO, had been rightly insistent that it be kept for its single purpose. He had told Andrew and the rest of his class at the crisis induction training "I don't want the wear and tear of other people using this equipment, traipsing in and out like it was just another meeting room. This room holds the key to our reputation. God forbid we ever have to use it properly, but if we do, everything and every person must work 100%. A failure in this room could wipe us off the map. I am not having my reputation or the reputation of this airline threatened by some numbers on a spreadsheet." And so, it was kept thus, the antithesis of the murdered teenager's bedroom - not a shrine to what was, but a pristine contingency ready for what might be.

Around the long central table were a dozen places each with a designated job title sign hanging above. To some that may have seemed a bit theatrical, like something on a movie set, but Andrew knew it was essential in the heat of an incident to understand exactly what each person was responsible for even if you did not recognise the individual incumbent.

The sign above his own chair proclaimed 'Go Forward Investigation Liaison', a role that would keep him here in this room as a generalist, only until the fate of the aircraft in question was established. After that it would either be back home if all was well, or alternatively he would be heading off to the closest airport to the scene of the incident. He looked down at this 'grab bag' and hoped desperately that it would not be the latter course of action.

Until things became clearer his responsibility in the room was to keep on top of any unfolding situation and continuously brief those in PR, as well as those in the adjacent Emergency Call Center, the ECC, whose unlisted number could be flashed on websites and television screens around the world in a matter of seconds. He knew that his very generalist responsibility meant he could easily be pulled away to assist other functions doing virtually anything such as answering phone calls from the public in the next door Emergency Call Centre.

Each position was furnished with a screen, a desk phone and its own cell phone. In addition, Dave had a second cell phone with a number known only to the CEO. He also had a satellite phone as a back-up in the event of a local cell phone failure which could so easily happen if hundreds of anxious friends and relatives suddenly swamped the network trying to reach the ECC.

Along one wall was a bank of TV screens. BBC World, Sky, CNN, Fox News and Aljazeera were all already online but so far not a whisper about Blue Yonder. That journalist attempting to enter the room earlier must have been a freelance stringer with some Blue Yonder insider on his payroll, Andrew thought angrily.

He looked at the facing wall, another bank of screens, the first one displaying the airline's website, the next their Facebook page, then a Twitter feed, a couple of prominent aviation chatrooms, and finally the Google newsfeed.

The room quickly filled up again with those who had left their half-smoked cigarettes stubbed out by the main door and their hastily drained coffee cups in the trash by the vending machine. No liquids were allowed anywhere near the keyboards.

The room fell silent. The occupants and their equipment were as ready as they could be.

Chapter 4

London time: Wednesday 15:50

Five minutes passed. No news was still no news. Andrew looked up as Dave cleared his throat.

"OK, folks, let's recap what we have got here. The aircraft is a Boeing 777, one of our newest, just under 3 years old. No known history of major damage, no bumps or scrapes on the ground. She went through the last major maintenance C-Check just 5 weeks ago. Pilot and co-pilot with more than 12,000 hours combined experience. The flight operated to time between here and Singapore and took off from there also on time after the usual transit stop for refueling and cleaning. Two on the flight deck, ten cabin crew and light passenger load, just 102. We will get the full name list up if we hear nothing further in the next 10 minutes."

One of Dave's two phones rang and the room hushed as he picked it up. Andrew was not the only one who instantly identified which one it was, and in the silence he heard even from several seats away the authoritative voice from the other end saying simply "I'll be with you in five."

"That was Tom," said Dave unnecessarily. "He is on his way."

To activate OCC, as had been done, was the contingency alert, the 'get ready' signal, the one that flashed amber and then more often than not went back to green. But for the CEO himself to put in an appearance was a foreboding. It was the next stage of readiness, an expectation of moving to red.

Jill, their seasoned P.R. lady, entered from an adjacent room and made straight for Andrew.

"Any update, kid?" Andrew was only two years younger. He knew the greeting was a response to the way he teased her about their age gap.

"Nothing yet. Tom will be here any moment."

"Yes, I heard."

"How much longer can we hold off saying something to the media?" For Andrew this was more just to say something than to seek an answer.

"Until we are asked directly, which unless we hear something positive will likely be any time in the next fifteen minutes. Or earlier if some plane spotter following the flight online starts tweeting when he realises it has not moved from the last known location."

The room was still hushed. Andrew pulled up his Facebook page on his phone. Why not? It was the calm before the storm. It lasted only two more minutes.

Aljazeera caught it first. Just a few words on the scroll bar at the bottom of the screen. '*A Blue Yonder aircraft has lost contact with Air Traffic Control two hours after leaving Singapore.*' The talking head above continued to pontificate on the weakness of the dollar.

"Damnit," said Dave, as all eyes followed his to the screen. "How the hell do these guys get it? Aljazeera of all people."

Along with everyone in the room, Andrew understood the inference. If the Arab world's premier news source was first on the case, who had given them the scoop? Aljazeera had long been suspected by the powers in the West to be the mouthpiece of terrorists. Paradoxically many in the Middle East thought exactly the opposite.

Jill caught the mood instantly.

"Listen guys, half the journalists working on that channel are former BBC and Sky News guys, senior people seduced out to Doha on dream tax free salaries. They are professionals. They know exactly what they are doing. A line like that would not appear without at least two reliable confirmed sources."

Within 30 seconds Sky News was riding on the coat tails with their banner reading starkly 'Reports of missing Blue Yonder plane appear on Aljazeera'. Less than a minute later the BBC limped into third place. The feeding frenzy had begun.

"OK," said Jill. We need a statement. And we need it right now."

All eyes moved to Dave as he gave his instruction.

"Pull the website home page. Redirect to the backup servers and amend the blanket text."

It was one of Andrew's tasks. With a nod from Jill he moved briskly back next door to the PR communications office and got to work on the website editor. Thirty seconds later with a minimum of word insertions it was done.

Blue Yonder confirms that flight number [010] en route between [Singapore] and [Brisbane] [has temporarily lost contact with local Air Traffic Control]. The plane, a [Boeing 777-300ER], is [3] years old and completed a major 'C-check' service with 100% certification [5 weeks ago]. The captain and first officer between them have over [12,000 hours] experience on this aircraft type. The aircraft is carrying [102] passengers, [10] cabin crew and [2] flight deck crew. Further updates will be issued as soon as there is any more confirmed news.

In under a minute the home page re-direct would be activated across the globe and all visitors to the website would be seeing the new message. The importance of using the present tense in the text was subtle but deliberate. The plane *is* 3 years old. Catastrophe would demand a single verb change.

Swiftly the atmosphere in the room changed. Not just because the amber was nudging towards red. More because of the man who had just entered. A few of the older contingent instinctively stood up. The lack of deference so common amongst the millennials in the workforce had not quite fully percolated upwards.

"No need to stand for me, we have work to do."

Andrew looked at his CEO. Tom Nichols was the kind of man you would pass in the street. For two reasons. One, because he preferred to walk most places rather than be driven, and two because he lacked any of the flamboyant affectations of some other entrepreneurial CEOs. No shock of unruly hair, no beard, no dark glasses. Average looks, slightly below average height, packaged into the easy charm of a chat show host. His trademark blue sweater and blue shoes the outward demonstration that he cared more for his company than himself. Brand consistency he called it when challenged.

The boss slid easily into the vacant seat at the other end of the oval table from Dave. From these positions the two of them could command the operation. Pilot and co-pilot. Not side by side as in a cockpit, but facing each other with their support teams buttressed in between. The layout was deliberately designed to suppress covert whispers and encourage full participation and transparency. Experience had taught the importance of clarity and shared disclosure.

The two men had worked together a long time and even although Dave was way more junior in the organisational pecking order Tom was smart enough to defer to him in operational terms.

"OK, Dave, what are the possibilities here?"

"I think our Chief Pilot is best placed to answer that one."

Andrew's eyes swiveled to the middle of the table ready to hear the response from the diminutive figure sitting there in a smart blue uniform with four broad stripes on the epaulettes and sleeves.

"At this stage it is hard if not impossible to rule anything out. But let's not forget that the most likely scenarios are the usual ones. Losing ATC contact on a long flight over water happens every day, at least for a few minutes or even up to an hour. Ninety minutes is not unheard of. Much more than that and we are moving from usual to unusual. Most likely, contact will be re-established in the next few minutes. But if not then we are left with just three possible scenarios. One, something is wrong with the communications but everything else is fine and the flight is continuing on course. Two, the aircraft is in serious difficulty of some sort, mechanical or hijack related, but is still airborne…"

"Yes, but why would they keep quiet if something is wrong?" Andrew could not stop himself interrupting.

"As pilots we all adhere to a simple three step sequence, drummed into us at flight school – 'aviate, navigate, communicate'. Not a lot of point wasting time talking to people on the ground hundreds of miles away if they are in no position to help you."

"And three?" Dave this time.

"It has come down."

"Thanks, Ana." Tom had every faith in the most senior woman in his organisation and was glad of her succinct no-nonsense appraisal of the situation. Ana Granata was originally from Brazil, the daughter of a crop-dusting father who had taught her to fly over the fields at the age of 14. Sensible, capable, and very experienced. She was the first one to voice the nightmare possibilities Andrew had been pushing to the back of his mind since the moment he received the call-out.

After a further few moments of silence Dave took over again. His original job application to Blue Yonder had been for pilot training but in that endeavour he got no further than the eyesight test. So, he had ended up on the commercial side of the business, consoling himself with week-end hours spent on Microsoft Flight Simulator. He and Ana spoke the same language even although Dave's vocabulary was only ever put into practice at ground level. Andrew listened intently as the two considered the possibilities.

"So, where exactly does that put the last known location, Ana?"

"Above the Java Sea, about 100 miles off the coast of Surabaya, Indonesia."

"Anything else in the area"?

"Nothing much apart from the tiny island of Bawean. And before you ask, the only airport runway there is just 3,000ft. Our Boeing needs almost twice that length to land safely." Clearly Ana had already done her homework

"And assuming scenario one and that everything is fine where will they be now?

"By now that would put them somewhere off the northern coast of Australia coming into range of Darwin ATC."

"And scenario two, if there has been a hostile takeover and they just keep going south or westwards where could that take them?"

"Eventually anywhere in Australia, but not as far as New Zealand. Or, with a change of direction, Indonesia, Papua New Guinea, the Philippines. It's possible with the remaining fuel, the plane could physically reach almost anywhere in mainland China or even North Korea."

"Possible but highly unlikely." Tom interjected a note of realism.

"At this stage we are only eliminating the impossible," said Ana, not afraid to correct her boss, "Until the facts prove otherwise it is best to assume that anything not impossible is possible. "

Andrew listened as a continuation of the exchanges listed out several more possible scenarios. With each one he could not stop his mind from conjuring up the implications. He liked scenario one the best, a cabin full of snoring passengers unaware, and a flight deck unconcerned by the length of radio silence over water in a remote corner of the ocean. Anything else put the dread that he was trying so desperately to subdue somewhere between likelihood and certainty.

Jill reappeared from the next-door media room.

"OK, the story is breaking big time now. We need to be seen to be on top of things. And by that, I mean you, Tom. I have announced an update statement on camera in 15 minutes. It's a good day weather-wise so we will do it at the front door. Andrew will gather the facts for you now and then both of you come next door and I'll give you the final prep."

Andrew was already on the task at his computer, knowing exactly what content would be required.

Tom nodded as Jill turned and left the room. "Right. Dave, Ana, anything else I need to know?"

"Nothing more than you have heard in the last few minutes," said Dave. "We will get you the passenger list before you go downstairs."

A list Andrew had been dreading. That would make things more real.

Chapter 5

London time: Wednesday 16:15

"I think Ana should be by your side," said Jill needlessly as Tom and Andrew entered the media room.

"Tá bom!" smiled the Chief Pilot as she stepped out from behind them.

"Great minds," said Jill. "This way we can show leadership from the top combined with gender diversity and female empathy."

"This is not a contrived PR exercise," said Tom, "we are talking here about the lives of our customers and our employees."

"In this situation *everything* is a PR exercise. But no need to tell you to be yourself, Tom. You always are. That is your strength and our strength as a company. So, I guess, no script. We have already stated the age of the plane, the passenger count and the crew experience so here is where they will go next. One, you will be enticed into speculation, *'what could have happened? What do you think has gone wrong?'* Don't go there."

"..anything not impossible is possible," Ana chipped in.

"Sadly correct," said Jill, "and that is what leads to sensationalist tabloid headlines such as 'Blue Yonder CEO does not deny that flight 10 could have been taken over by Martians.' So stick to the fact that at this time we have no evidence whatsoever of malfunction or threat to the aircraft and we are making all efforts to re-establish contact with the flight deck. That will bring us to their second line of attack which will be to probe the experience and capability of the crew. We need to release their details now."

"I have got those already from the despatch office," said Andrew. "Captain Simon Porter is one of our longest serving pilots with over 9,000 hours on the triple seven. Alongside him is First Officer Nabil Kahlil, one of our newer recruits who joined a while back from MEA, the Lebanese airline."

"How many hours for him?"

"Nudging 3,000"

"OK, don't break that down for the press," counselled Jill, "just re-iterate 12,000 hours in total as per our web statement. We don't want them homing in on a lesser experienced Arabic co-pilot."

"Andrew, I'll need you and the others to get the crew families on the phone right now," said Tom. "I want every one of them to hear from us first before they pick up anything from TV. Start with the Captain's wife. I will talk to her personally."

Andrew nodded. He had already retrieved the contact numbers.

"And the last line of questioning will be the *'how many Brits onboard?'"*

"That's the easy one," said Tom.

"Yes, maybe, but the best answer is to give the breakdown of all nationalities. We have a global customer base so it's important that we do not come over as Little England Airways. I have the summarised totals here. Mention the passengers, then move on to our crew. Most airlines make the mistake of putting their own people first."

"Right, anything else I need to know, Jill?"

"Yes, we have one medical case on board. Nothing life threatening, not a stretcher case, just a young man with a respiratory problem. He is Ecuadorian, travelling with a male nurse and has enough oxygen for the flight. Not worth mentioning to the media at this stage, that would only give them even more of a human-interest angle."

She handed Tom and Andrew each a sheet of paper. "This is the only time you should need to look down at notes."

Flight 10 is carrying 102 adult passengers, no children and no infants. Among the nationalities onboard are 18 British, 16 Australians, 15 Singaporean, 10 Chinese, 8 Ecuadorians, 7 Indonesians, 7 Malays, 6 Americans, 3 Russians, 3 Qataris, 2 Israelis and 7 others. In addition, the aircraft is being operated by 2 flight crew and 10 cabin crew.

16 Australians.

Just numbers? thought Andrew.

Fifteen plus one.

Chapter 6

London time: Wednesday 16:30

As Ana and Jill left the room, Andrew was already tapping numbers into his phone. Only three rings and he had an anxious female voice on the other end.

"Yes? Who is this?"

Andrew took a deep breath.

"Mrs Porter?"

"This is she." A very correct voice.

"This is Andrew Barnes. I am one of the managers at Blue Yonder."

"Is anything wrong?" The instinctive reply of a pilot's wife receiving a call from an unheard-of work colleague.

"No, not exactly. But I have Mr Nichols here who would like to speak to you."

He handed the phone to Tom, mouthing as he did so the identity of the recipient.

"Mrs Porter, Tom Nichols."

"Oh my god, what has happened? Has he been fired?"

"No, no, nothing like that. It is just that your husband, as you know, is in command today of our flight from Singapore to Brisbane and, well, we have not had any contact over the radio for a little while now. It is nothing to be alarmed about, but I wanted to tell you first because in a few minutes I will be giving a press briefing and after that some of them will try to contact you. I wanted you to be prepared for that. And to give you my personal assurance that as soon as we re-establish contact with your husband's aircraft you will be the first to know."

Tom paused to let the news sink in, and was not surprised by the long silence from the other end before Mrs Porter responded.

"From Singapore to Brisbane you say? Are you sure?" The woman sounded more concerned about the route than the news itself.

"Yes indeed, Mrs Porter. Once he is rested and turns around in Australia he will have another brief layover in Singapore and be back with you in a week's time. Look I am really sorry to cut this short but the press are waiting for me."

"I understand. I will switch on the television right now. Goodbye and thank you for letting me know."

"How was that?" asked Andrew.

"A bit strange. She seemed not to know her husband was commanding that particular flight. I guess some people don't talk much about work when they get home. She also asked if he had been fired."

"OK, next one." Andrew tapped and entered the number HR had provided for Nabil Kahlil. As the First Officer was unmarried, this was his brother Jamal. He counted the rings and as they reached six he waited for voicemail to kick in. But none did. Not at seven, eight....or even eighteen. He hung up.

"No answer from Nabil's family."

"OK, we will have to go ahead regardless," acknowledged Tom. "Let's get this show on the road. Tell Jill and Ana we are ready."

Chapter 7

London time: Wednesday 17:00

As Andrew, Tom and Jill stepped out into the early evening sunlight they were met by a barrage of camera lenses and microphone booms, with more journalists arriving by the second.

Tom was well used to being followed and door-stepped but Andrew could see that even he was taken aback. "My god, how did they all get here so quickly?" the CEO whispered to Jill.

"Some of them will have been on their way as soon as Al Jazeera posted," she replied. "Most of them will have already been hanging around the airport in any case. There are always enough celebrities and politicians flying in and out to warrant a permanent contingent of media passenger spotters."

Ana arrived seconds later and took up her position at Tom's side.

Andrew always relished watching his leader in action. Jill stepped forward.

"Ladies and Gentlemen, thank you all for coming at such short notice. In our business we always appreciate people who turn up on time."

The remark elicited a few brief smiles which Jill noted intuitively. Setting an informal tone was part of the brand.

"At this time, we will hear from Tom."

'Tom.' Again deliberate. Again important. Never Mr Nichols to the media.

"Please keep your questions until he has finished." Knowing this remark would be redundant did not stop her saying it.

All booms and lenses swiveled to Tom. Andrew shifted slightly to get a better view, and also to ensure he did not end up like one of those nerds caught staring in the background.

The CEO looked straight into the phalanx of cameras. "I know all of you and the many friends and family of our valued customers, flight and cabin crew are right now anxious to hear news of our Blue Yonder flight 10, on its way to Brisbane. As of now I am afraid there is no news. What I do have is facts. Flight 10 had its most recent contact with Singapore Air Traffic Control at 22:30 local time." Jill had reminded him to use the phrase 'most recent' rather than the implications of using the word 'last'. "That was now some hours ago. We have received no reported sightings of an aircraft in distress and until we learn otherwise our working assumption is that the flight is continuing on its intended flightpath suffering from a communications malfunction. While we remain concerned, there has been no indication that the flight is in any difficulty."

The inevitable interrogation began.

"How many British people onboard, Tom?"

"Eighteen."

"You report only just over one hundred in total. That is very low. Are the glory days of Blue Yonder over?"

"No, not at all. We have a very heavy cargo load on the flight so we had to cap the passenger numbers. This is, in fact, good news for us. Cargo pays very well."

"Why were Al Jazeera the first ones to break the story? Do you think they know something from the inside? Does this imply a terrorist angle of some sort?"

"Look, in the absence of any hard facts at this time, there is no reason to jump to wild speculation." Tom was keeping his voice steady despite his irritation at the question.

There followed a few more perfunctory exchanges as each enquirer fished for a headline. Andrew was on the point of returning upstairs when he noticed one of the foremost journalists edging forward to speak for the first time. A short man in jeans and wearing a sweater that might even have been rejected by a thrift shop.

"I understand there are also three Russian nationals onboard. Can you tell us anything more about their itinerary? Was it one-way only?"

Andrew's mind raced back to the comment he had heard from the security guard less than an hour ago. 'Scruffy little bugger'. As Tom had only so far mentioned the number of British passengers it was obvious someone on the inside of Blue Yonder was feeding information, probably for more than just beer money.

Tom glanced down at this paper. "Hopefully we will hear something from the flight deck very soon. A further statement will be released as soon as we do. Thank you all for coming."

"Just one last question." The same guy. "Is your Chief Pilot able to assure us that there is no known history of antagonism between the Captain and First Officer onboard this flight?"

Ana stepped forward. "Without exception the crew of Blue Yonder are all professionals. They conduct their operational duties to the highest standards in the industry. Such a question is not only irrelevant it is also insulting."

Jill groaned. She could already see the headline 'Tom's feisty Ana refuses to deny cockpit feud.' It was definitely time to close.

"That will be all, ladies and gentlemen."

Chapter 8

London time: Wednesday 17:10

Andrew decided to linger a moment before returning upstairs. After last night as the first shift on the night roster he was feeling a little bit like being jet-lagged, especially having had a shorter sleep and such an abrupt awakening. It was good to be out in the fresh air.

The press contingent were dividing up into those who were already heading off to chase the next story and those with the instinct that the better move was to hang around a while longer in the hope that no news became bad news.

He glanced down at his phone to check the time. Just after 5pm. The warmth was disappearing from the late afternoon sun. In the background planes were taking off and landing. Taking off and landing with the same metronomic frequency that they had done so every day for decades. Taking off and landing time after time. Safely. At any one time around half a million of the world's population would be hovering several miles above the earth eating chicken or beef. Andrew knew they were more at risk from salmonella than of falling out of the sky.

Briefly he closed his eyes in the hope that he might also close his mind for a few moments. He had to hope that the plane was still airborne and that everything was alright. Wherever the plane was right now it would be the early hours of the morning, and dark. But how and why might an aircraft lose ground communication and disappear from radar yet still be flying safely across some kind of communications black hole?

Anything not impossible is possible. Ana's words. That left open pretty much everything he did not want to think about.

Possible? A mid-air catastrophe caused by mechanical malfunction. But surely impossible without some kind of communication that something was wrong? Fatal mechanical errors at cruise altitude were almost unheard of. He knew take-off and landing were by far the times with the greatest potential for something going awry. Especially take-off when the pull of gravity had to be tackled and overcome.

Possible? Pilot error. But this crew were fresh, only a short time out of Singapore. And no one so far had mentioned any concern of bad weather.

Possible? An aircraft explosion due to a bomb onboard. But surely impossible that the sight of a 250-ton fireball would not have been witnessed by some vessel below or even on faraway land. But then again, he did not know how faraway that land might have been. And also the vessels in that region of the ocean were likely to be fishing boats manned by fairly unsophisticated men, more interested in hauling nets than looking skywards.

Possible? A deliberate change of course by someone in the cockpit for reasons unknown. None of them good reasons. A suicide mission? Hijack? But surely impossible without any of the passengers or cabin crew noticing something amiss and using the onboard Wifi or their cell phones to relay their concerns to the ground.

Surely impossible? But not absolutely impossible.

Thoughts of the terrible possibilities outnumbered the optimistic ones. *It's not impossible that everything is alright.* That was the one he had to cling to. Until something more was known the only way he could function was to concentrate on the facts and shut out the speculation whirring round inside his head. Trouble was, there was only one fact. *The plane was missing.*

He went back upstairs, hoping his colleagues might have some more news.

Dave looked up as Andrew entered the room. "How did it go downstairs?"

"No worse than expected. They are already fishing for a flight deck feud or a Russian conspiracy."

"Which means they have no more clue than we do," said Dave. "Good in some respects I guess."

Andrew walked over for a closer look at the wall holding the bank of screens. One of them was gently scrolling down through blocks of text. No images. No graphics. Just text. He moved closer.

"What's this one?"

"Roger Nigel." said Ana

"Pardon?"

"Rogernigel.com It is one of the most popular pilot chat room sites. We all use it, especially down route when we are holed up in some boring hotel room and just want some gossip.

"Why Roger Nigel?"

"Pilot humour. All British pilots are thought of as 'posh Nigels'. Take a closer look. They have been on to us from the start, even before Aljazeera picked up the story. These guys will give you a much more accurate assessment of what might be going on than you will get from some retired wing commander pontificating on TV."

Andrew peered closer at the screen and read quickly. As usual, Ana was right.

Joystick93 17:15

I know that stretch well. Flown it dozens of times. At the last known point of contact they were above an ocean pretty crowed with fishing boats. There are so many lights that some nights it looks like a fairground down there. If it ditched someone would have seen it. My bet is it is still flying.

Bobthedriver 17:18

I'm with you Joystick but how do you explain the radio silence? And the blank radar?

4stripes 17:20

Roger joystick. I don't think we are looking at a ditching situation here. The 777 has an Emergency Locator Transmitter (ELT) on the aft fuselage and that thing starts emitting as soon as it is submerged in water.

Joystick93 17:22

As mystified as you guys. Flightradar24 shows it off the coast of Surabaya at 22:56 local and then…nothing. That is a while ago now. How could something that size evade radar for that long?

FlightRadar24. The openly available website tracking all of the world's commercial aircraft. Andrew cursed himself for not thinking of that sooner. He returned to his position and punched in the URL he had used many times before to establish real-time flight positions. Instantly the screen lit up with a map stretching across the skies of southern England and north west Europe. He could see hundreds of little yellow plane images like a swarm of flying insects, nudging forward every second or two, heading in all directions of the compass. Heathrow itself was barely visible under the thick cluster of planes arriving and departing, like a stop motion movie of wasps around a jam pot.

He scrolled right, over the densely packed skies of Europe, past the cluster of Arabian Gulf airports, the empty spaces above Syria and Iraq and quickly on to centre over Indonesia. He zoomed in on Surabaya. A very different picture from Heathrow. Off the northern coast no more than half a dozen aircraft. He hovered over each one and a quick flick revealed more detail. Singapore Airlines, Garuda, Lion Air, but no Blue Yonder. Of course not. That was hours ago now.

He started to scroll further south east looking for where fight 10 might be now. Not thinking straight. As if a hundred others might not already have done so…and come up with nothing.

"It's time to change the assumption that everything is still OK. Our passengers' families are already beyond that. We need to open the ECC." Dave's voice brought Andrew back into the room. More jargon. The ECC, the Emergency Call Centre.

"And the press is certainly not helping." Jill had re-entered the room and pointed to the Sky News screen where the scroll bar proclaimed 'Off into the blue yonder. Why the silence over flight 10?'

Andrew knew his role. He picked up his phone and rang through to the airline's reservations office manager.

"Hi, Richard, I hear you are pretty busy there. We need to activate the ECC and get it up and running in the next ten minutes. We can't have our ongoing bookings disrupted by this other business. Let me know as soon as you can muster a quorum, and I will have Jill fire the phone number off to the media."

Richard acknowledged. Andrew put the phone down, confident that the well-rehearsed procedure would begin immediately. Using an automated call broadcast three dozen Blue Yonder employees across all departments would almost instantly be listening to a message similar to the one he himself had heard earlier.

This is not a test. Please attend the Emergency Call Centre immediately. If not available text reply NOAVAIL.

The first ones, the ones who were already at work within the building, would be in the ECC within a few minutes. Others would quickly follow. After thirty minutes, if needed, another three dozen calls would be made. Richard would hand over responsibility for the reservations office to his deputy and move to take charge in the ECC, a room across the hall from where Andrew was sitting.

"OK, folks," said Dave. "ECC will be up and running in 15. We also need to prepare the Go Forward team in the event this incident turns into an accident. We will need the standby aircraft refueled now."

Those in the room who were implicated in this next stage of readiness knew exactly what they had to do now. Quite a few left the room. As Investigation Liaison Lead Andrew knew that if the Go Forward team was activated he would be travelling with it. Some team members would be technical people, but most would be there to look after the next of kin who would inevitably want to be as close as possible to the last known location of their loved ones. In this case that would mean Singapore.

Andrew moved back to the video wall where the question uppermost in his mind was already being given a good airing by the Rogernigel community. He stood and watched as the chatter continued.

Bobthedriver 17:31

If Flightradar24 has not picked it up by now surely this plane must have gone down somewhere either by accident or design. it can't just go missing for 3 hours can it?

RadioLuke 17:32

As far as Flightradar24 is concerned yes it can. They rely on ADS-B technology (automatic dependent surveillance-broadcast). This is not the same as the primary radar used by ATC. The onboard transponder picks up the location using GPS and then transmits this along with other bits and pieces. The ADS-B receivers are mainly sited on the ground in the gardens and on the rooftops of a bunch of amateurs which is part of the problem around coverage. But the bigger issue is the range of these things. It is not much beyond 200 miles at best. The greater the distance between aircraft and receiver the higher it has to be flying. We are basically talking line of sight. Bottom line is much poorer coverage over oceans.

Flybywire52 17:34

Adding to RadioLuke. I took a look at the same flight for the past three nights using the history function and each time it disappears for around an hour or more around that same spot. But unlike tonight it then reappears closer to Australia. Definitely something fishy here.

Bobthedriver 17:44

it is unbelievable that in any normal situation the aircraft could have evaded civil or military radar for this long. So barring a sudden mid-air catastrophe the only other plausible explanation is that a person or persons with enough knowledge has managed to switch off the two systems that send signals to the ground and then descend to a low enough level to evade radar

RadioLuke 17:45

Anything below five hundred feet would do it. But much less fuel efficient down there.

Flybywire52 17:50

if so, Bob, where is it now?

Bobthedriver 17:51

Need to do some calculations. Get back to you on that one

Andrew moved back to his seat knowing it could be a long evening.

Chapter 9

London time: Wednesday 17:15

Inside the OCC room there simply was no more new information.

On the bank of TV screens speculation was ramping up as each channel dredged up its roster of so-called experts, ever ready to pontificate and theorise. Most of these talking heads were male, retired and over-used the word 'might'. Some talked cautionary sense. Most did not. And a few were plainly lunatics.

Andrew clicked back to the online threads on *rogernigel.com.* Here the conversation was more rooted in reality. Pilots are not known for wild imaginings. Reading on he was not reassured.

JumpseatJoe 18:15

Sounds like they are already getting hysterical on the telly. Just heard a wing commander on the Beeb spouting off about mid-air explosions. For God's sake, let's not get hysterical, people. Start with what we know. The aircraft lost contact. That's it. Other than that Nada! Here's my two pence worth. Take your pick from this lot

1. Cockpit crew suicide bid

2. Sudden oxygen failure, then for whatever reason the aircraft veers wildly off course and continues on autopilot

3. Serious malfunction of something or other demanding the crew's full attention to wrestle with it combined with complete loss of communications.

4. Shot down by military by mistake. No one likes to admit this sort of thing

5. Hijackers with a well thought out plan to incapacitate the crew and passengers, knock out the communications and fly goodness know where. But how are they evading radar? And why no demands?

6. Pilot disorientation. What if the pilots took the plane off autopilot and for whatever reason went off course without realising it. The plane could keep going for quite a while which would mean it is miles away by now

What d'ya think? Any takers?

BobtheDriver 18:22

Like your thinking JJ, but how come still nothing squawking, nothing from the cockpit and nothing from the self-loading freight with their dozens of cell phones? Even with 9/11 we got calls from the planes

Techtuner 18:23

Bob with 9/11 the bad guys did not need to fear anything about the passengers making calls. They were doomed from the start. Letting others know about it a few minutes beforehand would have changed nothing. I can think of several possibilities to answer a 'why no cell phones' line of thinking. A handful of cell phone jammers smuggled onboard by bad guys would do the trick.

Or sudden loss of oxygen could incapacitate the whole cabin. at that altitude it would take only 15-30 seconds. Take away the oxygen and its like pulling a switch, nothing gradual...the lights just go out in your brain.

Cheery thoughts. Can we keep this real, guys?

Andrew clicked off. With the TV offering sensationalism, the pilots in left brain overdrive, and his own mind anxiously trying to suppress both he was desperate for something to actually do rather than just absorb...and worry.

"I have just had a call from Richard," said Dave. "The Call Centre ramp-up is going more slowly than we need. Five minutes with the number on the TV and we are being swamped already. Andrew, appreciate if you can get in there to lend a hand for a while until we get more agents in."

"Sure." A firm reply belied his hesitation. He had done stints in the Call Centre before. He knew the drill. Gleaning information from anxious friends and family. Building a picture of the caller's connection with a passenger onboard. Listening, listening all the time while radiating empathy, not sympathy, the latter being instantly taken as an admission of tragedy. Simultaneously scanning the passenger list hoping not to be able to match up the name being enquired about.

But those other times were different. Empathy was hard enough, even when the passenger was just a name.

How hard would it be this time, when he knew that one of the those onboard was someone he loved?

Chapter 10

It was only three weeks ago that Andrew had first met her. Not on Tinder or in a singles bar, but at a party, the old-fashioned way. Both a little drunk. Both in a 'let's get out of here' mood. And so, they had. Andrew quickly discovered that Kimberley was a traveler, an Australian. Same thing he reckoned. In the three weeks, they had barely been apart. It just seemed right.

"I want to know everything about you," she said. So he told her his stories, each with a little gilding. He desperately wanted to impress this woman, but at the same time to be true.

"Now I want to know everything about you. How long have you been on the move?"

"Haven't been back to Oz in three years. Spent the last twelve months in London, working. To be honest, I kind of like it here."

Two hours later he asked, "And that's everything?"

"That's everything."

Neither of them had used the 'L' word yet but Andrew had quickly come to the realisation that it was there.

Only two days ago, he had been by her side when she got the phone call. It was only a couple of minutes, but as her face became more and more serious it was obvious this was not good news.

"It's my grandmother," she told him as soon as the call ended. "My cousin reckons she doesn't have much longer. Not quite at death's door but 'shuffling down the corridor' was the way he put it."

"Sorry to hear that." Andrew felt sheepish as soon as the cliché left his mouth. Even more so when he added "Anything I can do to help?"

"As a matter of fact, yes. You can get me on the next flight to Brisbane. I need to be there." Her eyes moistened. "Gran was always there for me when I was a teenager. Not the happiest of times for me. Now I need to be there for her."

Andrew had already opened the Blue Yonder app on his phone. Flight 10. The deed was done.

Chapter 11

Singapore time: Wednesday 20:15

The doors finally closed, the lights dimmed for night time take-off as the giant Boeing lifted up again into the darkened Singapore sky. Kimberley did not know if she was hungry. Did not know if she was tired. Did not know if she wanted to watch another movie. The jetlag aliens had taken over her brain.

Only yesterday they had had their first goodbye. No precedent. No practice. "Once I am ready to go, I just like to go," she had told him, "so don't expect backward looks."

"That way I will never know if you cry," he had teased.

Later on, that first leg she had called him.

Hi, Stranger, are you missing me already?

Where are you? What happened? He sounded worried.

On the plane, silly. Free wifi, remember, like you said.

So how is it? Your first Blue Yonder experience.

It's wonderful. I have got four seats to myself, able to really stretch out. Not a single baby onboard either. No crying.

I'm jealous. She could tell he was.

I peeked in front of the curtain before returning to my rightful place. Pretty empty too. Bunch of weird guys in black T-shirts. Better go now. Goodnight, my love.

'My love?' The endearment had just slipped out.

Goodnight Blue Yonder.

The fasten seatbelt sign pinged off. Kimberley picked up the inflight magazine from the seat pocket. 'Go Yonder' was the usual airline glossy PR publication, opening with a message from the CEO. Ghost written, of course, but congratulating the airline on taking delivery of their 21st aircraft and the opening of a new route to Morocco. She quickly flicked through the dozens of pages, mostly written by the founder's glamourous friends describing snatched week-ends and business trips, not surprisingly all to destinations served by Blue Yonder. With titles like '24 hours in Rio' and 'Berlin, No Expense Spared' she was hardly tempted to read on.

In less than a minute she had reached the back pages and the route maps. She drew her finger across the thick blue line joining London to Brisbane. Around now they would be crossing the equator. Tracing onwards across the fold in the middle of the page over Borneo, parts of Indonesia, somewhere called the Timor Sea and finally across the Northern Territories and down through Queensland to Brisbane. It all looked so easy. But that was on paper. Up here she knew the total journey time would be little short of 24 hours.

The other three seats in her centre block were empty. She glanced across at the male passenger on the adjacent aisle. Definitely a fellow Aussie she surmised, tall with beach-tousled hair and already in blue shorts and a sleeveless shirt in anticipation of spring in Queensland with its rapidly warming days. He caught her eye and she smiled across instinctively.

"It's a long way isn't it? I mean if you are going right through, of course. You're not one of those wimps who just got on at Singapore are you?"

"No, not at all," she shot back

"No worries, then. I was sitting way at the back on the first leg, but then I spotted there was far more space down here so I moved." He laughed easily and shot out his hand across the aisle. "Luke, pleased to meet you."

"Kimberley."

She could not help but notice the strength in his forearm. A handsome trustworthy face. In the days before Andrew she might already have been interested. And in those days she might have wanted the handshake to linger. She still might even have made it so, but a passing meal trolley en route to the front of the cabin put paid to any such notion and she withdrew her hand.

"And where are you from, Kimberley? Where we started from, or where we are going?"

"What makes you think I am from either? I might be from Nigeria or Norway y'know."

"Well I already saw the size of the backpack you loaded in the overhead bin, and now that you have said more than two words I can stop guessing. What part of Australia are you from? Don't tell me you are a Queenslander too."

"No, Melbourne. I am only heading to Brisbane for family reasons." She did not need reminding herself at this moment of the sad reason for her trip. No need to share that much. Not yet anyway.

She had always found that conversations on airplanes could go one of several ways. There was the perfunctory nod when first taking your seat followed by hours of silence and no further acknowledgement except if movement was required to enable a toilet break. She had had plenty of those. Then there was the gushing bore, probably a nervous flyer, who felt the need to take up the entire journey sharing far more than necessary about their uninteresting lives with never a single enquiry about what made the other person tick. And then, rarely, the truly interesting person whose company adds enjoyment to the journey and then the exchange emails before landing. But never follow up. She already had a hunch about categorising Luke.

At that moment the next meal trolley arrived between them and put an unwelcome stop to any further chat. It was feeding time. Tables down. Chicken or beef.

After the meal, which was better than expected, Kimberley selected a movie. The beginning was a bit slow and she was soon asleep, lulled by the cabin warmth and the quiet drone of the engines.

The emotional exhaustion of the past couple of days was beginning to catch up with her, and stretched flat across four seats she slept long, but not soundly. Somehow it was never quite possible to align the various seatbelt straps, buckles and raised armrests to avoid being prodded at every turn of her body.

She awoke with a dry mouth and the usual slight headache. She glanced at the journey map on the seatback screen in front of her and groaned. It showed the plane icon somewhere off the coast of Indonesia with hours still to go. She pulled herself upright and took a swig from her bottle of water. Looking across at Luke she saw that he too was asleep, feet towards her and head propped up by the window, his three seats not quite broad enough to accommodate his length.

By now Andrew would have finished his night shift, she reckoned, and was most likely long asleep in bed with the curtains tight shut to keep out the daylight. He would be lying flat on a proper mattress and without her there beside him. On both counts she tried not to think about it.

She freshened up in one of the bathrooms at the rear of the cabin. It felt good to use her legs again. A few passengers were stirring but most were still asleep filling the air with a medley of snores and snuffles audible above the background hum of the engines.

Back in her seat she resumed the movie. Not one of the best.

She was definitely in that state where the body has travelled faster than the mind. Just over a dozen hours ago she had been hugging Andrew goodbye at Heathrow and now here she was half way across the globe, disorientated, feeling tired but not tired

She felt happy that the back of the journey had been broken. But still hours to go, yet somehow in the context of the entire journey that did not seem like much. One or two more movies, a meal and a snack and she would be there.

She started to think about her grandmother again, hoping desperately that the old woman would hang on so they could enjoy a few final days together. She even dared to hope for a period of remission despite fearing this would be the most unlikely of outcomes. Yet this was a 90-year-old woman who had endured some harsh times earlier in life and until the last few weeks was living in her own house and driving her own car. Maybe there was still a few years left in her. However long there was it would not be enough. With the passing of her grandmother whenever it came would also come thoughts of her own life. So far, she had thankfully avoided any job interviews where she might have been asked the perennial 'where do you see yourself in five years' time?'. The answer to that would have eluded her. Much easier would have been her affirmative answer to 'are you happy right now?'

She closed her eyes and drifted off into a fitful sleep.

Chapter 12

London time: Wednesday 17:55

As Andrew crossed the corridor to the adjacent room, the thought he had been suppressing ever since he got the call came bubbling back. The rule was clear. Anyone with next of kin or other personal relationship with someone onboard a stricken aircraft was forbidden to participate in any element of emergency response. That was only common sense. Activity in the Operations room was one thing, but now in the Call Center he would be talking directly with others in the same situation as himself.

He knew he could easily have declared himself out. Easy, but difficult. Impossible, in fact. He could not leave and just go home to wait, to wait and not to know. At least here he would be doing something, helping, and be among the first to find out what was going on. Anyway, he reasoned, he had not yet spoken of Kimberley to anyone at the office. Things were too new. So, who would know? No one.

About half of the forty agent positions were already occupied and the wall display was flashing. Fifteen calls waiting. Andrew grabbed the nearest empty chair, and powered up the computer screen.

The man in charge of the room noticed him and came straight over. Richard Edwards was yet another of Blue Yonder's experienced and unflappable employees. His kindly eyes and beyond casual dress sense belied his rigorous, methodical approach to everything. Following behind him was a younger, rather nervous looking individual.

"Andrew, this is Josh. It's his first time in here. I want him to listen in to a few of your calls before we put him live. That way he can get the feel of things. I'll leave him in your capable hands."

"Sure."

Richard walked back to his command position as the newbie took the adjacent empty seat, plugged in his headset and looked expectantly at Andrew.

"I know you will have had the training, but just a few reminders before we get started."

Call lights illuminated the console on the wall in front of them, the flash of each one a cry to be heard.

"First, there is no accident. At least not yet. We have lost contact with the aircraft, that's all. The word is 'incident', not 'accident'. Don't get drawn into speculation with the callers. If they express their fears don't even murmur a 'yes' or an 'uhuh' or next thing they will be all over Twitter and Facebook telling the world that the airline has just told them the plane has crashed. Just remind them we have nothing that confirms a bad outcome."

Josh nodded, listening intently.

"Second, and I know this is hard, but when discussing anyone likely to be onboard for God's sake stick to the present tense. None of this '*did* you know him well?' or 'what *was* her final destination?' And finally, at this stage of the game don't use the phrase 'next of kin'. This is not the time for that. Conjures up immediate images of the man in the big cloak and sickle."

"Thanks, I get it."

"Just one more thing. If you get anyone claiming responsibility for bad stuff, or issuing any kind of threat press the red button in front of you. That sets off the recording and alerts Richard to listen in. OK, now let's do it."

Andrew plugged in a headset and pressed the flashing light on the desk console. 'Here we go,' he muttered as he jabbed the flashing button light on the unit in front of him.

'Blue Yonder, good evening, this is Andrew. How may I help you?"

"Is that Blue Yonder?" An older female voice. Worried.

"Yes." He had just said that it was but Andrew was not surprised by the plea for confirmation. Most callers would not be in a state of mind to register his greeting.

"My son is on that flight. Where is it?"

"I assume you are referring to our flight 10? At the moment we do not have a definite position but it should be in Indonesia airspace heading for Australia."

"Should be? What good is that? I always thought you were a one of the decent airlines, if there is such a thing! Why don't you know where it is?"

"I understand your frustration. Believe me, at Blue Yonder we absolutely share you concern. There are many reasons why a flight can sometimes lose contact for a while with Air Traffic Control. It is not unusual." He hated himself for sounding so formal. Lighten up. Show some empathy.

"For over THREE hours?! Surely THAT is unusual?"

"I agree it is not normal. We are doing everything we can to re-establish contact with the flight. If you let me have his name, your phone number and email we will contact you the moment we hear anything further."

Andrew toggled to another screen as she gave the details. He entered her name and relationship in the unspoken 'next of kin' field, phone number and email, then thanked her for calling.

Only one call and already Andrew could see Josh looking more nervous. On the wall unit the numbers were increasing. Twenty-three calls being answered, nineteen on hold…waiting, waiting. If he had chosen another job, a non-airline job like most of his friends, one of those lights would have been him right now. Himself, listening to some light orchestral music while imagining the worst for Kimberley, but really the worst for himself.

He jabbed the flashing button again. On the wall unit calls waiting momentarily reduced to 22. A second later it went back up again to 23…and then jumped to 25.

"You are through to Blue Yonder; my name is Andrew. I am sorry you had to wait." That sounded better this time. Hopefully more caring.

"My wife is on your plane." An older man this time

"Flight 10, yes?"

"Yes. I am so worried. I say 'my wife' but actually we have been separated for two years now. She just said she had had enough of me and walked out. I tried to keep in touch be she didn't want it. She kept saying she needed some space. I guess going to Australia will give her plenty of that."

"I am sorry to hear that. As far as we know at the moment if she is indeed on the plane she is still heading for Australia."

"What do you mean 'if' she is on the plane? Don't you have a passenger list?"

"There is a passenger list but it has not been released. We don't do that unless….." he caught himself.

"Unless what? You mean unless it crashes?"

"No, I was going to say unless we are legally required to release it to the police or the authorities. But nothing like that applies to flight 10."

"At the moment, you mean! Look, I was on hold for twenty minutes before I got through to you. Can you take my number and call me back as soon as you have some news, any news at all?"

"Sure. Let me have you wife's name and I promise we will do that."

Another screen. More details.

Another call politely ended. Getting into more of a rhythm now.

'You are through to Blue Yonder, this is Andrew. Sorry you had to wait." Shorter, punchier. Still empathetic.

"Tom Cruise."

"Pardon?"

"Tom Cruise, I know he is on flight 10."

"And you are?"

"Never mind who I am." A lady's voice. Middle-aged sounding. "Tom and I are very close. I always know what he is doing. I have met him many times. Many, many times. A lovely man, quite perfect. He doesn't always tell me where he is going but I know he is on that flight. I just know. I'm certain of it. I have got the feeling, the feeling I always have when he doesn't tell me but I still know where he is."

Josh's eyes widened. Andrew's did not. He had handled this type of call before.

"And your relationship to Mr. Cruise, madam?" Time for a bit more formality. He had always found that to be the best approach with the nutcases.

"We are lovers. But you mustn't tell anyone. Don't put that down, young man. It's private."

"Don't worry I am not writing anything down. This call is confidential." Might as well play along and get her off the line as quickly as possible.

"Some people say he is gay, you know? But I can personally assure you he is not!"

"Right then, thank you very much for your call. Just keep watching the television and you will know as soon as we do what is happening."

"Yes, thank you. You have been very kind."

"And if Tom gets in touch with you first, please call back in and let us know he is safe."

He cut her off.

"That's one we can laugh about later," he said to Josh. "But not now." With that he jabbed the incoming all button.

"This is Andrew at Blue Yonder. Sorry for the wait." Hard to be much shorter than that. But was it too abrupt?

"Hi, mate," obviously Australian, "listen I am really worried that my girlfriend might be on your flight. Y'know that one on Twitter that has been hijacked? What's going on, mate?"

"Well first of all, whatever you are seeing on social media, none of our flights has been hijacked. If you mean our Singapore to Brisbane flight then we are trying to re-establish contact with the flight deck."

"Yeh that's the one, mate. Do you have a passenger list? I hope she is not on it."

"At this time there is no reason for us to be too worried. The passenger list will only become available if there is cause for concern."

"Well if I give you her name and my number can you text me back when you hear something?"

"Sure, go ahead."

"Right, mate. She's a great girl. Love her to bits. Been working in London a while now, but she's heading home for some kind of family emergency, so she said. Her name's Kimberley, y'know after the region in Western Australia. But she's a Melbourne lass."

Silence.

"Are you still there, mate?"

"Yes….and your name is?"

"I'm Paul, Paul Nickson. And as I said, she is Kimberley."

He gave the surname too. Something Andrew definitely did not need to hear.

Had Kimberley really told him *everything*?

Chapter 13

London time: Wednesday 18:35

Andrew punched his 'busy' button. It was there for those who needed an emotional time-out, usually due to the relentlessly harrowing incoming calls. During the previous times he had worked in the call centre he had trained himself to be as emotionally detached as possible while still maintaining a degree of empathy. Hard enough when callers were weeping hysterically at the other end of the phone. Now he found that detachment suddenly impossible.

Two Kimberleys on the same flight, heading for the same place and for the same reason? Not even remotely possible. Therefore impossible. Therefore?

He felt sick. How come she had not said anything? Not even hinted about there being someone else, let alone someone in whom she had obviously also confided about her trip. Someone she must have contacted in the last 48 hours, so not just some long lost 'ex'. He had the guy's name. And his phone number. Should he just ring him back and ask outright? Bad move. Unprofessional apart from also being a bit pathetic. If this Paul person was an item with Kimberley, or at least knew her very well, this was not the time to start probing their relationship.

Now he had two things to forget about, to push to the back of his mind. Kimberley on the plane. And Paul, not on the plane. He put his headset back on and went back to the calls.

An hour went by. Still no further news from next door which made it increasingly difficult to talk optimistically about the fate of the aircraft. No news was no news. But no news could only be bad news in the minds of those calling in.

As the calls continued to pour in, two of the younger employees were assigned to begin filling names on

a huge white board at one end of the room ominously labelled 'confirmed onboard'. Each name had its own row followed by several columns, not yet labelled. But Andrew knew that in the event of catastrophe what the headings would be. Only one column would be headed 'survivor'. Please God that Kimberley's name would make that column. She HAD to be one of the lucky ones. Anything else would be unimaginable.

As Andrew finished another call and looked up Richard walked over.

"I think we have enough agents in now. Thanks for your help, letting Josh shadow you. I expect Dave could use you back over in the OCC."

"Sure, let me know if you need me again."

As he got up he turned to Josh. "Your turn now. Just remember 'present tense'. You'll be fine."

They both nodded. Neither was convinced.

* * *

Andrew reentered the room as Dave was about to give a briefing update.

"OK folks, listen up. I know it has been a frustrating hour or so but we need to change gear now. It's been more than 4 hours since the last contact. It is time to face up to the fact that something is horribly wrong. We need to say something to the media before they bury us completely. Tom will be back in a minute. Meanwhile, how much fuel could be left, Ana?"

The Chief pilot had been on the phone and her computer for the past 20 minutes working exactly in anticipation of being asked such a question.

"Assuming they are still airborne they would have used about five hours' worth leaving them another three to three and a half in the tank. However, the fact that they have obviously avoided radar strongly suggests they have descending to a much lower altitude, maybe just a few hundred feet. Down there, skimming the waves it would be far less fuel efficient but if someone wanted to avoid primary radar they would be doing exactly that."

"Right, we need to get an updated statement up on the website. Call Jill back in."

Twenty seconds later the Head of PR was back in the room. She stood by the bank of wall monitors while Tom paced the floor as spoke.

"There is too much we just don't know. What can we say, Jill?"

"We need to come off the fence. Continuing to admit we know nothing and refusing to speculate just won't wash. Look at this!" she pointed at the screens behind her. "It is getting worse every minute we say nothing."

'Airline silence is deafening. What are they hiding?' said one. Another was showing an animation of an aircraft exploding in mid-air in gruesome detail with bits plummeting earthwards above a map of Java. On a third channel weeping relatives were being interviewed in front of a besieged check-in desk.

Tom looked thoughtful for a minute before pronouncing. "You are right. We need to say something. *I* need to say something. Let's do it."

Tom and Jill left the room to face the press pack for a second time. Three minutes later their faces appeared on virtually every single one of the TV screens on the monitor wall above the legend 'live press conference'.

Andrew listened as the boss, eloquent and empathetic as ever, walked through the infinitesimal chances of some of the more terrifying scenarios. He concluded by stating that one thing that could definitely not be ruled out was the real possibility that everyone was still safe.

Andrew clicked back on to *rogernigel.com* and flipped back to catch up on the last 20 minutes or so of exchanges. On the screen a continuous dispassionate and mainly logical stream of comment and discussion from men whose professional lives gave them absolute trust in the reliability of their flying machines and absolute confidence in their own ability to deal with the unexpected.

Flybynight 19:57

Just watching Tom Nichols on the TV. He seems to be making the best of it poor bloke. Hard to admit you know nothing, especially when it is true.

Andrew realised suddenly just how tired he was. He closed his eyes only to be startled seconds later by his own phone ringing. He glanced down. It was Joanna, Kimberley's flat mate.

"Andrew, I can't stand this. Do you have any more news than we are getting online?"

"I wish I did. I am back in the office, naturally, trying to help where I can. We are still optimistic here. The reckoning is that it has not come down, but no one has any clue where it is."

Should he ask her about this Paul guy? Now was probably not the right time. It could wait.

"I have had some of her other friends calling me mostly asking if that is the flight she is on. I have had to tell them it is. It's just awful."

"Which friends? Anyone in particular?" He couldn't help himself.

"You wouldn't know most of them."

Or she didn't want him to know one of them?

"Listen," continued Joanna, "I hate to admit how worried I am. Can you come round here when you are done there? You can have the sofa if you like. It would just make me feel better to have you here."

"Yes, of course. It may be late. Don't wait up. You know I have a key."

"I'll wait up."

Chapter 14

Local time: Wednesday evening

Fifteen years since the man had last been here. Fifteen years tomorrow to be precise. And he was precise. The trip had been planned around the anniversary. No particular reason why a specific number of earth rotations should have anything to do with it but after all these years this seemed like the right time to revisit.

Coming back had started off as a vague notion around a year ago. But then the thought niggled and germinated until eventually it became so deep rooted it could not be dislodged. He did not quite notice at what point it had become 'The Plan'.

To come here had meant taking up all his vacation days. Two days to reach the country and then another day more to reach this place. This place where he wanted to be. Tomorrow. If he had come before, even just last year, he knew it would have been too painful. But somehow in the last few months he had come to terms. Now he was ready.

The village was smaller than he remembered. Maybe it had shrunk, depleted by the interminable move to the town only a few miles away. Although it was a small place his memory pictured it as always busy, always bustling. People outside, going about their business. Others, with no business to go about, sitting on doorsteps and standing on street corners. Children playing in the middle of the dusty roads, their mothers unworried, knowing that any traffic would have four legs and not four wheels.

Tomorrow he would go to the place. The exact spot if he could find it, about a mile from here. For now, he was content just to find somewhere to spend the night in the village. He approached an old man sitting cross legged and toothless in front of his one room shack. In his dimly remembered pidgin he asked about accommodation. There was a place around the corner that was available and cheap he was told. No surprise. Everything was available and cheap in this place because nobody came here anymore.

But why was the village so quiet? Deserted almost.

The old man told him.

Maarten froze.

Chapter 15

London time: Thursday early morning

Andrew remembered the first time he had ever stayed awake all night. Thirteen years old and his parents had agreed he could have a New Year's Eve sleepover at a friend's house. Until that time there had always been the end of one day disconnected to the beginning of a new one. What went on in between was a mystery to a child. Nothing joined the 'good night' to the 'good morning'. Except sleep, of course, which did not count. He knew there were people like milkmen and nurses and street cleaners who must know what the real night time was like. But not him.

That first all-nighter had been a rite of passage. An entry into the adult world of not having to go to bed when it was dark.

When he interviewed for the airline all those years ago and was told that the job involved some night shifts it had not phased him.

But this was the first night shift ever which had been just like a frenetic daytime, only it was dark outside. More and more people had turned up to work the call center, not just those who had been called in but many more who could not sleep and just wanted to do something to help. Eventually Richard had to start turning them away. Every phone position was full and there were a dozen people as backups drinking coffee, eating pastries and waiting.

Rumours and speculation continued to swirl around in the TV studios and on social media as those desperate for certainty could not accept the concept that no news is no news. Somebody must be hiding something went the logic. And if not, then it is obvious what has happened. Let's not pretend that the plane has not been accidently shot down by the military, hijacked by terrorists or deliberately crashed into the ocean or the jungle by a suicidal pilot. If there is no proof it did not happen then it could happen. Indeed, it *has* happened.

Only on *rogernigel.com* did Andrew find hints of any common sense. There was inevitable nonsense there, too, as the wannabe pilots piled in to the thread with their need for attention, but anything that was just plain daft was quickly removed by the forum moderator. In the absence of any visual evidence either in the water or from those on the ground or at sea the notion of a midair explosion or a ditching had been largely discounted several hours ago. Hijacking remained one of the not impossible possibles but all were mystified by the fact that no credible claims of responsibility were forthcoming. But what if they were being kept secret? The usual rationale for a hijacking therefore did not seem to apply. Defection in that part of the world did not seem to make sense to the pilots either. Who would want to seek asylum in Indonesia? Exchange of passengers for political prisoners or ransom would first of all demand a safe landing somewhere, and that would have had to have been negotiated with ATC hours ago.

Andrew also read guarded exchanges and discussions about the theory and practicality of how those with evil intent might variously disable the aircraft communications, power and oxygen supply. *Bobthedriver* even started thumbing through his own copy of the Boeing Triple 7 tech manual and had described the ease with which much of this could be done. The others quickly shut him up, not wanting to provide a lesson plan for future attempts at such activity. The moderator deftly removed his more detailed posts and warned him to change the subject but not before Andrew and no doubt countless others had time to digest the fact that it was highly feasible. It brought him no comfort.

Andrew was left surmising that there were still four not impossible possibles – sudden catastrophic failure, pilot suicide, terrorism, and finally, incorrect response by the cockpit to some abnormal situation. He had no clue in which order to prioritise the likelihood of these. He preferred the latter two which at least gave some hope. The first two did not.

He learned that affected family and friends of those onboard were congregating in increasing numbers at Singapore Changi airport and also at Brisbane.

Finally, at around 6:00am with no further news and mounting media frenzy Dave had instructed everyone to get some rest.

Andrew looked at the three wall mounted clocks, of the type seen in hotel lobbies the world over in an attempt to comfort their guests in establishing the moment. The type of clocks that actually have the opposite effect. The clocks that disorientate. Wherever we are on the planet, he thought, surely we all share the same time? This moment here now is this moment right now for Kimberley wherever she might be. Here in London one clock declared it was ten past six in the morning. In Singapore it was 7 hours later. And the one showing 'Time at incident site' showed an hour earlier, counter intuitive considering Java was further east, but in that part of the world the lines were not exactly straight. Between Singapore and Brisbane there was just two hours' time zone difference so wherever the aircraft was right now, even if at the bottom of the ocean what did time matter? It's all made up. Now was now. And now was exactly when no one knew anything more about the fate of Blue Yonder flight ten. Except those onboard.

Twenty minutes later Andrew had been relieved and was on an early tube heading for Shepherds Bush.

It was 6:30 am when he decided to exit the tube at Hammersmith and walk the final mile to Kimberley's flat. Twenty minutes in the fresh air would be welcome after a night in windowless air conditioning. Outside the tube station he ignored the opportunity to pick up a copy of the morning 'Metro'. *Blue Yonder Terror Plot?* was not a headline he needed to know more about.

It was still early but the throng of going-to-workers flowed against him as he crossed at the lights and headed up Hammersmith Grove. As he often did he wondered what kind of jobs they might all be going to. Some would have more responsibility than he did, many would certainly be better paid, further up the career ladder striving to see themselves elevated even further always 'in five years' time'. But how many would share his passion for the industry they worked in, helping thousands of people every day to jet around the globe to reconnect with friends and family, to see new amazing new places, to strike business deals?

And how many would be heading for work today struggling with the thought that a hundred of their customers might have been killed during the night?

As he got closer he paused a moment to text Joanna. If she was still asleep he would just go back to his own place. The reply took thirty seconds.

Of course I'm awake..what news?

Be there in 5 dont worry

Don't worry? How stupid was that? Everybody said it, reflexive, unthinking, useless.

As he approached the flat Andrew slowed down. What was he going to tell Joanna? It had been difficult enough in the call center during the night to reassure disembodied voices of people he had never met, to be almost clinical in the gathering and imparting of what little information he had. But this was Joanna, Kimberley's best friend and he felt guilty that he had nothing much to tell her either. Nothing except 'don't worry'.

Outside the door he paused, knowing what awaited him. Best friends usually come in two varieties – opposites, or clones. Kimberley and Joanna were definitely the latter. Apart from the fact that Joanna was a New Zealander, somewhat shorter than Kimberley, and with cropped red hair that contrasted with Kimberley's frizzy mop, the two girls could easily have been cousins. Maybe even sisters. Certainly, a shared DNA in the personality department. Equally practical. And equally attractive Andrew had thought at first meeting. Yet he had wisely not allowed himself to dwell on that aspect, even although Joanna was more outgoing than Kimberley in one respect. She was a toucher. The type of person who instinctively laid her hand on the forearm of whoever she was talking to. An intimate gesture that mean nothing beyond a huge potential to be misconstrued by men who were attracted to her. And as far as Andrew had seen, that meant pretty much all of them.

He reached for the doorbell but before his finger made contact the door was flung open and there stood Joanna red eyed and pyjamaed. She flung her arms around him and squeezed tight. No sobbing, no shaky voice just a very long hug. Anyone behind a twitching curtain might easily have taken the scene for something completely different.

Eventual release. "Come in and tell me what's happening. I want to know everything you know. Everything you can tell me, and especially everything you can't. After that I'll make you some breakfast."

"I'm afraid everything I can tell you is everything I can tell you, and sadly it is nothing more than you have probably been reading online....all night by the look of it."

"I think I might have had half an hour's nap, not more. I am so worried. Will she be alright?"

"We honestly don't know. But here's the thing. After all these hours and no reports of an aircraft coming down we are working on the assumption that the aircraft continued flying. Or else it may even have landed somewhere. I'm sorry, we just have no clue as to where it is. But as soon as we do locate it I will be among the first to know. And so will you."

"I so hope she is alright."

"Me too."

He held her gaze in a moment of terrible shared loss. Not actual loss, at least not yet. Just loss of any kind of explanation, any kind of understanding or clue as to what might have happened. A shared not knowing about the fate of their friend.

Joanna moved to the kitchen area and Andrew followed. Without asking she began to crack some eggs into a frying pan.

She had her back to him, engaged in the task. Now would be a good time to ask. Casually.

"Does she have other friends who might be worried too? People we should text?"

"Loads. She is a popular girl. I have contacted some already."

"Including Paul?"

She did not turn around. There might have been a short pause or maybe not. Maybe Andrew just expected one.

"Who?"

"Paul, I thought he is a good friend.......Paul Nickson."

"Not that I know of." If there was any shakiness in her reply the sound of sizzling eggs was covering it. "This will be ready in a minute." She turned to face him and smiled. "Coffee?"

"Yes please."

Andrew barely knew Joanna. In the three whirlwind weeks with Kimberley they had met only a few times, usually in the pub. Mostly Kimberley had stayed at Andrew's place. Now suddenly here they were sharing breakfast together, and her in her nightwear.

"How long have you known Kimberley?"

"We have shared this place for a few months, but I met her a while before that when we both had part time jobs in the same restaurant. We just clicked right away. Not just the antipodean thing, but she is so much fun, but much more practical than me. Tough too. One time we both forgot our keys, got locked out of the flat and she just kicked the door down. Then she called the landlord and told him we had been burgled and could he please send someone round to fix the door."

"And?"

"He came round himself within 20 minutes with a big toolbox. I think he quite fancies her!"

"Yes, she does have that effect. I should know." He smiled.

Joanna finished with the eggs, ladled them onto two plates atop some fresh toast. They sat down to eat.

"Let's get this while it's hot. I'll do the coffee in a minute."

They ate in silence, Andrew was still wondering how much Joanna really knew about other men in Kimberley's life. If the two of them really were as close as they appeared then Joanna surely did know everything and her rebuttal was good news. Either that or she was lying. Sitting here opposite the perky woman in pyjamas who had just cooked his breakfast he chose for now to believe the former.

A phone rang causing each of them to reach for their mobiles which were each sitting on the table between them like Colt 45s in a saloon bar truce. The call was for Andrew. As he picked it up to answer Joanna laughed sheepishly.

"Same ring tone!"

The look on Andrew's face quickly changed the mood in the small kitchen. He was listening intently, saying nothing. After less than half a minute he clicked off without a 'goodbye'.

"So?" she hardly dared asked

"It was a recorded broadcast. I have to get back to the crisis center. They say there has been a development."

"A 'development'?! For god's sake what does that mean? Is that code for something awful?"

"No, it is just neutral language to describe a change in circumstance." Andrew was saying the words but he did not believe it either. "Look, I have to go. Now. I'll hail a black cab outside by the Green. Thanks for the breakfast, it was great."

As she opened the door for him, another hug. And this time also a kiss. Almost a proper one.

"Call me as soon as you know what has 'developed'"

"Sure."

Chapter 16

Local time: Wednesday evening

In his faltering pidgin Maarten asked the old man to repeat what he had said.

It was a dialect with virtually no grammar just a jumble of nouns and adjectives with a single present tense.

"*Api bukit besok*" was what he heard.

"*Gunung berapi?*" he queried.

The man thought a moment and then nodded. He then turned and began shouting and waving his arm at a figure watching them from the distant corner of the street. Maarten saw that it was a small boy, about ten years old, watching them warily while slowly bouncing a very old and worn football. After a moment the child picked up his ball and disappeared quickly round the corner.

Maarten lifted his dusty backpack, heaved it onto one shoulder and headed around the corner in the direction the man had indicated.

Fifteen years since he had last been here. Here in one of the planet's least explored countries where more than 80% of the population lived in remote rural settlements.

Transport limited by the country's mountainous terrain meant that the capital, a virtually lawless city was not linked by road to any other major towns. Most villages and towns could only be reached after days travelling on foot or by small aircraft landing on tiny grass airstrips. Where he stood now had been a bit easier, but not by much.

The heat of the morning was already unbearable. Nothing stirred apart from a few supine dogs, indolent in the shade. He hoped to find accommodation close by. Then again everything was close by. It was only a small village.

He pushed open the door of what was little more than a shack, albeit with sturdy wooden walls and a corrugated tin roof. As his eyes adjusted to the dim light he saw he had entered a remarkably tidy office space furnished, unexpectedly roomy with light pine furniture which looked oddly familiar. A door at the side led into an adjacent small shop space stacked with hardware. Brooms, plastic buckets, tools, crudely made kitchen utensils, rope. Everything imaginable, and then more.

Behind the desk stood a tall figure. Then Maarten realised the man was actually seated. A very tall man indeed.

"*Rum?*" Maarten enquired, pronouncing it 'rhume'. He might as well dispense with the verbs. The language was not keen on anything involving action. "*Bet?*" he added.

"Sure, we have a room....and a bed. Several if you want more than one." The man smiled as he stood up.

"You speak English?"

"Better than you speak Tok Pisin."

"That's a relief." Maarten eyed the tall man. "Where did you learn?"

"At school. Before I moved here. Do you like the furniture? Most people are surprised to see it here."

"Yeh, all this hardwood around and yet you furnish the place with pine?"

"Ikea. I just liked the look of it for a change. Not easy to get it here, but worth it don't you think? I'm Arief by the way."

"Maarten."

"Have a seat then, Maarten. What brings you here...especially at this time?"

"Used to come here on vacation. My dad worked in the capital so we would come here a couple of times a year to get away from it all. You know, go camping and live the simple life on the edge of the jungle. My parents were keen on that kind of thing. I liked it too. I guess it rubbed off. Both my parents were keen bird watchers so what better place to come." It was not a question but Arief instinctively nodded as Maarten continued. "My dad was also a keen amateur botanist. He insisted on showing me as many different plants as he could, the ones to marvel at, the ones to eat and definitely the poisonous ones to avoid."

"Yes, even in paradise we have those too. So why did you come back?"

"A bit of a pilgrimage." Maarten chewed his lip. He need not have worried.

"How many nights do you need?"

"Let's start with two. Should be enough."

Chapter 17

Singapore time: Wednesday 22:30

Simon Porter had been flying the Boeing 777 aircraft for almost a decade. He knew the controls and the handling better than he knew his own car, an early 90s Lotus Elan. His car was a labour of love, totally impractical and inclined to be temperamental. By contrast the Boeing in thousands of hours of flying had never given him a moment's cause for concern. All the important bits, engines, ailerons, wheels, rudder, worked perfectly across years of service, maintained by a fleet of engineers who themselves were beyond perfectionists. They had to be.

It was the cabins behind him that contained the hardware and software that was more susceptible to the odd niggle. Seat recline was the number one problem area, especially those flat beds in the business cabin that had more moving parts than bones in the human body. On this trip, so far, things had gone smoothly except that the inflight WIFI had suddenly gone out shortly after take-off from Singapore. Julie had come forward to let him know and despite advice radioed back from base they had been unable to fix it.

Sitting here in the cockpit it felt like his cocoon. It always did. The land far below, now in darkness but soon to be again in light, was indeed a world away. Down there was a world far removed from where he sat high above and in comfort. For the duration of the flight he would relish this escape from earthly worries, something that too many could only look forward to in death.

The temperature was just right, the stillness and quiet hum belying the giant thrust of the powerful engines behind him. To the layman, or the eyes of any child lucky enough to be shown the cockpit before take-off the array of screens, lights, switches and buttons was beyond comprehension. How could one person possibly know what they were all for? But to Simon the purpose of each and every one of them was as familiar as the items in the toolbox of his Lotus. By contrast the contents of his wife's extensive kitchen spice rack were a complete mystery to him even although each jar and packet was labelled. Cardamom? Fenugreek? Sumac? Whatever was wrong with salt and pepper? He had his cockpit. She had her kitchen.

Under normal circumstances in less than a week's time he would be back in that kitchen, drinking coffee and reading his paper while his wife cooked. But this time he had determined it would not be so. Going back there would not be an option, not since he had met Julie. Somewhere behind him, beyond the locked door she would be serving coffee and drinks to any of the business cabin passengers who might still be awake. And at some point, soon she would bring him his meal. For some time now, due to the well-publicized tragic circumstances with other airlines it had become Blue Yonder policy never to leave just one person on the flight deck. So, his chances were good that his co-pilot might choose that moment to take a comfort break and a stretch by walking to the back of the plane leaving the two of them alone for a few minutes. That would be the perfect moment for the plan. He had bought the ring in the Gold Souk during his last trip to Dubai.

He looked across and smiled at the genial Lebanese man in the right-hand seat. They had not spoken for the past fifteen minutes or more but the silence between them was comfortable. He had flown many times with Nabil as his First Officer and spending yet another seven or eight hours alone together he did not feel the need to pass the time with chit chat. They already knew enough about each other's life back on the ground, their cars, their sports teams and all that important stuff. Not everything, but enough. He knew that Nabil had long ago left a troubled land, a roller coaster of strife both internal and external. His leaving for Paris and ultimately London yet with frequent return trips to his homeland was something Simon had never asked him about. Something which seemed to suit Nabil just fine.

On the personal front, as far as Simon knew Nabil did not suspect there was anything between him and Julie. But in the enclosed world of a small company you could never be sure.

It was 30 minutes or more since Nabil had last spoken to Indonesian ATC. Simon had heard them bid the aircraft a cheerful 'goodnight'. The silence was nothing to be concerned about. Sometime soon they would be picked up by Australian ATC at Darwin Airport in the empty Northern Territories. Until then there would be a little while longer to enjoy gliding through this radar black spot above the Timor Sea.

A while back Blue Yonder had been at the forefront of those airlines who had switched to allowing their passengers to use their cell phones at cruising altitude to connect to an onboard hotspot that then relayed the signal earthwards.

But for some time now, above this empty stretch of ocean there was no connection to be had. The passengers' devices would be silent. And with the onboard WIFI out as well they too would be totally off the grid. Do them good, thought Simon.

Chapter 18

Singapore time: Wednesday 22:15

There are only two ways to fly a modern passenger plane – manual or on autopilot. These days the former was reserved for a shorter and shorter time, just around take-off and landing. The longer the flight the less 'real flying' that takes place, something which had led some pilots to favour short haul aircraft. Blue Yonder flight 10 was on autopilot, with both men relaxing. Nabil was nursing an almost full cup of coffee waiting for it to cool.

A buzzer sounded, most likely indicating the delivery of Simon's drink, the one he had belatedly asked for as Nabil got his. Before opening the door, Simon was about to check one of the three galley cameras, but then remembered that this was one of the small things he had noted as unserviceable in the pre-flight checks. Annoying, but not a big deal. Not one of the many more serious faults that would have hindered the aircraft's dispatch.

Acknowledging with a nod to Nabil that the other man was the handling pilot, Simon unbuckled and rose to look through the peephole. He saw Julie, her head turned and facing back towards the cabin. No doubt momentarily acknowledging a passenger stumbling towards the forward toilet. He smiled, knowing she would always put the customer first even if it meant walking backwards with a tray of food and hot coffee.

Simon unlatched the door.

The force of intrusion immediately flung him backwards across the compact flight deck. He slumped onto the centre console, face upward. The door slammed behind the two men who burst in. Simon could see the one at the back had dragged Julie in with him, his hand clamped around her neck. He heard her scream out his name and then she crumpled silently to the floor. He did not notice the syringe.

Pilot training and refresher courses had kept Simon's brain alert to many dozens of contingency actions but all of them had been to do with actually flying the aircraft and not with being assaulted in a confined space. In a different occupation, one more concerned with bodily threat, he would have learned that success in close combat comes from three things all of which his assailants had just amply demonstrated – surprise, speed and immediate violent action. On such matters Simon had not read the manual. He had not attended the classes. But someone else in the cockpit had.

Nabil's head half turned the moment the door opened. As a pilot, the corner of the eye is almost as important as the centre - reading all of the instruments, noting all of the lights and toggle switches across the expanse of the instrumentation panel.

As Simon looked over at his co-pilot, he saw Nabil give a quick flick of his left hand and direct a cupful of scalding coffee into the face of the forward assailant. As the man instinctively wiped at his eyes Nabil used the moment to unbuckle his seatbelt. Rising from his seat he closed the gap between himself and the intruder. A short guy. Black T-shirt. Half a second. Nabil was staring at the gun in the man's right hand. No time to think about how such a thing might have been smuggled onboard. A quarter second. A deft cross body kick from Nabil's right leg separated the weapon from the fingers that were clutching it. The look on the guy's face showed that surprise could work both ways.

Neither of the intruders had made any attempts to conceal their faces.

As Simon lay across the console his first thought was for Julie. That in itself was a huge change from a year ago when he would have been thinking only of himself. Maybe a distant ten years before that a vision of his wife might have been foremost.

Barely two seconds since the men had entered. Simon stared up as Nabil landed a right hook centre on his assailant's face. The look of surprise changed to anguish as blood spurted down the man's chin and he crumpled to his knees.

One down and one to go. Not even three seconds now. The larger of the two men, a huge guy, standing right behind his crouching comrade also had a gun and that one was pointing straight at Nabil's head. Smart guy. Smart enough to have shielded himself on entrance with the short guy whose black T-shirt was already staining.

Further heroics suspended.

"Don't even think about it, my friend."

Who are these guys? Simon recognised the accent as somewhat Germanic sounding.

As his co-pilot half raised his hands in a gesture of compliance, Simon slowly picked himself up and edged back towards his seat. On the floor Julie remained comatose. Mr. Bloody Nose wiped his damaged face with his arm in the sleeve he didn't have, and looked angrily at Nabil. In a larger space he might have followed through his anger with physical retribution.

"What do you want?" asked Simon. An instinctive question. A stupid one. Like asking the same thing to the man with his head in a stocking mask, marching out of your house clutching your flat screen TV.

"All we want you do what we say," said the large one at the back, "so back in your seats and take this thing off of auto-pilot."

'This *thing*'? Not this *plane* which would have been the British word, or this *airplane*, the American. Both men looked Asian. Simon speculated that this one had learned his English from being around Europeans. As for the other one, he had not uttered a word. He could have been bleeding in any language.

Simon regained his seat. As captain it was his rightful place. The one with the damaged face retrieved his gun from the floor. Simon flicked the aircraft back to manual control taking back command from the computer that was better at flying the plane than he was himself.

Nabil edged slowly sideways away from the instrument panel. If the bad guys did resort to using their weapons on him a single bullet exiting out through the side of the fuselage was unlikely to be catastrophic. Unlike in the movies, a small hole would not erupt immediately into a gaping chasm that would suck them all outside in an instant. A bullet through the instrument panel was more of a risk, but with the array of failsafe backup systems, certainly manageable. The displays would detect their own failure and reconfigure. Least understood would be a shattered cockpit windscreen. Definitely best avoided. If he remained at the side then the current trajectory of an exit headshot would be virtually harmless for the aircraft. But not for him. This was the sort of thing Nabil knew. Simon did not.

"Sit down. Now!" As Nabil obeyed the gunman moved forward, standing over the two pilots with his weapon aimed diagonally downwards.

"OK, switch off the transponder. Now."

Simon gave Nabil a look that acknowledged what both knew. With no transponder signal being sent out and at this position above miles of empty ocean the aircraft would become instantly invisible.

"And if I don't, what then? You shoot me? You shoot my co-pilot? Do either of you two actually know how to fly a plane?"

"We know good. We can do anything we want with the plane. If you do not help us it does not matter."

Simon complied. Switching off the transponder was definitely not in the rulebook but doing so was not going to kill anybody he reasoned. Not at this point anyway.

"OK, now same with ACARS." Simon had hoped this was not coming. These guys had done their homework. ACARS stood for Aircraft Communications Addressing and Reporting System, basically a system which transmits data on location, altitude, heading and speed. With ACARS as well as the transponder off it meant the double whammy for Flight 10. Invisible, location unknown, and heading who knows where?

Reaching down to the lower ACARS screen, Simon obeyed, knowing that in two seconds the digital footprint of a hundred and fifty tons of flying metal would vanish.

"Now maintain FL350, nice and steady so we don't wake up sleeping peoples."

* * *

Across the aisle Nabil was continuing to process information, his brain whirring. He reckoned it was a better than evens chance that one of these two guys actually did know how to fly a plane otherwise as Simon was intimating, the guns were useless as an implied threat. Useless unless? What else? A pause. Unless there was another person or even several others in the cabin behind them who had the skills and the training to take over the controls. In that case it would not matter to them if he and Simon were lying on the floor full of bullets.

Adding to the evidence was the use of the term 'FL350'. As a trained pilot Nabil knew this was shorthand for 'flight level 35,000 feet'. Not only did the bad guy know the jargon he had also known what instrument to look at to establish the fact. And that made him what? At the very least it made him someone with a very definite plan about what was to happen next.

"Whether or not we cooperate I assume you plan to shoot us both at some point anyway?" A calm Nabil voiced his logical conclusion.

"I sure you will cooperate because if you do not the first one to suffer will be Captain's girlfriend. Before she dies. Maybe long before she dies. After that it will be your passengers. Ninety-four, one by one."

Nabil's thoughts continued in over-drive. "But if one of you goes back into the cabin the one left here will be outnumbered. In your shoes I would not risk it."

"There is no risk. Do you think we two are alone?"

Bingo! The inference confirmed the answer he had already calculated. The total passenger count was 102. But the guy had said 94. In addition to the two now in the cockpit they must have six more guys back there. There was no further harm in double checking.

"How many of you then?"

"Enough. So don't try any more kicking and punching. It will get you nowhere."

More than enough, thought Nabil. Eight in total. Two to cover the business cabin and then two for each of the two economy cabin sections. Whatever these guys were after this was a very well-planned set-up, certainly not a spur of the moment thing. Figuring out their motivation could wait. For now the important thing was to keep calm and keep flying safely.

Simon, flying the plane, was clearly demonstrating rule number one - aviate. Meanwhile Nabil was thinking both forwards and backwards.

Forwards. All but two of the cabin crew were female so if things got physical the male tally would be no better than four against eight. And how many of the eight had weapons? A fair bet it would be all of them. As for the passengers there would not even be a nail file or a pair of scissors among them. It would be too much to hope that they might have a rugby team onboard.

Backward. These guys really know what they are doing. Who are they? What has motivated them to do this? How long did it take them to plan this operation? And where was it planned? Yemen? Pakistan? Iran? Libya?

* * *

"OK, now you will vent the aircraft" barked the lead bad guy. Simon turned to object only to find that it was *his* head that was now the target. By now he had regained most of his composure and was back to thinking of himself as the captain of this ship and not some kid in the playground obeying the dictates of the school bully.

Simon considered the consequences of the demand. It effectively meant to depressurise the passenger cabin by manually opening the outflow valves, something that would have the same effect as opening all the windows, as if that were possible. At this height, equivalent to one mile higher than Mount Everest, that was a life-threatening proposition.

There was a lengthy silence.

"No more delay," yelled the front man. "Put on your masks."

The Big Guy at the back easily hoisted Julie's inert body onto one of the jump seats and quickly reached for the adjacent oxygen mask, slipping it on her dazed face. The smaller man likewise took care of himself on the second observer seat. It was only then that Simon noticed the Big Guy had also dragged in one of the cabin crew oxygen units for himself.

"Vent the cabins now or your co-pilot, your girlfriend and two passengers will die."

"And if we vent the aircraft with more than enough oxygen masks for this light load don't you think that makes your threat kind of empty?" Simon knew his co-pilot would be thinking the same thing.

"You know as well as I do that each passenger mask will supply oxygen for around 15minutes."

"Yes," said Simon, taking a modicum of comfort from the fact that with such a light load it would probably stretch closer to 20 minutes. "That gives sufficient time for us to descend safely to 10,000 feet," he added.

"Except that we are not going to do that. Not yet. Maintain FL350."

Reluctantly Simon obeyed the order to vent the aircraft, knowing that as he did so the passenger cabin masks would immediately deploy.

The flight deck oxygen mask air supply ran off a different system isolated from the passenger cabins for the very reason that they were now encountering. The four of them plus the comatose Julie would be fine, at least for now.

Shutting off the cabin oxygen mask supply was not something that could be done from the flight deck, otherwise surely the bad guys would have planned for that. But maintaining high altitude until at least the passenger cabin oxygen ran out was easily achieved if backed up by the threat of force. Simon had already worked the scenario through to its deadly conclusion. A conclusion that would become a reality in just over 15 minutes.

Shit, who are these guys? They clearly know their stuff. It was a few months since his last refresher but Simon carried the figures in his head the way a learner goes for his driving test knowing braking distances in the wet and the dry. At 35,000 feet, where they were cruising now, the average person would survive less than half a minute once the oxygen ran out.

Blue Yonder flight 10 maintained altitude.

Chapter 19

Singapore time: Wednesday 22:05

A short stocky man, walked down the aisle of the Blue Yonder aircraft. He was bulkily dressed and clutching a small carrier bag. Approaching in the other direction from behind was one of the flight attendants moving forward with the duty-free trolley vainly hoping for a few sales to boost the commission pool that the crew would share at the end of the month. As the two reached the same spot the man made to squeeze past the trolley. In doing so the bag snagged on the armrest of the seat. The passenger in the seat, a girl with frizzy hair, looked on as a couple of small pieces of wood fell from the bag to the floor. Instinctively she bent down to help retrieve and return the items to their owner. The man took them back from her proffered hand with barely any acknowledgement. His eyes quickly shifted away as he dropped the pieces back into the bag. Two tiny triangular wedges of wood no thicker than a matchbook.

The man with the carrier bag continued his progress and entered the rear economy cabin. Stopping a moment by the exit row central bulkhead, he continued to stare ahead down the aisle, the hand at his side resting firmly against a small door in the wall. If anyone was watching they might have wondered what he was looking at. But no one was watching. They were all asleep. And the man was looking at nothing. After a few more seconds he was done looking at nothing. Two cabins, two nothings looked at. All complete, nothing left in his carrier bag he returned to his seat in the middle cabin. Front exit row, middle cabin, just behind business class. He had paid extra to ensure that. The exit row had no seat in front. Instead he sat facing two empty jump seats where the crew sat for take-off and landing. His tray table was folded back into the arm rest, his meal tray long since cleared away. But unnoticed the man had kept his knife, metal not plastic. In the other economy cabins two other men had also kept their knives.

The man had not entered the Business cabin. There was no need for him to go there. His friend in the black T-shirt would already have taken care of that section.

In addition, he also knew that the medical case was in the Business cabin, the young man with breathing problems. Julie had initially fussed after him recognising that he might need reassurance during take-off but he had politely brushed off her enquiries after his well-being. If she had the time to look at him now, she would have seen that he looked surprisingly healthy.

* * * *

It was not a loud thump. For a second Kimberley thought she might have imagined it. Did she also imagine a fine mist starting to drift through the cabin? And the quiet, almost imperceptible hiss of air. Suddenly the ceiling was full of yellow as if someone had decided to hang the cabin with bunting. Sunflowers growing upside down from the sky and not the earth. Surreal. There was a pungent smell not unlike burning.

A full two seconds. She felt light headed. Euphoric almost. Somewhere from the back of her brain came the words she had heard and ignored a hundred times. *'Pull the mask towards you. Place it firmly over your nose and mouth, secure the elastic band behind your head and continue to breathe normally.'*

She did as no one was telling her.

At the front of her cabin she saw a flight attendant, stumbling to the galley bulkhead. Her destination was a wall closet, one of several throughout the aircraft with green stickers above the catch. One sticker showed a picture of a cylinder with the symbol O2.

The closet door was swinging open, the contents empty. The man who had only moments earlier passed Kimberley's seat was holding a cylinder in one hand and a gun in the other. The mask over his face had a tube that snaked downwards to the cylinder ensuring that he could continue to breathe normally.

The flight attendant staggered back to the jump seat and made a desperate grab for the mask that was hanging there.

Kimberley felt dizzy.

'Although the bag does not inflate, oxygen will flow to the mask.'

Thank goodness it was true.

* * *

A similar scene was playing out elsewhere on the plane. Some of the cabin crew back there found the door to their oxygen closet jammed tight shut by a small wooden wedge pressed in between the door edge and the frame.

Others found only an empty closet, and also a man with a gun. Unnoticed on the floor nearby lay a small piece of wood and a meal tray knife.

In all cases the portable crew masks were inaccessible. For the crew there was no alternative but to regaining their jump seats.

In the Business cabin the young man with the respiratory problem simply activated his oxygen supply. His nurse smiled as he himself reached for one of the two other extra bottles they had been allowed to bring with them.

Chapter 20

Singapore time: Wednesday 22:30

On the flight deck Julie had roused drowsily just as Simon had seen her do a few hours earlier in the comfort of the Fairmont hotel. Now she was seated at the rear of the flight deck, uncomprehending and zoned out.

The instant Simon had depressurized the cabin, the smaller of the two gunmen had pulled out and clicked a stopwatch. Now the man looked at the dial. Eleven full minutes had gone by. It was time for further instructions.

"In a moment when I tell you. I want you to start a steady descent to FL270." A few more seconds silence and then the command was given. "Now."

Simon gently nudged the control wheel and the aircraft began smoothly losing altitude.

As Simon watched the altimeter he was doing the mental arithmetic. He glanced over. The co-pilot was obviously doing the same. The pointer marked in ten intervals of a hundred feet was steadily rotating at the rate of one rotation every 30 seconds, a descent rate of 2,000 feet per minute.

To descend to FL270 from where they were at 35,000 feet would take just four minutes. That would be getting very close to the time that the emergency oxygen supply to each mask in the passenger cabin would run out. Someone had got a gold star for their maths homework.

* * *

The full fifteen minutes had gone by as they levelled out at 27,000 feet.

Even at this lower altitude they would still be almost two miles higher than Kilimanjaro, a mountain conquered by 99% of climbers without oxygen. But these were people who correctly take several days to acclimatise on the way up.

'Time of Useful Consciousness' had been just a chapter heading in Blue Yonder flight training routine. For Simon it was now a reality. At 27,000 feet the average person could sustain less than 90 seconds oxygen deprivation before being unable to function rationally. Cut that altitude in half again and almost everyone would be fine. To be perfectly safe without oxygen would require being closer to 10,000 feet.

Simon surmised the situation behind him in the passenger cabin, confident that the masks had deployed automatically. But now it was imperative to go lower to get anywhere close to a properly safe altitude where normal unaided breathing could resume. To his great relief the Big Guy gave him clearance to go lower. "Down to 17 thousand as fast as is safe."

* * *

With the depressurisation of the passenger cabins and the plane now dropping rapidly all but the shallow breathers were starting to gasp for oxygen. Apart from those on the flight deck, only six pairs of lungs were functioning at full capacity - one very healthy-looking medical patient plus five others. Each now with their own portable oxygen supply. Six people who knew exactly what they were doing and had little time to waste. Six people who had less than five minutes to secure control of the cabins before a further descent to a lower altitude would enable the rest of the passengers to breathe unaided.

Most of the passengers would be too old, too young or otherwise too weak or frightened to be of much concern to the hijackers. But an earlier reconnaissance of the occupied rows had shown that around a third were marked out as able-bodied males of an age and strength to put up resistance. Just as planned, a manageable number.

On a signal from the Big Guy, one of the captors stepped through into the main cabin and barked an order. "OK, do it!"

Ninety-four passengers remained in their seats unable to move. Anything beyond a half crouch would relinquish the lifeline that was delivering their precious oxygen. One elderly man stood up fully and stepped into the aisle. As he did so the mask snapped from his face. Within seconds he crumpled to the floor gasping. Another passenger tried to use his feet to shove him back towards his seat but the older man no longer had the strength to raise himself up to grab the mask. A few seconds later seven decades of life experience expired on the aircraft floor.

The six men quickly went to work. These were not large men but five of them were solidly built. Low, squat featured, strong armed. The sixth, the medical patient, the exception with a slenderer torso and bright alert brown eyes.

From the seatback pocket in front of them, each pulled out a small bag of nylon straps. To an untrained eye they would resemble nothing more than cable ties. To the airport X-ray machine they had appeared as innocuous strands of plastic. But to the company who touted them on Alibaba, imported from China, they were sold cheaply in packs of a hundred as zip-tie hand cuffs. Easy to pass undetected in hand luggage. But no doubt after this escapade cable ties would be joining badminton rackets, tent pegs and packing tape on the long list of banned items.

The men worked silently and fast, moving from row to row identifying any adult male passenger who might be a potential trouble maker. If Kimberley had been more alert, she would have been indignant that she was not considered a threat.

In a matter of seconds one cuff was zipped to a wrist and the other end to the adjacent seatbelt bracket. The cuffs were advertised with a breaking strength of 240kg. The seatbelt fixings would withstand several times that force.

The lifeless body on the floor of the cabin was more than enough to alert most of the passengers to the futility of resistance. But one, in blue shorts and a sleeveless shirt had other ideas. As one of the captors reached to restrain him Luke stood up to his full height and made a wild swing. The smaller man stepped back, deftly avoiding the blow. At the same time the hijacker at the front of the cabin grabbed the nearest passenger and thrust his gun to her head. "Sit down." A redundant order. The threat was obvious

* * *

It did not take long for the strongest looking passengers in all three cabins to become 100% secure. For good measure the female flight attendants had been restrained too.

In the business cabin with the smallest number of genuine passengers the medical patient had finished his work easily. He had taken more care than the others not to be too rough nor to tighten the cuff to the point that it might constrain blood flow. He walked back through the curtain. Once he received a silent thumbs up from his compatriots to indicate they had also completed their tasks in the more populated parts of the aircraft he moved forward again to give three decisive knocks on the cockpit door.

The Big Guy made his exit from the flight deck leaving his compatriot to guard the pilots. The medical patient was the first to speak.

"Are they alright in there? Did you have to use force?"

"Only a little. But one is dead." The Big Guy showed no disappointment as he whispered to the other. "Listen, if we are to do what is best for the cause then some people are going to get hurt. This is your plan, remember?"

"My plan does not need us to kill people, my brother. If we do that in the struggle to re-unite our homeland, we become no better than those who stole it from us in the first place."

"We shall see." With that the Big Guy re-entered the cockpit and shut the door.

* * *

"What's our altitude now, Captain?"

"17 thousand. Holding steady."

"OK, start the descent again but this time drop much faster. No one is going to give us any trouble now."

"How low are you planning we should go?"

"Right down until you can smell the sea. I will tell you when you can stop."

Now Simon had an incentive to increase the rate of descent. He knew that the faster he could bring the plane down lower the less risk there would be of running out of oxygen at unsustainable altitude. Two or three minutes or so in steep descent and most passengers should be able to breathe fully again without a mask. But after that? What then? So far these guys were not giving anything away. He left a short silence before being compelled to ask.

"Once we are flying low, what then?"

"Then I'll give you the new flight plan and you can switch back to autopilot and have a rest."

Simon did not turn around, but he imagined the guy was definitely smirking.

"And if we don't?" Nabil this time.

"Oh, you will." Nothing more than that. A threat without specifics. The most terrifying kind.

Chapter 21

London time: Thursday 08:00

It should have felt like a new day. But it did not. He had only been away for less than 2 hours yet it seemed that time had ceased to be behaving properly, like having jet lag but without the journey. As Andrew walked back into the Crisis Centre he also pondered time of a different sort. That extra second before Joanna responded to his question about the Paul guy. And also, the length of her parting kiss. He was too tired to think straight about the implications of either.

He regained his seat and moments later Dave called them all to attention.

"OK, folks, we all know that speculation is just that. But ABC News Australia has picked up a report from a lady in Perth. Now before you all tell me that is too far away to be remotely close to any projected flight path, just hold on. This woman, Judi, owns a fleet of fishing boats that ply two stretches of water, one in the south Indian Ocean and the other in the Banda Sea."

As he listened Andrew started tapping away on Google maps eager to pinpoint the latter location. He noticed he was not the only one doing so.

"We recorded this twenty minutes ago." Dave waved a remote at the bank of screens on the wall and the sound instantly unmuted on one of them showing a rather earthy looking middle-aged woman standing outside a suburban bungalow. Quite a large suburban bungalow, with at least 4 cars parked in the background. The banner underneath read 'Judi Ferrier: captain reports possible Blue Yonder sighting'. The woman was speaking in unhurried conversational tones clearly unruffled by the fact that her words were being beamed to millions across the planet.

"Bob is one of my most experienced captains in our fishing fleet, Ferrier's Fish. On this trip he has already been away for 10 days with a crew of 6. I like to keep in touch with my boys and Bob and I were chatting over the radio about 11 o'clock last night when he suddenly broke off and started to describe what he was seeing. An aircraft overhead, about five miles north was heading east and very quickly getting lower and lower in the sky. The way he told it sounded like it was coming down quickly on a steep diagonal," she paused as if considering and then, "what he actually said was 'Christ, Judi, it's coming down more slopey than a Chinky's eye'. Sorry if that is offensive but that's the way he told it. I didn't think much about it at the time, but now with all the news about that Blue whatsit plane I thought I had better say something."

As she spoke the woman remained quite placid and could hardly have been more matter of fact. It was clear to Andrew that earning obvious wealth from sending her men out into lonely darkened seas had not given her any airs and graces. Nor any great degree of fashion sense, judging by her faded shirt and jeans.

Dave flicked the sound off. "There's nothing more. After that she just reports that it disappeared in the distance. What do we think?"

It was Jill who was first to answer. "Doesn't matter what *we* think. Everyone who sees that will now have a mental picture of a Blue Yonder plane plummeting towards the ocean."

"But if that were the case don't you think that this Captain Bob would have relayed witnessing such a scene. If he was that close sure he would have seen it?" Andrew voiced what he knew would be the shared thought of many in the room.

"I am sure you are right but a mystery does a better job of hooking more viewers than does a fact. They will want to keep this one running as long as they can," said Jill

"It's 18 hours now since the aircraft left Singapore. At the very best it would have run out of fuel about ten hours ago. Until we learn otherwise we need to assume it kept flying. So where the hell could it be now and why and how did it get there?" Dave this time.

Andrew, along with the rest of the room, turned to Ana eager to defer to her experience.

"It's not rocket science, guys. Only two possibilities. If the plane was on auto-pilot and the crew for whatever reason were incapacitated then it would have continued to head generally eastwards and could have reached anywhere as far as the Solomon Islands before running out of fuel. Whatever has happened it is still likely to be in that general area, or possibly even further north, maybe around the Philippines. But anywhere else, further south or even turning around would bring it back into pretty solid radar cover."

"So why don't we don't know where it is?" It was Chris, the IT technician who kept the Crisis Centre boxes and wires humming. In his world technology was the answer to everything. "With all these satellites up there surely something would have seen it, Ana?"

"Yes and no. Yes, because the people who could theoretically see it are military, but that is only if they are looking for it, which they are not. Not yet anyway. It's like CCTV in a sweet shop. If you are not looking when the kid steals the candy you can only re-wind later when you realise the chocolate is gone. But, no, because we know the transponder and ACARS are both switched off."

"ACARS?" Andrew heard Chris asking. He could have answered this one himself, but held back, deferring to Ana.

"It means Aircraft Communications and Reporting System. Basically, it is the electronic version of the old voice radio messages. ACARS transmits data such as the aircraft position, altitude, speed and direction. So when it is switched off we lose all that.

She paused. It was worth waiting.

"But there is a kind of yes. Primary ACARS can be switched off, but our aircraft also carry a second terminal called Classic Aero which operates independently and cannot be switched off so long as the aircraft is under power. Classic Aero is a lot less useful. All it does is send out a ping to the Inmarsat satellite system once every hour to synchronise timing information and keep the connection to the satellite network alive. But at least it would establish that the plane is still operational."

That one was new to Andrew.

"Right, we need to get Tom back in here, now," said Dave.

Andrew admired the fact that his CEO always appeared to be on top of things. Always anticipating. Even so, he was as surprised as the rest of the room when Tom walked through the door even as Dave lifted the phone to call.

"Hello again, everybody, I know it's been a long night." Their leader looked as fresh as always. Andrew knew he would not have slept either.

"Did you see that Australian lady on TV just now?" asked Andrew.

"Yes indeed. It's time to notch up a gear. Jill, I need you to draft a statement in response to that speculative report. Focus on the message that we have no confirmed reports of an aircraft coming down. At this point the plane will most definitely have run out of fuel so it must now be our working assumption that the flight is on the ground somewhere. Cautiously optimistic, you know the style. Also, I have given the order to activate the Go Forward team. The back-up flight leaves for Singapore in 75 minutes. Our local manager down there is really struggling. He does not have that many staff in the first place but he has already had to send some of his people down to Brisbane. Friends and family are starting to gather at both ends of the route."

It was Jill with the inevitable question. "Any chance we can keep the Go Forward team deployment under wraps from the media? You know what they will make of it if they find out."

"Pointless," interjected Andrew, "those guys on Rogernigel will be on it within minutes. As soon as they see unscheduled metal with our tail plane taking off and heading east on Flightradar24 they will be all over it."

Tom turned to Andrew. "I see you already have your Grab Bag. Get over to the terminal as soon as you can."

"Sure." Andrew's adrenaline kicked up a notch. He had trained and rehearsed for the Go Forward routine regularly since shortly after joining the airline. But now it was real and he was he was ready for it. With a nod to Dave he picked up his bag and purposefully headed for the door.

"Safe travels, Andrew."

He turned to acknowledge the cluster of other faces looking after him.

"Good morning, Blue Yonder."

Chapter 22

Local time: Wednesday evening

"A bit of a Pilgrimage," Maarten repeated, more quietly the second time Arief enquired. He stopped at that. He did not feel anywhere near ready to share with a stranger the torment of having lost his mother and father all those years ago. Somewhere a mile or so from this very spot was the place where his childhood had abruptly ended as he scampered up a tree, agile as a monkey, and then watched in fright as his parent's tent was flattened beneath a hail of debris. Two days he had spent up that tree, hungry and thirsty…but never cold. Two days for a sleepless frightened orphan to wonder why he had not done more to warn his parents. Even a simple yell would have been something. "Wake up, mum, quick, dad, get up this tree here with me." Just because parents are supposed to look after their children did not mean it cannot work the other way around. For years he had cursed the fact that his first instinct had been to save himself. Self-preservation at its most primal.

Two days until the whirr of helicopter blades announced his rescue and a return first to hospital in the capital and then after a few weeks packed off to his aunt's house back in Rotterdam. The thoughts he had had during his time in the tree branches had never receded. Rather they had grown and engulfed him in a wave of guilt. Why had he not done more? Why had he not done anything at all? Would returning to the scene lead to any sort of closure? Was he a lucky boy? He did not feel it.

"What did you mean by asking me about coming back 'at this time'?"

"Well, it's been a bit crazy around here these past weeks, what with all the changes. And now everyone has been terrified about the volcano."

Maarten flinched. "Yes, the old guy on the corner mentioned it. What did he mean?"

"They reckon it is going to blow again. Pretty soon. Most likely sometime this week. I am told they can be pretty accurate about these things nowadays. Some guys who said they were from the university showed up a couple of months back and set up a monitoring station just outside of town. Scientists, I suppose. Scared the people half to death with their predictions."

Maarten gazed into the distance at the peaceful apex of the mountain. "Looks pretty calm to me."

Arief nodded. "Last week they told us there was a 95% chance it would happen within a week. Then a couple of official looking government guys showed up and ordered everyone to leave the village and get into town. Now as you can see pretty much everyone has left. Apart from that one old man and a few dogs, there's no one else here."

"One old man, and a kid with a football," corrected Maarten, remembering the child he had also seen."

"Yes, they call that one Kema. No one knows his real name. Poor kid is an orphan. When everyone else left he just kind of stuck around. No one to go with."

"And you stayed too?"

"Hope I'm not wrong, but I just plain don't believe them. Neither do the dogs and that's the main thing. My grandfather always reckoned that the animals sense it first. They pick up some kind of vibe in the atmosphere. I am sure you saw them outside. So long as they are not worried then I am not worried either. So, I hid out the back for a morning when the government guys came yesterday for a final check. I'm staying put, not that there is much going on here. My main business, incoming tours, is back in the town. We get cruise ships coming in a couple of times a month. Huge monsters with hundreds coming ashore who need to be fed, watered and ferried around the sites. I have a fleet of buses and two restaurants to cope with that lot."

Arief gestured round the empty room. "Accommodation in the village was never our strong point, just a few volcano nuts from time to time. It's the hardware that keeps me going. Everyone needs this kind of stuff," he gestured through the open door, "makes life easier if you have decent tools to chop wood and carry water. I was doing great business with the scientists, they cleaned me out of spades, saws and axes. But most of them left a week ago. Only a few there now as far as I know."

"How come they needed the tools?"

"I don't think the monitoring part of their job took up too much of their day. I took a look once when I was making a delivery to them. Just a tent with a few machines with dials that didn't seem to need much watching. To pass the time they roped in a bunch of the local kids to clear some ground for a football pitch. I guess that is what the tools were for. I think they got a bit carried away. They cleared a huge swathe. Ended up being more like a straight running track than a soccer field. But it has been great for the teenagers. There is not much to do around here and they are all football mad, watching every English Premier League game on the only satellite TV in the village. Bit of a squeeze in the hut so we bring it outside whenever it is not raining. Now after a game on TV they can go off to their own proper pitch and act like their heroes, falling about the place every time they get tackled."

"Sounds like a win-win. Both sides got something to counter the boredom."

"Anyway, about the 'rhume'. You can take your pick. The best one is directly opposite, across the street. It's even got running water. It's yours for 30 kinas."

"Thanks, I'll take it." Maarten quickly translated the amount to the rough equivalent of the price of two good coffees in Amsterdam. "If you are certain about the volcano I plan to take a little walk out that way tomorrow."

"Sure, come over first and I can point you in the right direction."

"No need. I think I can remember."

It was a short journey that he had seen many times on the ground.

And once from a helicopter.

Chapter 23

Singapore time: Wednesday 22:40

Simon glanced at the Altimeter screen as he had been doing every 30 seconds for the past few minutes. Seven thousand feet and continuing to drop fast. Still blue sky up here but he could see the cloud cover a couple of thousand feet lower. At this height it should now be perfectly possible for the majority of the passengers to survive on the cabin air. Simon had skied at much higher in the Pyrenees without difficulty. A few of the more delicate souls might still struggle but two or three minutes more and even they would be alright too.

Chapter 24

Singapore time: Wednesday 22:45

The gunman at the front had ordered them all to remove their oxygen masks. Kimberley did so and was relieved she could breathe normally. She noticed others were more tentative. She had only had one glass of wine after take-off from Singapore but her head was throbbing and her mouth was dry. She looked across at Luke, her new Australian friend.

"Alright?"

"Not really. My mouth is like the bottom of a parrot's cage, my right wrist is tied to the bloody seat and my fingers are tingling."

"Tied?"

He looked down. "Yeh, some bloody plastic strap. It's pretty tight. There is no way I can break it. What about you?"

Kim raised both arms. "Free as a bird." She pressed the call button on the console in front of her.

No one came. She looked forward and saw two crew members facing towards her, fixed to their jump seats. One male, one female. Kim stood up unsteadily and stepped into the aisle ready to move forward and report this most bizarre of circumstances. Two rows in front of her someone else also stood up and stepped into the opposite aisle. A man. He turned to look at her. Despite her groggy condition she was still able to recognise a gun.

"Sit back down, Miss, you are not going anywhere. Stay in your seat. If I see you moving around again someone will get hurt". He turned again and headed for the front of the cabin, obviously confident that she would obey. For a moment he disappeared behind the curtain. The female cabin attendant, stuck to her seat, mouthed a 'sorry' towards Kim. The male had nothing to contribute except a despondent face.

Kimberley looked across the aisle at Luke.

"What the hell is going on? "she whispered.

"No more idea than you have." He turned his head to survey the rest of the cabin. "It looks like all the other blokes are in the same situation as me. Tied to their seats with these damn plastic things."

"I still feel quite woozy," said Kimberley, "I remember the oxygen masks coming down but then a bit fuzzy after that."

"How far do you think we have gone?" Luke asked her.

She stabbed a finger at the seat-back screen in front of her hoping to find the route map with the flight position. Nothing. She reached over the screen in the adjacent empty seat. Same. Looking around there was not a flicker anywhere.

"No idea. The inflight entertainment system is out so no way to tell where we are now."

"Hold on a minute, there might be."

Kimberley watched Luke as he struggled to reach the right-hand pocket of his jeans with his free left hand. At last, he managed to drag out his cell phone and a dull glow lit up his lap.

"Have you got a signal?"

"Nope. We lost it when the WIFI went out. And even if we were low enough to catch a ground base, either we are in the middle of nowhere or these guys, whoever they are, may have activated a jammer. Probably both."

"A jammer?"

"It's not that difficult. Down in Oz several pubs and restaurants do it to encourage their customers to actually talk to each other. I'll explain some time but right now we need to figure out what all this is about."

Luke stabbed his phone screen a few times and then held it up to the window.

"What good will that do? No signal is no signal."

"Different technology. I have a map app that works off of GPS so all we need is a satellite or three. Up here that should not be a problem." He grinned weakly.

They sat briefly in silence. All around them other passengers were beginning to stir and question their circumstances. Several pressed their call buttons. For a few moments no one spoke. Then several of the men found their voices simultaneously and the cabin filled with cries of confusion and anger as they tugged at their wrist restraints to no avail.

"Bingo." Luke shouted across above the din. Kim was still staring and leaning towards him.

"So where are we then?"

"Over a lot of blue stuff. The Banda Sea, north of East Timor. Heading more west than south west so not exactly making a bee-line for Brisbane."

"Hijacked." A statement, not a question.

Luke looked down and tugged despondently at his right wrist. "Can't argue with you there."

A few of the females in the cabin began to stir and stand up moving into the aisle. The man with the gun reappeared.

"Shut up, all of you. And sit down." There was no point in refusing.

"What's going on, pal?" An impotent yell from the middle of the cabin.

"Nothing to worry about. Everyone stay in your seats and no one will get hurt." Hardly reassuring with one already dead, thought Kimberley.

"I have to pee." A plaintive cry from the back. Female.

"So do I." Kimberley this time. She did not need to but quick thinking told her it would be worth testing the situation sooner rather than later. Quick thinking that was also formulating a plan.

"OK, you first," the man motioned at Kimberley, "but don't try anything. I will be waiting for you."

The crew had not had time yet to clear away all the meal trays. Kimberley scooted across her row of seats to the aisle opposite Luke and as she did so she picked up a piece of cutlery and slid it into her pocket. The man waved the gun in her direction and motioned her forward towards the bulkhead toilets.

"In there, and don't be too long. Make it quick, two minutes. You only have to pee."

He stood back into the exit doorway to let her pass, keeping one eye on her and one on the rest of the cabin where most of the passengers were still staring blankly, trying to grasp what was happening.

Kim pushed the centre of the door which folded in the middle into a V-shape. She moved in quickly and closed the door. She slid the bolt across on the inside, half expecting a shout telling her to keep it unlocked. It did not come.

Kim had not wanted to pee. But now she was inside she did. *Must be Pavlov's toilet.* Maybe in a moment, but first there was something else. The plan was still formulating.

She had remembered that after a particularly good bout in bed she had cheekily asked Andrew if he had ever 'done it' on an airplane. He denied it, but in a way that made her not so sure. Instead he had launched into one of his many passenger stories. He had lots of those. Some of them were probably true.

With a lot of embellishment and even more grinning he told her of a couple who were caught in the act. They had met onboard and after a few hours of drinking and giggling it was more than just their seatbelts that had clicked. The woman was a very frequent flyer and knew the inside of an aircraft better than her own home. She nuzzled into the man's ear and told him exactly what to do. They left their seats, one to the right aisle, one to the left.

Two adjacent toilets mid-cabin with doors opening onto opposite aisles but with a movable partition between them. With a quick flick on each of only two clasps the party wall could be folded back to provide ample combined space for a wheelchair….or a mile-high tryst. The couple had tested the concept and found it most satisfactory. The appropriately named 'party' wall had served its purpose.

Kim looked up at the top of the partition wall and immediately spotted the clasps. At least that part of the story was true. So was the bit about the quick flick and the opening up. As she moved through into the other space she reached into her pocket for the cutlery. A knife. Not made of plastic. Not particularly sharp, but good enough.

Quietly Kim opened the door opposite and crouching low crawled into the cabin. A few rows back and staring straight ahead sat Luke. He saw her immediately. Puzzled. She made the universal finger to the lips with one hand and with the other held aloft the knife so he could see it. Then with a waving motion she indicated what she was about to do. Luke nodded his understanding.

Kneeling to the floor Kim gave a few warm up swings and then sent the knife sliding along the cabin floor towards Luke. Like skimming a stone into the water. It only took a second but in the slow motion of her mind she saw it falling way short. In the real world it landed only a few inches from Luke's row. As she disappeared back into the toilet he reached out and quickly scraped it across into the seat well with his right foot.

The whole thing had taken less than 30 seconds. Kim replaced the partition. She reckoned she deserved a pee. No reason not to keep the guy waiting.

As Kim returned to her seat, Luke was busy trying to reach down for the knife. Taking his mobile phone out of his pocket had been easy compared to this. He gave up trying to stretch across his knees with his left hand to reach the floor. Gently sliding the knife to his left side with his right foot made it less difficult. Not easy but less difficult. Moments later he had the knife in his left hand and was sawing away at the restraint around his right wrist. It was not going to be quick. The knife may have been metal but it was designed for chicken or beef, not tough plastic. He had still not managed it when he saw Kim returning to her seat.

This was going to take a while.

Chapter 25

Singapore time: Wednesday 23:00

Flight 10 had broken through the cloud cover and was now fast approaching the sea. At this low-level Simon had already re-set the altimeter to properly gauge the true height above sea level. Dispensing with 'flight level' the instrument now showed that they were a mere fifteen hundred feet above the waves. His eye told him that too. The water was clear and flat. An airplane could land on that, skim across the surface and float awhile before finally sinking under. His mind flickered to the famous 'Miracle on the Hudson' episode back in 2009 when two pilots safely brought 155 passengers onto the river just off midtown Manhattan. He did not fancy entering the record books as 'the second most successful ditching in aviation history.' Far worse was the thought of being among the least successful.

"What now?" asked Simon.

The big man pulled a scrap of paper from his pocket and thrust it forward.

"Program these waypoints into the flight management system"

Simon scanned down to the end of the list of printed map coordinates. Longitude and latitude. South and east, S4340.3 E15237.9.

One fifty-two east was good news. Almost exactly the same latitude as Brisbane airport. Only one-degree difference, so in terms of continuing their easterly flight direction no problem on the fuel front. But the airport they had been heading for was on a longitude of twenty-seven degrees south, not four. Four degrees south would put their destination very close to the equator and still way above the Australian coastline.

He began punching the numbers beneath his right hand into an oversized keypad that looked like a 1970s calculator, or a telephone for the elderly and confused. Where on earth were they heading? Hopefully it would be 'on earth', or more accurately on concrete. He hoped for lots of that, hard smooth and flat. Strong enough to withstand two hundred tons of aircraft hitting it at 140 knots.

"So not Brisbane then?" Simon enquired

"No."

"Where then?".

"You will find out when we get there."

"And when will that be?"

"If you do not do anything stupid, about 3 hours."

Simon instantly assimilated that revealing the remaining journey length showed a high level of confidence. Confidence that nothing would or could be communicated beyond the cockpit, confidence that nothing stupid would be done and that the big guy figured the prospect of military fighter planes coming alongside or worse still shooting them down was a non-starter. Relief, but worrying.

Chapter 26

Singapore time: Wednesday 23:00

Back in the cabin Luke was nursing 5 numb fingers. The knife Kim had skimmed to him had taken several minutes to weaken and eventually snap the plastic restraint. During his exertions the amount of blood pulsing into his right hand had been next to nothing. What now? He reckoned he was definitely a match for the gunman at the front of the cabin who was shorter by several inches and not particularly fit looking either. But common sense told him that there would be more than one guy onboard. Even just one in each cabin and one in the cockpit would mean four. Probably more like six.

He looked across and smiled weakly at Kim. For now he would bide his time.

Chapter 27

Singapore time: Thursday 02:00

About three hours the Big Guy had said. It had been almost three hours. The aircraft was still on auto pilot and for the first two hours had flown over nothing but sea. Then for the past 45 minutes or so they had been overflying the land mass of Papua New Guinea. A place Simon knew nothing about. A place most commercial pilots other than a handful of Australians would never have to land in reality or even in simulator practice. On one of the many screens in front of him he could see the only sizeable dot was Port Moresby, the largest city, situated on a finger of land jutting out south east from the bottom of the island. But the waypoints in the flight management system were taking them to the north of there and heading further east still.

As he looked down Simon saw the east coast of the main island slipping behind them. 152 degrees east was the last latitude he had been ordered to program. He hoped the destination was not much further than that. Ahead lay the Solomon Islands and then after that nothing but 9,000 miles of the Pacific Ocean until the coast of Peru.

"So it is the Solomon Islands then?" he ventured. "Hope they have somewhere big enough to land this thing."

"They do not," muttered the Big Guy.

Simon had long realised that these guys, whoever they were, had clearly done their homework and lots of it. This was no spur of the moment action. More likely something that had been a long time in the planning and something that involved more than just the 6 or 8 men onboard. They definitely knew what they were doing. Hopefully that would include knowing that wherever they were indeed heading would be somewhere they could land safely.

But where? They were leaving Port Moresby behind and well to the south. Anywhere else with enough concrete to land a Boeing 777 would have to be somewhere with the existing infrastructure to accept large commercial aircraft. And that would mean somewhere where the plane would be parked on the outfield, most probably surrounded by armed police and soldiers itching to storm the cabin with stun grenades while some sort of lengthy negotiations took place? Simon was well aware of such instances in the past. Mostly they did not end well.

"We are getting close to the final waypoint." A statement from Simon. A short pause, followed by a question. "Where after that?"

"That's it. After that you will switch to manual and keep going until I tell you to bring us down."

"Down where?"

"You'll see. Don't worry everything is prepared."

At this point in a normal flight Simon would be doing the wrap-up spiel over the intercom, thanking everyone for flying Blue Yonder and going on about local time and outside temperature. No point in that now. And if only he knew it, no point either in 'cabin crew, 30 minutes to landing' directed at the team behind them who were cuffed to their seats.

Chapter 28

Singapore time: Thursday 02:10

Back in the cabin Kimberley could feel the change in air pressure on her ears as she intermittently went deaf and then swallowed hard. She looked over at Luke.

"I think we are coming down to land. Can you see anything out your side?"

Luke took advantage of his unrestrained wrist and scooted over to his window seat. It had been light for a while a now.

"Coastline. A lot of sea. Maybe some sort of island or peninsula. We are heading over land, thank goodness. But there are just trees. Lots of them. A few clearings with some huts or something but I am not seeing a runway. Not anywhere."

"That doesn't sound good." Kimberley stated the obvious. "Let's hope there is an airport up ahead somewhere."

She watched Luke swiftly moving back to his aisle seat as two gunmen appeared at the front of the cabin.

One was a big man. A man in charge. He made no announcement about upright tray tables, upright seatbacks and taking a moment to be reminded of the nearest exit but his pronouncement in a loud voice without the intercom, conveyed all they needed to hear. "OK, we are going to land soon. Sit tight."

Kimberley reflected ruefully that all the males in the cabin had no option but to obey and 'sit tight'. Except one.

The Big Guy turned to leave as his smaller accomplice came forward. As he drew level with their row Kimberley watched Luke spring out of his seat. With one blow he knocked the gun out of his captor's hand and with a kick to the guy's stomach sent him faltering to the floor. The gun landed three rows back. Luke leapt over the prone body and started towards the weapon. Three seconds and he would have made it. But he only got to two before the Big man, standing in the other aisle yelled across.

"Leave it!"

Luke ignored the shout. One second more and he had leant down, picked up the gun and half raised himself back up to a crouching position.

"Drop it!" Louder this time. Kimberley looked across in the direction of the sound. The Big Guy was glaring at Luke, and at the same time pointing his weapon at the head of his nearest female passenger, a terrified elderly Asian lady. The implications were obvious.

Luke dropped the gun and returned to his seat. The Big guy came over quickly and slapped him hard in the face before producing a new cable tie from his pocket.

Chapter 29

Singapore time: Thursday 02:15

The one who had posed as the medical patient sensed that he was about to be blamed for the actions of the unrestrained passenger. He was right.

"Next time, be more careful, brother," the Big Man snarled at him. "We need to do this right. This may be your plan, but it is my operation."

"Sorry, Zar, I thought he was still tied to the seat."

"Don't speak my name. When this is all done we don't want to be identified."

"When this is done, it won't matter. We will have our country back," he replied.

He was the one who the other would have called Zico before they boarded the plane. The one who was the smarter of the two and had always let his bigger brother protect him in happier times as boys.

It was decades now since the farcical 'Act of Free Choice had ceded their birthright to another nation. Half their former homeland had been lost as the country was sliced in two by a perfectly straight line, save for the wiggle of a river at its centre. It was he, Zico, who had pointed out that the appearance of the enforced new border on a map resembled that of a dying vital signs hospital monitor. He was the one who said that the blip in the middle of the line was like a flicker of life, a small sign of hope.

He was the one who had studied International Business with a minor in tourism, a non-existent activity in their remote and backward country. One day people might come there, but for now there was no compelling reason to do so. No 'unique selling proposition' as the jargon in his textbooks had taught him.

And then there were people like his brother, Zar, eager to fight in the hopeless struggle against superior forces. But early acts of armed aggression were easily repelled especially as some of the arms were little more than spears and clubs.

Zico was the one who saw best that neither the political overtures nor the low-key armed struggle was getting them anywhere. Advancing their cause was being hindered by that universal lubricant – money. Being poorly funded lay at the root of their stalled progress. Without expensive professional PR to pump a continuous stream of stories to the global media, without properly financed delegations to trawl the worlds' institutions, without something more than sharp sticks and ancient rifles Zico feared that another half century could easily pass without resolution It was from these thoughts that Zico first mooted a new approach. A well thought out strategy that properly executed would provide more than enough funds to accelerate their journey towards freedom for their homeland. A plan which was now, at last, unfolding.

Chapter 30

Local time: Thursday 07:00

With the advantage of a forward view Simon was struggling to conjure up any optimism about an airport ahead. They were still over the island of New Britain, but only just. A few miles in front he could see coastline. After that there would be nothing but thousands of miles of Pacific Ocean. He looked downwards. Just trees. The aircraft was now lower than a thousand feet above ground level. And even closer than that to the tree tops.

He had practiced and practiced many hours in the Blue Yonder simulator a huge variety of emergency landings. But not one that brought a wide-bodied aircraft to nestle gently on the tops of a forest.

"Where exactly?" Simon asked as calmly as he could. "I kind of need to know that now right now."

"A minute more and you will see."

Simon strained his gaze ahead for any signs of a runway. Nothing. Another thirty seconds went by. Still nothing.

Then both pilots saw it at once. A clearing. A clearing among the trees. A clearing with no huts in the middle. Wide enough and probably just long enough. But not by much. The surface was green, not gray.

"Is that it?"

"Yes. Take her down."

"You realise we have got more than two hundred tons laden weight here and that is just grass?"

"Grass on top maybe. But you will be fine. Trust me. Take her down. Now."

Grass on top? What did that mean?

"And if I do not?" Simon already surmised this was a pointless question.

"Then your friend here does it. Otherwise we shoot you both. There are others with us who can do it. So you might as well do as I say.

With horror, Simon realised the Big Guy was right.

Chapter 31

Local time: Thursday 07:15

Maarten's father and mother were both keen birdwatchers which was part of the attraction for them of this part of the world. With over 700 exotic bird varieties from flowerpeckers, honeyeaters and parrots to the vibrantly colourful birds of paradise his parents only had to sit on canvas stools at the door of their tent, binoculars and notebooks in hand to be quietly content for hours on end. It was during such times that Maarten would wander off and play at the edge of the surrounding jungle. At first, he would just chase off the monkeys, climb the lower reaches of a few trees to see if he could get high enough to glimpse the sea which lay in a bay a few hundred meters away to the east.

But on this, the second morning of their holiday together he came across something more exciting than a few creepers and the exotic birds that were keeping his parents so raptly entertained. He nearly missed it at first, passing over to scurry up a tree. Then on the way down and jumping the last few feet he stumbled and fell to the ground grazing his shin on a piece of rock. Squatting down to nurse the bruise he took a closer look at the stone. It was oddly square. In fact, not stone at all but a corner block of concrete jutting a few inches above the ground.

Brushing away the covering vegetation was not easy but the more he pulled and tugged the more smooth concrete was revealed. The sheath knife his parents had given him for his last birthday came in to its own as he used it to hack and slice away more and more of the tangled green undergrowth. It took him more than twenty minutes before his labour was rewarded with the realisation that the concrete formed a framework. A horizontal framework for a heavy metal door almost a meter square.

The door was unlocked and heavy. But not heavy enough to defy a healthy 12-year-old boy using a strong knife as a lever. On the third attempt it swung through 180 degrees and hit the ground with a thump. He was breathing heavily with the exertion as a wave of cool musty air invaded his nostrils. He put his head into the newly opened space and stared down into the darkness. It was a moment he never forgot. The treasure beneath that door became his secret and for the rest of the days until the holiday was cut short he visited every day.

* * *

Maarten thought about the trapdoor again now. Would it still be there? Of course it would. Perhaps later, once he had completed his pilgrimage to the memory of his parents, he might see if he could find it again. After the passing of so many years the rainforest would not make that an easy task. It would be hard enough to satisfy the prime reason for his trip by finding the clearing where his holiday had ended and the tree that had saved his life.

It was definitely a well-worn path from the village to the place he was heading. No vehicles, but many feet had certainly trod this way. Frequently and recently, otherwise within days the vegetation would have started to reclaim its natural space.

He had been walking for almost an hour and reckoned it would not be much further now until he reached the area where he and his parents had camped during that last holiday together.

The air was full of noise with a cacophony of bird calls merging together to form the Muzak of the forest. It was just beginning to get light. Maarten stopped and listened intently to see if he could single out his favourite, the aptly named Superb Bird of Paradise, with its tack-tack-tack rhythmic call. An impossible task to identify any single call amid the wall of chatter, squawks and trills emanating all around. Then gradually the sound grew louder. Louder and deeper. But not from the bird song. At first a distant drone, but then followed by an increasing rumble that he easily identified as the engines of an approaching aircraft. Louder still. He looked up beyond the treetops and there it was, flying low. This was no small propeller plane of the type that had brought him only yesterday to the tiny local airport. This was a huge commercial jet more like the one he had flown in from Amsterdam. The plane was descending rapidly and was now dangerously low.

The birdsong stopped and the air shook around him as the plane passed directly overhead casting a fleeting shadow across the ground where he stood. For a moment Maarten was puzzled. Puzzled and scared. He knew little about aeronautics but it was obvious this plane was very close to landing. Landing on the treetops of a dense rainforest, considering there was no proper commercial airport within miles.

Then suddenly it struck him. He *knew* where it would come down. There was only one place possible. And it was very close.

That last summertime Maarten had played there for days on end. While his parents sat by the tent he had roamed this secret kingdom. Every day a new direction, and every day a new discovery. At first this area had seemed like the middle of nowhere but very quickly he had realised that people had been here before. Lots of people. Long ago people and not just the natives from the huts and villages.

Gradually he had figured it out. He had never told anyone. In the aftermath of his parents' death he had almost forgotten about it. There were plenty of other thoughts then to fill the mind of a twelve-year-old orphan boy. It was only years later in the university library when his studying was going badly that something jolted his memory and after thumbing through a few books in the historical section he had been able to confirm his theory, his childhood conjecture of what this place had been.

The plane had disappeared from sight but it could only be seconds now until it came down. Maarten had imagined the scene many times in the days he had played here. A big fat bellied machine dropping out of the sky and thundering across the forest floor. He wanted to close his eyes but did not.

Any second now, surely?

Chapter 32

Local time: Thursday 07:17

Simon felt the wheels meeting the grass. First the undercarriage then the nose wheel. The thump was more muted than that on concrete but the feel was surprisingly firm. Two seconds… three, four, five, six…. The aircraft continued moving forward. Smoothly. Surprisingly smooth, but far too fast. On either side and frighteningly close, greenery whizzed backwards. Up ahead more greenery. *How far ahead?* Close enough that the plane would smack into it in another twenty seconds. Simon's mind flashed to difficult landings, especially fun ones on the simulator like the old Hong Kong airport, or the one airport in Bhutan ringed by Himalayan peaks that seemed to reach out in an effort to puncture the fuselage. For those ones it was the coming down that presented the challenge not the efforts to decelerate fast enough to avoid hitting a line of trees. The spoilers had automatically deployed, reverse thrust was at maximum. His foot on the hydraulic brake pedal was flat to the floor. There was nothing more he could do.

* * *

Kimberley felt the thump, moved to the brace position and waited for the bang. It did not come.

* * *

Maarten ran forward. Not easy in the heat but he knew only a few seconds would take him to the edge of the clearing. And moments later when he broke through the tree line, there it was. The scene he had imagined so many times in his games. A giant aircraft juddering to halt at the very far end of what had once been a runway. Gently rolling towards what Arief told him had very recently become a football pitch.

Chapter 33

Local time: Thursday 07:19

Simon felt the sweat beneath his light short-sleeved shirt. He looked across at Nabil who returned a nod of congratulation. An appropriate response to the man who had just succeeded in safely landing two hundred tons of airplane in a jungle clearing with no external guidance

The Big Guy with the gun had expected nothing less. "Well done." Perfunctory. No hint of admiration.

This is how it had been planned. And now this is how it was. They were on the ground with the captive passengers and crew having left the outside world completely clueless as to their location. To the rest of the world they were lost. Off the grid, off the radar. Out of sight, but if things in the outside world were also going to plan then they would definitely be front of mind.

Simon peered forward through the windscreen. The horizontal treeline was less than 100 metres ahead, just slightly more than a single plane length. And in that space the vegetation at either side was little more than the width of the wingspan for about half the distance but then it tapered closer and closer towards the end. Thank goodness he had managed to pull up as quickly as he had done.

"OK," the Big Guy tapped Simon on the shoulder, "get on the intercom and tell your passengers to stay calm and stay in their seats. So long as no one tries anything stupid there is nothing to worry about. "

Simon flicked the intercom on and paused a moment. Hundreds of times he had spoken to those rows of passengers behind him, the unseen crowds who paid his wages. But always before it was when he was in full control of the facts. The weather, the altitude, the time of day, the outside temperature…all things known. He was used to being the reassuring purveyor of the situation in the world they were about to step into when disembarking. This time was different. He was as clueless as they were. Not even sure if they would disembark.

"OK folks," he started with the familiar form of address so beloved of American pilots. Under the circumstances, better than the more British 'ladies and gentlemen'. Whatever was about to happen they were all in this together. 102 passengers infiltrated with 8 bad guys plus 2 flight deck and 10 cabin crew. Those were the facts he knew.

"As you will have realised we have now landed, but not in Brisbane. We have some people onboard who apparently don't want us to go there.......yet. There is no cause for alarm." *Stupid*, he realised as soon as he said it. The very words that instantly make unimaginable horror imaginable. Better recover quickly. "We are safely on the ground and as soon as I can I will get back to you with an update on our situation. Meanwhile please remain in your seats with your seatbelts securely fastened until the engines are switched off and the seatbelt sign is off."

Behind him fifty or so males tugged at their wrist restraints. The one who had enjoyed brief freedom was among them. Luke had long since been re-tied.

"Good" instructed the Big Guy. "Now ease this thing forward as far as you can go until the nose is up against those trees ahead."

Simon looked at Nabil, knowing he would be thinking the same thing. Airplanes are amazing feats of ingenuity. They can hurtle across the ground at over 150 mph, they can ascend to almost 8 miles high and transverse the widest oceans with impunity. But the one thing they cannot do under their own power is move backwards. Not in the air, and not on the ground. An insect stranded on its back has more chance of righting itself. Not so much a design fault, just that there is no need. And wherever they were now there was not an aircraft tug in sight. Simon knew that if he kept his aircraft sitting where it was right now there would still be enough room to turnaround and at least in theory take off again. Moving any further forward into the chicane of vegetation would condemn the machine to remaining earthbound unless they were to be rescued.

There did not seem to be any point in arguing. Simon eased

the throttle and the giant aircraft crawled forward until the nose was only a few feet from the trees. On either side some of the overhanging branches had gently brushed the wing-tips in passing.

"Shut down the engines but keep the cabin APU running." Simon obeyed. More flight deck jargon from these guys who knew what they were doing. APU meant the auxiliary power unit, in simple terms a generator housed by the tail plane that would keep the cabin power and air conditioning running almost indefinitely, for as long as there was fuel in the main tanks.

"What now?" Simon asked.

"Doors to manual, then we will get some of the people off this thing."

'Doors to manual' the refrain heard by every arriving passenger, every day, everywhere, simply meaning to disarm the inflight status that determines that should a door be opened the evacuation slide would automatically inflate and shoot down to the ground almost as quickly as a car airbag in an accident.

"And how will we deplane people without a ground crew?" Nabil this time.

"No problem, we will use one of the slides."

Chapter 34

Local time: Thursday 07:25

Back in the cabin everyone was now awake. There had been a crescendo of chatter until in each section the men in charge had told everyone to shut up. Kimberley could hear a range of anxious exchanges quietly connecting pairs of confused faces. *What is going on? Where are we? Who are these guys? Are you alright? Can you get a phone signal? I have no bars. Nothing! Are you tied up too? Don't worry. Stay calm. I love you.*

At the front of the economy cabin Kimberley saw one of the two armed men moving towards the door. He turned to the flight attendant, the one who had seemed to be in charge but who right now was looking a bit spacey as she stood by her jump seat.

"OK, arm the door."

Kimberley watched as the woman flicked a switch. Then the guy who had spoken pushed her aside and as indicated in three languages in red font on the door panel he pulled the huge lever in the direction of the red arrow and the door obligingly thrust outward. A blast of hot humid air rushed into the cool cabin and as Kimberley looked out of her window she saw the evacuation slide unfurl like a party blow-out noise maker and then drop to meet the ground.

"OK, the first nine women towards the front gather some things quickly and come forward to this door. Bring only your passport, one blanket, one pillow, one sweater and whatever toiletries and medicines you can carry in the sick bag. Also take the sim card out of your phone and have it in your hand. You have two minutes." The man waved his gun to indicate the appointed nine.

Kimberley was number eight. As she quickly gathered together the allowable items she wondered about the sweater. She had not packed one in her carry on, thinking it the last thing she would need this side of winter. Why might they need one here?

Wherever they were it was certainly not cool outside. The humid jungle air was already percolating the cabin and fighting the AC to some effect. Locating the sim card and removing it from her phone was fiddly. Not something she did every day. She had already established that there was no signal onboard so deactivating the phone was hardly going to make any difference.

She looked across at Luke. She could see the phone in his hand hoping he might still have its GPS app activate. "Where are we now?" she whispered.

"Nuburton," was what she thought she heard.

"No talking," barked the man with gun.

Kimberley moved away to stand along with the others in the aisle by the door, like sky-divers waiting to be pushed.

The gunman moved along the line and took the sim card from each of them. "I doubt you will get a signal down there. But just in case. Throw your stuff down ahead of you. Fold your arms across your chest and don't grab the sides. Go, go!"

The woman at the front, a middle-aged Asian lady who looked terrified hesitated a moment before being given an abrupt shove. Off she went screaming like a child on a helter skelter. The others got the message as each one voluntarily sat quietly down and slid earthwards. Five, six, seven…..and then Kimberley. She threw her belongings in front of her but instinctively kept hold of the pillow and used it to sit on. Why she did that she had no idea. The warm air rushed past and the sweet smell of vegetation filled her nostrils, a welcome change from the stale dry atmosphere of the past few hours. If it were not for the horror of the situation she might have been enjoying this.

She hit the ground and stepped up to gather her belongings and move forward. Within seconds the last two behind her had joined the group. Ten? What happened to nine? Then Kimberley realised that the final woman was the flight attendant who had been standing by the door. She too had been commandeered. She too had a small bag of belongings. A tall woman with a no-nonsense look about her. Kimberley gave her a slight nod. It was returned. As if to say *'so we are the only two Caucasians in this lot. We might have to trust each other. We might have to see what we can do about this situation.'* A primal recognition of another like herself. The type of instinct that would be totally redundant in a homogenous shopping mall crowd back in London or Brisbane. But here, in this place, in this particular small group, in this reality it was different.

On the ground a man Kimberley had not seen before started to usher them into a tight group. He was not dressed like the men on the plane. Instead he was wearing long khaki trousers, stout walking boots and a long-sleeved camouflage shirt stained with sweat. He carried a gun.

The man waved the gun in the air, unthreateningly. Looking round Kimberley realised the wave was an acknowledgement to one of the hijackers from the plane who had quietly launched himself down the slide and was now dusting himself off. He was a small man. Compared to the other men in black T-shirts, Kimberley thought his face less harsh. If not kindly, then neutral, like someone ready to lead a group of ramblers for a Sunday hike in the Blue Mountains. Moving together the gunman embraced the other with a smile and Kimberley heard an obvious greeting in a foreign tongue. '*Zico, temanku.*' The small man acknowledge the greeting with a nod.

It was obvious to her that their arrival had been expected. This landing in this place was no accident. *Why not make a run for it? There are ten of us and only two of them. Yes, but where to? Which direction? Where was the nearest habitation? A hundred meters, or a hundred miles? Two with guns.* For now, it seemed there was nothing else for it but to follow instructions.

The group moved off towards the tree line along a narrow pathway that appeared to have been recently hacked through the dense vegetation. For two or three minutes they walked in single file with the man in khaki taking up the rear. Then just as suddenly as the vegetation had begun it ended and they were standing in a clearing about the size of a tennis court. The ground was flat and featureless apart from the far-left corner where there was a small stone wall about a meter high and ten meters long. Behind it stood another man. Visible from only the chest upwards Kimberley assumed he was either very short or else sitting down. From the look of his shirt she could see he was dressed in similar fashion to the other man who had already awaited them on the ground. Raising his arm above the wall the man beckoned them over.

"Go. There." The man in khaki instructed from behind. The group moved forward tramping over the hot earth. Kimberley realised it was less than an hour ago that she was dozing in a cocoon of safety and now here she was, on the ground, separated from the rest of the passengers in some desolate place being herded to goodness know where. The bling of Singapore Changi airport was surely not just a few hours ago?

The group reached the other side of the clearing and was ushered round behind the low wall to where a thick metal trap door lay open revealing a large square hole in the earth. The man who had beckoned them over was standing a couple of steps down on a stone stairway leading into the gloom. Neither short nor seated, Kim realised.

The group hesitated. None of them had yet spoken to any of the others. Ten of them, a group only in the sense of numbers. So far, apart from one exchanged smile, no interaction, no sense of shared situation or destiny. Kim wondered if she should act alone and simply break away from the two unarmed men. *How would they react to that? Would one of them chase after her and strong arm her back? Would they shoot? Would others join her?* Looking around at the other mainly Asian women she doubted it. A lifetime of group conformity would most likely keep them all together.

The last few paces Kimberley had deliberately walked slowly until number nine overtook her and she was now left standing in front of the flight attendant.

"I'm Kimberley," she whispered over her shoulder.

"Julie."

"Yes, I saw your name badge just before I jumped."

"Quiet" came the command. "No talking. Go down." In single file the ten women entered the darkness.

As eyes became accustomed a weak light was switched on. And then with thump the door above them closed.

Chapter 35

Local time: Thursday 07:35

Now, all these years later, as he crept forward Maarten watched as the giant aircraft came to a halt against the far tree line. A landing befitting his boyhood imagination. What on earth was going on here? Had there been some sort of inflight technical emergency which had forced the captain to land immediately in whatever terrain he could find? If so it was an incredible stroke of luck to find somewhere that had even the semblance of a runway.

Maarten saw a door open on the nearside of the aircraft. A brightly colored slide shot quickly outwards and then down to where another waiting man nudged it into position. Within a few seconds people began leaping away from the plane and careering earthwards. Even from this distance he could make out that they were all female. *Women and children first?* It kind of fit his emergency landing theory.

But just as quickly as it had started the evacuation stopped. Not even a dozen people were on the ground, brushing themselves off and picking up scattered bundles of whatever it was they had thrown down in front of them. All women. *Surely there were more people on the aircraft? Why only this number coming off?*

The women formed into a single file behind one of the men while the other took up the rear and began to cajole them forward towards a narrow gap in the trees. Maarten could easily make out that the two men were armed. He knew nothing of weapons but he could see each had some sort of rifle. A moment later they had disappeared into the forest.

Maarten's first instinct had been to rush over and help but now he was not so sure. It might be better to figure out exactly what was going on before making anyone aware of his presence.

From his vantage point the aircraft lay almost directly ahead with the path taken by the women off to its left. Rather than reveal himself by crossing the open ground in front of him

Maarten took a few paces backwards and then began his clockwise journey round the perimeter of the undergrowth. At first the going was pretty tough but then luckily, he stumbled upon a faint path, not great, but recent enough to make progress a lot easier. It had been a long time ago but he knew exactly where he was heading.

Chapter 36

Local time: Thursday 08:00

Back in the cockpit Nabil watched through the window as the last of the women disappeared into the rainforest. The big guy standing behind him reached forward and picked up the handset from the central console and flicked the on switch. Unaccustomed as he surely was to public speaking his voice carried an undoubted authority. Those listening would certainly realise this guy was in charge. No polite 'ladies and gentlemen, girls and boys' and no 'this is your captain speaking.'

"Attention. You do not need to know where we are but you do need to understand how you must behave until we get what we want."

This was one announcement that everyone was going to listen to, Nabil thought grimly. One they had never heard before. And one they would never forget.

"It is not our intention to be here very long, just until we get what we want. If you behave properly no one will be harmed and our well-prepared plans mean you will not be too uncomfortable. In a moment we will need help from some of you. Please cooperate when you are told. But first you need to realise that some of us are with some of you in each cabin as well as here in the cockpit. Also, our friends on the ground have a group of female passengers outside in the forest. Any bad behaviour from any of you in one group will bring immediate punishment to those elsewhere. Anyone trying to be a hero will cause the death of another."

Nabil's brain was already clicking into military gear. Back in the Lebanon, prior to entering civil aviation, his Special Forces training had been far more about quick assessment of dangerous situations than the brute force of taking out the enemy. And what he had just heard left him in no doubt that these guys, whatever they wanted, definitely knew exactly what they were doing. Dividing their hostages into different groups in two different locations was smart, very smart. That would vastly increase the difficulty of any future rescue attempt. Any two-pronged assault that was not meticulously synchronised would quickly lead to disaster for one of the groups. It would also subdue any heroics from those still in the cabin knowing that some of the women were being held elsewhere.

So far, no demands but the phrase 'just until we get what we want' had been said twice. Nabil thought he might as well ask.

"What exactly is it that you want?"

"For now you do not need to know. If all goes well you will find out later."

"And what if 'all does not go well'?"

"It will. Unless someone does something very foolish."

There was a pause. Not a long one, before Nabil heard four knocks on the cockpit door. Any normal knock would be twice or three times. No one gives four knocks. *Another sign of a well-rehearsed signal.* The Big Guy turned and motioned to his compatriot to open it. The two pilots swiveled round and saw bad guy number three facing them in the doorway. A shorter man much smaller. Shorter, thinner but with strong arms. He was wearing a headband flashlight of the kind worn by night hikers.

"Ready, boss?"

"Yes. Go down now."

Nabil looked through the flight deck open door as the short, muscly guy stepped back into the cabin, bent down and stripped away a square of carpet. He raised the flush handle in the floor beneath and with a quick tug opened the trapdoor. Reaching in he flicked the light switch to reveal the short metal ladder leading down into the space below. He entered quickly. The reverse action of going up into an attic. Not much room, but that was of no consequence. He had been picked for the job.

* * *

As he reached the bottom of the ladder short muscly guy looked around the cramped space. It was just as it had been on the YouTube video. The one he had watched over and over again. He was in the Avionics Bay, a place housing much of the electronic wizardry that supports the magic of flight. Not somewhere ever normally accessed inflight but a place visited frequently by the maintenance ground crew. But small guy was not here to marvel at the circuitry. His destination was elsewhere. He moved past several large cylinders racked on the wall, bottles containing the oxygen that had kept Simon and Nabil alert and flying while their passengers relied on a less exhaustive separate supply behind them.

He knew the nook where he stood had three doors. One he had used to enter and one was in the floor leading to the outside. This was far from being a game show but his interest was definitely in what was behind door number three. In such a small space he found it easily and stepped quickly through to find himself in the darkness of the forward cargo hold.

Ahead of him, in the beam of his headband flashlight, stood rows of baggage containers. His homework had told him that a Boeing 777 has space to slide in up to 32 of these aluminium cubes in the forward hold. And, just as in the video, the guy was relieved to see that only one row of containers lay between the Avionics Bay entry door where he stood and the external unloading bay.

He looked at the containers, essentially square pegs in a big round hole, leaving just a small space between their perpendicular sides and the curvature of the aircraft frame. Small but just wide enough. The little guy squeezed in and wriggled through towards the loading bay door. Each container had a fabric entry flap that comprised one side of the cube. As he stood there he was able to unlatch the one adjacent to the open door. *Yes, this was the one.* The two accomplices at Heathrow Ground Handling had done their job well. Without them this load might have ended up being buried at the very back of the container rows leading to a much more difficult and time-consuming exercise. The guy peered inside and saw exactly what he expected – four enormous cardboard boxes with the words 'Pitch Perfect -Your weatherproof soccer field covering' stamped on the side. He re-tied the flap then turned to activate the mechanism for the external door from a panel on the wall. Slowly the gull-wing structure rose on its hinges giving a slight jolt to the airframe. Looking out from this vantage point three meters above the ground the man had a wide view of the thick foliage that enveloped the narrow space in which the plane now stood. Beyond the treetops and in the distance he could see the smouldering top of the nearest volcano. Wisps of smoke against the pale blue sky. No reason to be alarmed. He had been briefed. Fifteen years since the last outpouring. But then again volcanoes were hardly known for their predictability.

Shifting his gaze downwards the guy saw that all sides of the small clearing below were stacked high with piles of cut brush, some of it still quite green, but most already having turned brown in the heat. Branches, leaves and creepers of all kinds.

Two other members of the team were waiting in the clearing below and as they both looked up one of them called out.

"Ready?"

"Ready."

He knew what to do.

Chapter 37

Local time: Thursday 08:15

Back in the cabin Luke sat gazing at his numb fingers. Having been hit once, he was itching to try again. Not sure what, but something. No clear plan yet but his thoughts were interrupted by the approach of one of the armed men.

"We need four of you outside now. You, you, you and you."

As he pointed out the selected four, all male, the man moved forward brandishing a retractable blade knife and proceeded to cut each one free. Luke noted that the chosen quartet were clearly among the biggest and strongest in the cabin. Himself plus three others, but he was not going to try anything while ten of the women remained out of sight elsewhere on the ground. As far as Luke was concerned it was Kimberley plus nine. More than enough of a deterrent until the odds could be changed.

The four were ushered forward towards the open plane door. This time no one was told to bring anything with them. Their strength would be all that was needed. Luke jumped on to the slide, second last, and hurtled down. Only a few seconds in motion but the rush of warm air both invigorated and relaxed him. He hit the ground and instantly jerked onto his feet just as he had learned to do as a practiced skydiver. Seconds behind him was the last man. Luke looked around at the others, all similar in age and physique to him. A posse of muscle.

"Stand away, stand away." Luke turned to see two khaki clad men, one of whom was gesticulating wildly for the group to move away from the foot of the slide and towards the forest. The two were already heading that way. The four hurriedly obeyed and made towards what looked like piles of brushwood. There was no reason not to.

Standing to the side of the cargo bay door above them he noticed a guy with his hand on a joystick protruding from a side panel on the interior wall. As the man flicked a switch, Luke could see a small light turn green. For a moment, nothing but then slowly a large container rolled gently forward towards the gaping entrance. Under normal circumstances at a proper airport Luke had often watched as a ground handling flatbed hoist nudged the side of the aircraft waiting to receive the baggage load. But in this case there was nothing save for a three meter drop.

The container continued a few moments longer until almost half of it was protruding from the side of the plane. The metal box teetered on the edge of the bay door like a hesitant teenager standing on the brink of a high diving board.

"OK here it comes" The yell came from atop as Luke watched the container launch inelegantly off the side of the fuselage. A single summersault and it crashed firmly to the ground, the flap side perpendicular and facing the forest. Like the throw of the giant dice.

"Right, all of you, get these boxes out of the container." An easy command. A difficult task. It took Luke and his three compatriots several minutes of heaving and straining to get enough purchase to start moving the first of the giant boxes forward and prise it free from the cargo cube. The second and third were the same weight but a lot easier once they had got the hang of things. The last one, which must have been almost empty came out in a trice.

When the job was done one of the two men who had stood by watching the exertions reached into his backpack and threw each of the quartet a bottle of water. Luke gulped it down. Not chilled, but still welcome.

While the group sat sweating and panting on the ground greedily slurping the water, Luke watched as the other guy moved forward with a box cutter in one hand and began to slash at the nearest cardboard wrapping. One of the heavy ones. He sliced away at the thick card in order to gain enough purchase to pull open a strip and rip it to the ground. Then another. And another, until Luke could see what was inside. It appeared to be a tightly folded stack of thin green material. Like a gigantic box of tissues. Except it was not a stack, but a single integrated sheet of thin plastic.

"What the hell is it?" Luke thought he might as well ask.

"What it is, is not what it will be. Finish your water and you will find out soon enough."

Chapter 38

Local time: Thursday 08:30

The Big Guy stepped out of the flight deck back into the business class cabin which by now was completely empty. The handful of real passengers had been moved back into the adjacent economy cabin. Easier to control one group than two. Also, it meant that the most comfortable quarters could be left for the private use of the team.

The Big Guy reached into one of the overhead bins and retrieved a soft side bag from which he quickly produced a handset. Not a sleek smartphone slimmer than a slice of gum, but not the size of house brick either. Somewhere in between, closer to the gum than the brick. No motif of bitten fruit on this thing. Not a household name. *Thuraya.* To the uninitiated the clue was in the the last three letters of a sticker on the back - *Inmarsat.* A satellite phone that could shoot its connection up beyond the atmosphere and did not rely on a jammed or otherwise weak terrestrial WIFI signal.

The guy dialed a long number. It was picked up immediately.

"Yes?"

"We are here. Everything is going to plan."

"Good. Keep it that way. Do you have cover yet?"

"We are about to start. Maybe two hours."

"And how long for it to settle and look natural?"

"In this heat, a few hours"

"OK, nothing more until tomorrow. Let them wait."

"Agreed."

Nothing more. Nothing that would alert anyone or anything listening in. No trigger words. No clues. And even if someone was interested then devilishly difficult to detect the source of a satellite phone to anything more specific than a wide region. And that is assuming anyone listening already knew when and where to expect the call. Completely safe for now.

The call to London would be made soon but not from here.

The middle man would make it, the one the Big Guy had just spoken with. The one with far better English. An untraceable accent as well as an untraceable call. He would use a burner phone routed via a second one that would forward the call to London. The second one would never be found. The account for that intermediate one was still active but the handset itself lay smashed and broken at the bottom of a river.

Chapter 39

Local time: Thursday 08:35

"Time to go to work"

As Luke heard the command it suddenly struck him how bizarre his situation was. By now he should have been almost in Brisbane, in the real world, ready to meet his mates for a riotous lunch probably merging into a riotous afternoon and evening swamping his jetlag with beer. And yet here he was sitting on the forest floor with three other guys he had never met, being watched over by two armed guards.

The four of them reluctantly got to their feet and moved to survey the now opened packages already glistening with a thin film of dewy moisture as the humid air hit the cool surface of the plastic material.

One of the two guards approached. He was carrying a very large ball of string and a thick coil of rope.

"OK, which one of you plays cricket?"

A redundant question to an Aussie. With a curt hand motion the guard indicated Luke with his raised arm. Walking over he handed him the ball of string, the rope and a small rough stone.

"Let's see how well you throw. Tie one end of this string to the stone and the other end to the rope then come with me."

Luke quickly obeyed and then followed the guard under the belly of the plane to the other side where his next instruction was to throw the stone with string attached up and over the fuselage back to the other side. He stepped up for the first attempt ready to take a swing. It looked to be about thirty feet to the top of the aircraft. Easy. He took the throw and both of them looked ahead waiting to see the stone plummet to the ground at the far side. Nothing. The stone made several bounces on the plane roof and then settled atop.

"Pull back and try again."

Clearly Luke had underestimated the width of the giant aircraft. He retrieved the stone by tugging on the string. Two more attempts before his effort was rewarded.

They watched as the guard at the other side reached for the string and began pulling and pulling. It took some time until eventually the connected rope had also snaked over the aircraft roof leaving one end dangling at each side.

Looking in the distance to the open luggage container Luke could see one of the others from the group begin to work with the rope and one of the huge plastic sheets. At first it was not clear, but after a minute or so it appeared that he was tying the rope to one of the corners of the material. While this was happening the other two passengers were motioned to come and join Luke who nodded silently to them as they approached. They still had not spoken. Time for that later.

When the rope tying task was complete the two guards exchanged a thumbs up.

"Right you three. Start pulling on the rope."

Six arms did as they were told and began to pull on the rope easing the start of the plastic sheeting up towards the far side of the aircraft. To start with it was easy but as more and more material left the ground and billowed upwards the weight increased. And as it slowly met the wall and roof of the aircraft the friction increased the resistance. If this was a tug-of-war it seemed like there were ten men on the opposing end of the rope. Not fair.

It took the three strong men a half hour of exertion before they finally got the first giant plastic sheet entirely pulled over the forward section of the plane and spread to cover it from the nose to the front of the wings.

It took the rest of the morning to complete the task, repeating the procedure first at the aft section and then again over each wing and finally the tail plane. At sixty feet high that last bit had been the biggest throw challenge to Luke's by now aching right arm.

Finally, the aircraft was completely shrouded in the swathes of plastic sheeting, like the furniture in a summer house abandoned at the end of the season. From prying eyes in the air it would still look a bit odd, but not like a hi-jacked plane.

The guards allowed the group a short break for lunch consisting of the contents of what would have been the prearrival breakfasts, thrown down from the plane wrapped in duty free bags. Luke and the other three ate greedily, washed down with more bottled water. So far there did not seem to be any worry about shortage of rations. The activity with the string and the rope and the coverage of the aircraft had shown a great deal of forethought. Hopefully the simple matter of sustenance had been equally carefully planned for.

During lunch a third man they had not seen before appeared from out of the forest carrying a long rudimentary ladder made from two wooden poles with variously sized sticks acting as rungs, lashed together with what looked like the same rope as had been used to haul the polythene sheeting. Quickly sizing up the height he proceeded to prop up the ladder against the edge of the wing. Leaning at a slight incline it fit nicely with about a foot to spare at the top.

"For the next job we will need more of you."

The way out had been down the slide. But now there was a way back. The guy who had brought the ladder clambered up the wooden rungs and across to the over-wing door. Once there it was a matter of seconds to use his box cutter to slice a flap in the plastic sheeting, give four knocks on the door then stand back as it swung open.

Luke watched, sitting cross legged on the warm earth. It was not long before he saw a single file of male passengers emerging from the plane, crossing the wing and making their way down the ladder to the forest floor. He counted six. 'And now we are ten' he murmured.

The guard with the gun went over to join the man who had brought ladder and they began to speak together. The guard had spent the whole morning with a bunch of strangers who did not share his language and who might even try to attack him at the first opportunity. He began to speak, at first in serious low whispers but then quickly more loudly as he relaxed into welcome conversation after his isolated morning. After a while the two men separated. The one with the gun taking several steps away from the group to a spot where he turned and leant comfortably against a tree. A vantage point from which he could easily watch ten men and aim at anyone that was stupid enough to try anything.

The one who had brought the ladder then instructed Luke and the others in halting English.

First, he pointed to the piles of brushwood which he and the other 'scientists' had spent the past several days hewing and stacking.

"Take these, carry much you can and go up there." He motioned to the ladder. "On top put everywhere. Come down. Take more again. Same same."

So not only was the plane to be hidden beneath a giant sheet, there was to be a layer of forest foliage on top of that. Luke moved first and scooped up an armful of branches.

"More, more." came the instruction.

'It's alright for you, mate', he thought, 'you're not the one who has been throwing stones and hauling sheeting all morning.' Reluctantly he picked up one more branch and moved over to the ladder. His arms may have been tired but now it was time to punish his legs. He quickly reached the top and climbed on to the flat of the enormous wing. Walking to the very tip he dropped the load, roughly spreading it with a kick of his foot. Behind him the next guy was already doing likewise. And another. He moved back to the top of the ladder just in time to wait for the final passenger to step off on his way up.

And so it continued. Like an army of ants moving bread crumbs back to the nest the ten of them toiled up and down the ladder bringing the branches up onto the covered plane. Luke quickly lost count of the number of trips he was making. The wings were the easy bits. Nice and flat, all you had to do was drop and kick.

The roof of the fuselage was more of a challenge. First of all, to scramble up there, clinging to the loose folds in the material was hard enough, but then to drop and spread the foliage onto a curved surface where some of it simply dropped off and landed back on the ground seemed futile.

When they were finished it would look from the air like nothing more than a clearing of uneven ground covered with the detritus of the forest. Luke found the repetitive circuit of labour immensely boring. Until the task was interrupted by one piece of excitement.

Chapter 40

Local time: Thursday 07:45

Maarten had moved surprisingly quickly. Now he crouched down at the edge of the undergrowth from where he looked across the clearing to a low stone wall. It was a silhouette that somehow instantly clicked in his mind. Like the overlay of a negative on top of the original photograph, his childhood memory fused onto the view in front of him. He knew this place. His secret hideout.

He had arrived just in time to see the final three women in the group disappear behind the wall. That could only mean they must be going down into the ground. Two western women and one Asian. He knew this area was deserted due to the real or imagined imminent volcanic activity. He had seen no one on his walk since he left the village. These women could only be the same ones he saw exiting the plane a few minutes ago. In the stillness of the forest, above the bird calls, he heard the familiar but long forgotten thump as the trap door closed behind them.

What now? He had no real idea what was going on here. A plane landing on a runway after decades of abandonment. Some passengers being taken off and marched to his secret hideout, the disused underground labyrinth. He decided this was definitely not the time to rush over, open the trap door and shout down the hatch.

For now, he would wait. He settled down just on the very edge of the forest. If anyone emerged from under the ground in front of him he would not be seen. The morning was warming rapidly and he had been up early. He closed his eyes.

Chapter 41

Local time: Thursday 08:15

In the cool stillness beneath the ground Kimberley's eyes were adjusting. Somewhere in the background she could hear the low hum of a generator that was powering the dim electric light. The group had been ushered through two small chambers into a third much larger space where there was seating around three walls. The fourth wall was covered in floor to ceiling metal shelving, rusting in places, but still robust enough to hold rows and rows of tinned and dried foods. The labels were in a language she could not read but the pictures showed a range of vegetables, fish and fruits in the cans while the bags held rice by the sack full.

"Sit. You have a rest now while we prepare this place for your stay." It was the guard who had brought them from plane. He was less muscle-bound than the others. He had an almost courteous manner as a host might invite guests to be seated in a restaurant. As well as his companion at the trapdoor Kimberley had counted four of them in total.

The group obeyed, each of them clutching their small bag of possessions on their lap. Kimberley moved closer to Julie on the cool hard bench. Her eyes were fully adjusted now. She looked at the flight attendant beside her. A face that looked maybe five years older than herself. But the hands and neck nudged more towards ten years older, she thought. No facelift, just a woman who had taken care of herself in the places that showed most. And despite their shared bewildering predicament, a woman who looked like she would always know what to do next. A self-assured, kindred spirit.

"Not exactly the Fairmont Hotel, is it?" said the woman in the Blue Yonder uniform.

"Wouldn't know. Never been there, but I'll take your word for it. Any idea at all what is going on here? This was not exactly a planned stop on my itinerary. Do you think your guys in the cockpit will already have sent a message? Radioed for help or whatever it is they do in these situations?"

"I wouldn't count on anything like that. I was on the flight deck when these guys took over. There was no time for any mayday call. It all happened very quickly. And then I blacked out. Very clever of them to split us up. I don't think Simon will try anything while he knows some of us are in the cabin and some are on the ground, wherever this is that we are."

"Who is Simon?"

"Oh, yes, sorry, he is my….I mean he is our captain. Actually, he is not that much of an action man, not that kind of action anyway. His co-pilot, Nabil, is more in that mould. Simon told me that he used to be something in the Lebanese military. Certainly, he looks pretty tough to me."

"I wish we knew what was going on back there on the plane. What do you think these guys are after? Why are they doing this? "

"Whatever they are up to I don't think it is about the destination itself. Hijacking a plane just to get to this isolated place doesn't make sense in itself. Judging by what we saw walking over we seem to be a long way from anywhere. Assuming we kept going in roughly the same direction we must be somewhere in the Pacific"

"We're in New Britain."

"How do you know that?" Julie's eyes widened

"A guy on the plane has a GPS app on his phone. He kind of told me. At least I think that is what he said. But I still have no idea where that is."'

"It's part of Papua New Guinea."

"How come you know that?"

"One of my heroines, Amelia Earhart, took off from this country on the last leg of her attempt to be the first woman pilot to fly around the world."

"And?"

"She didn't quite make it. Disappeared into the ocean…..or not, depending on which wild theory you believe. It was a long time ago."

"What do you think these guys want?

"Probably money."

"In exchange for us?"

"That would be my guess, but at this stage who knows? Do you have anyone else travelling with you?"

"No, not really. There is this guy, the one with the GPS, Luke, an Australian I met on the flight. I don't exactly know him but he is pretty athletic looking. A useful guy to have on our side but last time I saw him he was in his seat like all the others. At one point he was not tied up."

"How did he manage that?"

"It would take too long to explain at the moment. I'll tell you later. Let's just say he had some help."

"From you?"

"Yep"

"Clever girl." The older woman was clearly impressed. "Do you think he is the sort who would take a risk?"

"Definitely"

"Then it could be useful to speak with him. At least set up a line of communication. Someone in the passenger cabin will be easier than the flight deck where they will be watched more closely in a smaller space"

"Are you forgetting the little matter that we are down here, trapped beneath the ground with no sim cards in our phones and in any case no cell signal out there onboard?"

"Yes, I know that." Julie paused. "But there could be a way."

Julie rummaged in her sick bag and after making sure neither of the two guys were looking in her direction she surreptitiously extracted two plastic rectangles each slightly larger than a cell phone.

"More phones?"

"Not exactly. They are walkie talkies. I bought them in Singapore for my nephews. They don't need a cell network as they only talk to each other. According to the guy who sold them to me the range should be around 3 km. So easily from here to the plane."

"Only one problem then. How do we get one of them onto the plane?"

It was clear to Kimberley that it would need someone to

return to the plane to deliver one of the devices to Luke. For that they would need an excuse. The two women took several minutes of discarding a raft of impractical options before Julie suddenly declared, "Got it. Did you buy any duty free on the way here?"

"Only a litre of Johnny Walker Blue in Singapore. I bought it for my uncle, the favourite whisky of my grandmother's favourite son."

"Perfect. In a minute I am going to call over that one." Julie pointed to one of the guards, not the almost kindly one. "I will explain to him as best I can that if he takes you back to the plane there will be nice liquid prize for him."

"Do you think he will go for it?"

"Definitely. Trust me, I have been flying long enough to spot a drinker as soon as they board. It saves a lot of trouble later in the flight if you know what you are dealing with from the start."

And with that she motioned the guard to come over. At first he looked puzzled as Julie launched in to a combination of pidgin English, miming and pointing but eventually he seemed to understand what was being proposed and he smiled at the thought of a longed-for drink of premium scotch. The words 'Johnny Walker' seemed to need no translation.

The guard wandered back to impart the news to his compatriot. The other one did not seem too sure at first but eventually nodded. An armed man looking after eight female prisoners should be secure enough. Kimberley looked down as she felt Julie slipping one of the two devices into her pocket.

"OK, A walkie talkie for this Luke guy, and a bottle of booze for our friend here. Fair exchange I'd say."

* * *

As they walked back to the plane in silence. Kimberley noticed the guide occasionally smiling to himself in anticipation of his present. He did not seem too concerned that she would bolt away, probably figuring a woman would be too scared to thwart his authority. And his gun.

They reached the clearing and for a brief moment Kimberley was taken aback. The plane had gone. Or to be more precise the shiny metal fuselage was no longer visible. In its place she quickly took in the monster shrouded shape and surmised what lay beneath. Scanning the group who were trailing back and forth with armfuls of foliage she quickly recognised Luke. He was taller than the rest, and despite the heat moving more quickly, his sweat drenched T-shirt clinging to his muscular torso. Looking up from his labours as he was gathering branches for the umpteenth time, Luke seemed startled to see Kimberley approach. Their guards were a bit slow on the uptake and before they had time to intervene the two were standing facing each other with their backs shielding the view of their respective captors.

Kimberley shot out her arm towards Luke. "Quick, shake my hand, act like you are pleased to see me."

As he obeyed she slipped him the walkie talkie. "Take this. Hide it in your pocket. We will talk later. Listen for two short buzzes" And with that she turned and marched on towards the foot of the ladder.

As she walked the fresh smells of the forest were ever present. A wetness. A sweetness. And then faintly but increasing with every step towards the plane, a fetid note. As she reached the ladder the smell mushroomed into a fetid stench. It was not difficult to locate the source. Under the shadow of the wing lay the rotting corpse of the elderly passenger who had expired from lack of oxygen. His body had been tossed there without any sense of human dignity. Lacking the decency of even a rudimentary covering, nature was taking its course. The face was black and bloated. Kimberley stifled a retch as she looked at what a few hours in the heat had done. The head was almost completely covered with insects.

Turning quickly away, Kimberley signalled to her guard to wait at the foot of the ladder as she ascended onto the wing and then made her way across to the flap covering the doorway.

Inside the cabin the scene was much as she had left it. Most of the passengers were sitting silently, still trying to fathom where they were and what was happening to them. At the front by the bulkhead one of the guards stood, solemn and bored, his rifle butt resting by his foot. Moving to her seat area she reached into the overhead locker and retrieved the Changi Airport duty free bag containing the promised whisky. For a moment she considered not bringing it out to the guard, but then thought the better of that course of action. Might as well keep them onside for now.

She was quickly back on the ground and presented the prize to her captor. His face broke into a smile and at that moment she could definitely have made a run for it. He was so pleased he would probably not have bothered to go after her. But where would she go to?

Chapter 42

Local time: Thursday 09:00

It seemed like only minutes shut-eye, but in fact it was almost an hour before Maarten awoke, drenched in sweat and a bit stiff from lying awkwardly on one arm. He looked over towards his old hideout. Still no one above ground. He settled down, not sure what he might be waiting for.

In the oppressive heat he might easily have dropped off again, but it was not long before he once again heard the thump of the opening trapdoor hitting the soft earth. Looking over he saw two figures emerging, one of the Western women, the one with frizzy hair, and one of the armed men. The guard did not look particularly vigilant nor did the woman look like she was about to make a dash for freedom. The two of them headed off in the direction of the plane.

* * *

Maarten slunk back into the trees behind him. Circling round he was soon back at his original vantage point. But now the scene was very different from earlier. The plane, as such, had disappeared from view but it was obvious from the shape of some giant sheets of material where it had gone. A makeshift wooden ladder was propped against what was definitely a covered wing. The girl had descended the ladder carrying something in one hand. A party of males scurried around in the undergrowth gathering brushwood. A hive of activity.

He watched from his cover as the girl sat down to rest on a low rock. Her captor standing some short distance away lit up a cigarette as he examined what looked like a bottle he had just been handed by the girl. Whatever was going on here it was clear from the armed guards that the women from the hideout and the other men on the ground by the plane were not here by choice. Were there more people? How many were in the hideout? Inside the aircraft?

Common sense told him that approaching the girl without

attracting the attention of any others might answer a few of his questions. Hopefully she would understand English. Or Dutch.

Silently he crept forward on his belly until the girl was just a few metres in front of him, looking sideways. Luckily the guard has turned his back and was facing towards the plane.

"Psssst! Do you speak English?"

The girl turned her head quickly in the direction of the voice. At head height there was nothing to see but then looking down she saw Maarten's prone figure, a tall body topped with an unusually square face. A face with glasses. The head jerked and smiled briefly up at her.

"Don't be afraid. And turn your head back, don't look at me."

She obeyed. "Who are you?"

"Introductions later, but whoever these other guys are I am not one of them. What's going on here?" He almost added 'do you need help?' but decided that was stupid and obvious.

"We are from the Blue Yonder flight. The one I hope everyone is looking for. The plane was brought down here hours ago by these guys with the guns."

Maarten had no idea what she meant by 'the Blue Yonder flight' but for now that was not important. "Why? What do they want?"

"No idea. Your guess is as good as mine."

"How many of them are there? And how many of you?"

"As far as I can make out there are 8 or 9 of these guys, maybe more. Right now there is one guarding us here, one in the bunker and the rest on the plane. We are ten women including me in the bunker and then apart from these passengers you can see on the ground there are dozens more onboard. I have no idea exactly how many in total, maybe a hundred."

"Who knows you are here? Have you called anyone to get help?"

"None of us on the ground have working cell phones and onboard there is no signal at all. There has not been for hours before we landed. We think there is a jammer."

Maarten noticed the guard turning his gaze back in the direction of the girl. Pressing himself even closer to the ground he lowered his voice to a whisper. "There is no phone signal out here. But back in the village I could call someone for you."

"Easiest if you take this. It's no use to me without a sim card. The battery is almost flat too You'll need to charge it then look in the contacts. His name is Andrew."

"Thanks."

"You had better hide now." As she spoke, the girl glanced over to the man with the cigarette and the bottle. "I think it's time for me to go back."

Looking over, Maarten saw the other guard approach and start remonstrating with the smoker. It was loud enough to hear. To his ear the language sounded vaguely similar to Indonesian. He could pick out only a few words, made easier by the fact that many of them were being repeated. It took him a few seconds to realise that the man had a stutter. Either that or he was just very angry. The smoker stubbed out his cigarette, put what appeared to be a bottle in his pocket and moved in the direction of the girl. He was getting close.

"Look for me again tomorrow. By the bunker," whispered Maarten. With that he slipped the girl's phone into his backpack, wriggled slowly backwards and disappeared snakelike back into the undergrowth. He slithered off, not noticing that the man with the bottle had glanced over and seen him.

Chapter 43

Local time: Thursday 09:15

After the confines of two flights and the artificiality of Changi airport Kimberley found it refreshing to be outside again as her guard wobbled his way with her back towards the bunker. The rest of the women had now come out from underground and were variously either stretching or sitting on the low wall.

Heading towards Julie, Kimberley opened without preamble, "I met someone."

"Very nice for you, but we can discuss relationships later."

"No, I mean, here, on the ground. A guy. Just a few minutes ago. I have no idea who he is but I gave him my phone so he could call."

"Call who?"

"Someone I know who works for Blue Yonder. His name is Andrew. He will know what to do."

Their conversation was cut short by one of the guards. Not the one who was already slightly drunk. It was obvious from his arm waving and gun pointing that it was time for the group to return underground. With only a little help from the wobbly one, the group of women was rounded up and marched back to the trapdoor opening behind the small wall.

Kimberley took one last wistful look at the sky before following Julie down into the gloom.

"And you say he works for us, for Blue Yonder? What is his surname?"

"Barnes. Depending on the time of day he will either be sleeping or else holed up somewhere on the end of a telephone speaking to people who are worried about us. Probably in London," Kimberley paused, "or from the tales he has regaled me with about something called the 'Go Forward Team' I suppose he might even get to Singapore at some point. "

"Yes, I know all about the Go Forward Team. Ironically I am trained up as a member of that myself. I guess I have already 'gone forward"', she paused. "and you are right, the airline is likely to have flown an additional support group to Singapore to help out our local team there. Your Andrew may well be with them."

The conversation broke off as the two women reached out to the others in the group. After a few minutes chat Kimberley discerned that the rest of their group contained two demure Indonesians, four Singapore Malays and two Chinese women who had not a word of common language with the others.

Suddenly, the sober guard reappeared and spoke to the two Indonesian women in a tongue that they seemed to at least partially understand. He then motioned for one of them to impart the message to the group. The younger of the two stepped forward.

"He says that we must take some of the boxes of food supplies over to the plane. The two Chinese ladies will stay here as he says they do not look strong enough but the rest of us must help now."

Kimberley asked the obvious question. "What language was he speaking to you? Indonesian?"

"Yes, Bahasa Indonesian, but very badly. We have so many dialects. I don't think he is one of us."

"Of course I understood him too, as our languages have much in common" said one of the Malay women," but I agree it was terrible. He is definitely not from our country either."

Julie led the way as one of the guards ushered them back down into the bunker and through to the second chamber where the far wall held a stack of shelves loaded with boxes, cartons, sacks and assorted containers. The writing and labels were not in English. Kimberley watched as Julie motioned to the nearest guard pointing at the shelf with one hand and showing him an upturned palm with the other. A universal 'which one?' signal. He indicated a shelf of identical boxes. "Take boxes," he commanded in faltering English. And then on the shelf below to some plastic containers, "Take water".

The women, minus the Chinese ladies, each came forward and took either a box or a water container.

"Now we go." A superfluous command as the guard ushered them back along the way they had come in and once more out into the open.

* * *

The struggle up the ladder onto the wing made her glad to stoop down and once again enter the cool confines of the aircraft where the air conditioning was still working well off of the auxiliary power.

"How are things holding up in here?" she heard Julie asked one of her colleagues. From the name badge she could see this one was Emma. "How is the mood?"

Emma's head moved side to side. "So, so. Pretty subdued, considering. Everyone is tired, of course. The women who are able to move about have formed into little clusters of conversation. The men are clearly frustrated at not being able to do anything with their hands now being metaphorically tied. How about outside, down there, where have they taken you?"

"Some kind of underground bunker, close by," Julie answered. "Not sure what the place is but it is cool, well equipped with supplies and plenty of room to lie down."

The women spoke a while longer, still trying to make sense of their situation. But as the guard ushered them back to the exit door for their return to the bunker Kimberley was no further forward with the two main questions.

'What exactly is this place?'

'Why have we been brought here?'

Chapter 44

Local time: Thursday 11:00

Maarten was sweating from his hurried journey back to the village. Keen to re-charge the girl's phone and call this Andrew guy he had slurped water on the way without stopping.

A couple of time he thought he heard a noise behind him, the crack of a branch, the swish of a bush being jostled. With birds and animals everywhere, he paid it no heed.

The village was even quieter than when he arrived yesterday. Was it only yesterday? He headed straight for Arief's shop and entered. No tall man behind the makeshift counter. Instead there was a scribbled note. *Gone in to town for more supplies. Back later tomorrow.*

A quick search uncovered Arief's solar power unit with its row of sockets. It was behind a stack of neatly folded dish towels. From one of the sockets trailed a solitary charging cable. It was only then it hit him, of course he would need such a thing. He had already clocked that the girl's phone was a different brand from his one, so his own cable would be no good. It was difficult to see in the gloom if this one would fit. He switched on the phone. After a few seconds it showed only one bar of charge. Gingerly he inserted the cable. At least it went in, but the fit seemed a bit loose.

Ten minutes should be enough time to test if the connection was working. That would give him enough power to find this Andrew guy in the contacts list and make the call.

As he waited, Maarten stepped outside into the deserted street. After a few moments he made out a stooped figure hobbling toward him. It was the old man he had met on arrival.

"Selamat pagi," Maarten reckoned the Indonesian 'good morning' greeting was probably a safe bet.

The old man raised his arm in silent acknowledgement.

"Pria tinggi?" Maarten enquired after Arief.

"Dia tela pergi" *Gone away.*

Maarten's pidgin did not stretch to enquiring further. In any event the old man had already shuffled off with the air of someone unconcerned about his destination.

Waiting for the phone to re-charge Maarten looked around at the empty village. Here he was back again.

Rabaul. Papua New Guinea, or PNG as Maarten's parents called it. This is where they had spent their holidays. Happy, until that last time.

Maarten had not known it at the time. It was only later that he had read up on the real history of the place which far from diminishing his boyhood fantasies had made his memories even more special. He learned that at the beginning of the war the Japanese had overwhelmed a small Australian defense force and proceeded to develop Rabaul into a massive Army and Navy base, among the largest in the South Pacific theatre.

Above the ground they built runways while beneath they dug tunnels and caverns where various supplies and even barges were once hidden. This was the wartime hideout that Maarten had uncovered - a subterranean labyrinth of low ceiling chambers many retaining their wartime furnishings and basic comforts. He had played happily down there, staying cool underground, sheltered from the afternoon heat.

Here was the most magical of places for a young boy's imagination, darting around waving sticks as pretend guns, and fighting off enemy soldiers by the dozen.

Now, he had read, that apart from scuba fanatics, only the occasional tourists and WW2 buffs returned to Rabaul. No doubt they would gingerly keep an eye on the peaks still periodically smouldering in the distance as they wandered along the disused runways of what had once been a key Japanese air force base spearheading the war in the Pacific.

This all made sense as to why this spot had fit the bill. The old runway had somehow been cleared sufficiently for a large aircraft to land. *But why?*

When he first saw the Blue Yonder plane under its blanket of foliage, only yesterday, he instantly connected the image to something else. Revisiting the haunts of his boyhood games held one more secret apart from the underground labyrinth. For as well as the single remaining exposed example of a Japanese aircraft Maarten had found a second plane. It had happened on the first day of the trip. Only a hundred meters from the overgrown runway but so completely invisible under such a thick mass of jungle growth that at first he had thought it to be nothing more than a small hillock. He had rushed to the top of the mound to gain a better vantage point for some imaginary shooting at more enemies and there just below the summit he had tripped on a protruding loop of metal. Scraping away the topsoil with the stick he was using as a pretend gun he discovered it to be a small circular antenna.

Over the ensuing days he had returned with the camping spade his father always brought along to dig a latrine. After only a short time of shoveling aside the debris he had uncovered an easily openable hatch leading down into what was the cockpit. Looking down revealed nothing but total darkness. The next day he dispensed with the spade and returned with a torch to investigate further.

The cockpit was a boy's dream of dials and switches made all the more magnificent by two huge steering wheels. Unlike the traditional U-shaped joysticks these were complete circles akin to those in a car. Thus, from one moment to the next as Maarten sat there, in his imagination he could switch from being a pilot to a racing driver. Whoever had last flown this aircraft had left nothing behind but a few very old and very rusty discarded tins of tomato juice.

Maarten had spent many hours alternating between exploring below ground and playing in his secret abandoned airplane. He had been planning to revisit the latter on this trip until his activity had been interrupted by the sight of the landing plane.

Ten minutes had surely passed. Maarten stepped back inside and picked up the phone. Still just one bar on the battery. *Damn. The charging cable must be a mis-match. Maybe just enough power for a short call?* As he went to stab the Contacts icon he felt a sharp blow to the back of his head. His nose flooded with smell of distilled spirit as he slumped to the ground. Pain fleetingly preceded the darkness.

Chapter 45

London time: Thursday 10:00

Stephanie Walsh had already been at her desk in the City of London for three hours. From her fourth-floor window she looked out at what was now just a trickle of latecomers scurrying to their offices. Among a forest of glass towers, she enjoyed the fact that her company had taken up residence in a refurbished Victorian building with its cornice work and other design details that served no function other than to look splendid. Also, it meant she was on the top floor.

In the near foreground she could see the iconic bullet-shaped Gherkin building. Might just as well have been nick named the Suppository she had thought at first sight all those years ago. And beyond that the Lloyds Building with all its service ducts and entrails on the exterior as if the architect had been Jack the Ripper.

Her employer, 'Richardson Alliance', was sited deliberately close to the Lloyds Building, home of the world-famous insurance institution. She liked the fact this signaled to the outside world that she worked for a serious player in the market.

Ten years in, Stephanie still loved her job. At dinner parties no one quizzed her beyond her initial response, naturally assuming that a role in insurance equated to boredom. That was most definitely not the case since yesterday when they had first heard the news about Blue Yonder.

As Stephanie took her first sip of morning coffee and settled down to scan through the overnight emails her desk phone rang. She reached to pick it up with one hand as she toggled her screen with the other.

"Good morning, Richardson Alliance, this is Stephanie."

The voice on the other end was muffled and heavily accented. The message was brief. "We have the plane."

"Sorry, could you repeat that? What aircraft are you referring to please?" A redundant second question. Along with the whole office she knew there was only one.

"Blue Yonder flight 10. I am sure you know it is fully covered. Do not contact the police if you want to avoid a claim payout. If we find out you have involved them it would be a very expensive mistake. I will call back at the same time tomorrow when you have had time to think about what a safe return is worth to you. Give me your mobile number. I will not call again on this phone."

Instinctively Stephanie responded to the request and gave the caller her number.

"Wait, who are you? I need more details than that……."

No one there.

Stephanie put down the phone and reached for her keyboard. The screen flickered back into life, showing the file she had already been looking at since her arrival. It contained the entire Blue Yonder fleet list showing each aircraft registration, type, age, total premium and three columns for the insured amount of cover. Each of their 777 aircraft showed varying amounts in the first column for hull cover, and then multiples of that for passenger liability and for third party liability. Ever since 9/11 she had seen that last column throw the entire industry into a panic as claims started to flood in for the massive damage to infrastructure on the ground, totaling billions.

The unfolding Blue Yonder drama had enveloped her ever since the news had broken yesterday when she and selected others had gathered in a meeting room to discuss their exposure. Richardson Alliance was a major player in the syndicate of firms underwriting the Blue Yonder fleet.

Stephanie scanned her eyes down the fleet list in front of her. Towards the bottom was the missing aircraft, already heavily asterisked. As she clicked on the appropriate row a pop-up window confirmed what she knew already.

Aircraft: G-BAXY Boeing777-300

Operator: Blue Yonder Airways

Cover: hull $200m; passenger $1bn; third party $1.5bn

Richardson Alliance exposure: hull 25%

Status: Missing

Everyone in the office had done the maths. One quarter of two hundred million dollars. In the event of loss Richardson

Alliance would be liable to pay out fifty million dollars equal to over thirty-five million British pounds.

* * *

Thirty minutes later Stephanie was standing with the company founder, Gareth Richardson, in the paneled boardroom awaiting the arrival of Tom Nichols. They had, of course, offered to rush over to Heathrow to meet the boss of Blue Yonder Airlines but luckily Tom was already in the City on other business and had readily agreed to come immediately to them.

Stephanie's boss, Gareth, was a patrician of the insurance industry now close to retirement age although she doubted that he would ever permanently leave the firm he had founded over thirty years ago. Grey haired, elegantly dressed in a Hackett suit he was the epitome of that old adage that an English tailor provides the best cut in the world for the body you have, rather than the one you wished you had. From day one Stephanie had always found him a reassuring presence. Which in the current circumstances with fifty million dollars at stake was just as well.

"So that was all he said? 'We have the plane….and don't go to the police'?"

"Yes, exactly that."

"And what impression did you get from his voice? Old, young, British, foreign?"

"Age, hard to tell. Could be anything really. Definitely not British but the accent was weird, it was kind of all over the place. Maybe a bit like I heard some of the people speak when I was on holiday in Bali last year, but with a slight Australian influence. Not really something I have ever heard before."

Further discussion was interrupted by a brief knock on the door as Tom Nichols was ushered in to join them. Stephanie noted that she was first to receive his brief handshake as she returned his genuine smile. Perhaps the world *is* moving on she thought.

"Good to see you again, Tom," said Gareth. "Pity about the circumstances. Stephanie here is the one who took the call I told you about. Less than an hour ago."

"There is not much to tell," Stephanie took the initiative without being asked to speak. "The voice just said that they had the plane and not to contact the police if we want to avoid a pay-out. Also, to expect a call back later when we have had a think about the value of a safe return."

"The value of what they have is pretty clear. Worst case it could be well over a billion dollars in total spread across a number of insurers." Gareth spoke methodically as if these possibilities were everyday occurrences. "It will depend on the extent of any damage to the plane, the fate of the passengers and the injuries to any third parties."

Tom countered quickly. "If they have the plane and they are telling us its return is worth the insurance cover value, then it must be undamaged. If the aircraft is intact then we have to assume for now that the passengers are too. Wherever they have come down let's hope everyone was strapped in, then barring a few bruises or a heart attack most of our customers should be OK. At least for the moment."

"But where could they possibly be, out of sight and off the radar?" Gareth voiced what Stephanie was thinking.

"South-east Asia is a large area with lots of islands, more than 13,000 by most reckonings and less than 1,000 of them inhabited." Stephanie was remembering her Geography A-level focus on the area and the hours she had spent memorising the topography, culture, populations and commerce of the countries in the region.

"And spread across these islands are over 300 airports," added Tom. "Our folks back at Heathrow are already trawling through the list for likely candidates with runways long enough to take a triple seven and yet remote enough to be taken over without the whole world already knowing about it. They are still looking but I am not convinced anywhere qualifies on the latter count considering our planet has more cell phones than people."

There was silence for a few moments. Stephanie pondered the situation. If the plane and passengers were safe for now how long would that last? How desperate were the people who had done this? The lengths they were prepared to go to in order to seek millions of dollars was already impressive – taking over and bringing down an aircraft with over a hundred people onboard in some place remote enough to remain off the radar. But what lengths would they go to if things did not go to plan and they did not get the money?

Tom again. "OK, let's think logically. We have no idea who these people are or where they are holding our aircraft. We all want the safe return of the passengers and I also want my plane back in one piece. You, Gareth, would certainly prefer not to have to pay out your quarter share of two hundred million dollars. And lastly, we don't know if they are calling other insurers or just here."

"If they are calling other insurers in the syndicate I think I would hear about it pretty quickly. As a courtesy I think I should make some calls myself and let others know what is about to hit them."

"No, don't do that yet, Gareth. My hunch is these guys will prefer to deal with just one channel and right now the fewer people who know about this the better. By all means make some courtesy calls and shoot the breeze with your industry colleagues but wait for them to bring it up. You will know pretty damn fast if any others have been contacted."

"Whoever else they might have called we all operate under the same code of ethics," said Gareth. "We do not negotiate with terrorists, we bring in the authorities. I'm afraid it's the British way of doing things. If these guys were smarter they should have picked on another nationality."

"Like the French?" said Tom.

"OK I'll hold off for a few hours while I make some calls around the business." With a grim smile to Stephanie and a handshake to Tom, Gareth left the room sharply.

As the door closed Stephanie spoke first. "So we do nothing? We don't go the police? Remember I am the one they called and I am the one they will call back, maybe tomorrow, possibly sooner. What do I say?"

"You assure them that you, your boss and I are the only three people who know about their call and that it will stay that way for now. Tell them that nothing will happen until they can prove that the plane and the passengers are safe and well. Then most importantly, ask them what they want and why they want it. I doubt they will answer the latter. I have to get back to the airport now but let me know as soon as you hear from them again."

With that they exchanged phone numbers and moments later Stephanie was alone in the room once again staring out the window at the Gherkin. The routine of her day could wait.

Chapter 46

London Time: Thursday

Andrew looked out of the window of the relief aircraft at the Alps far below. The gigantic chunks of rock stretched endlessly, and miles high, yet the illusion of distance across the crisp clear air made them look no more real than a relief map made out of papier-mâché.

Upfront in the cockpit the plane was under the command of Blue Yonder's most experienced pilot, Ana Granata. Tom had insisted on it. Andrew felt reassured, knowing that there was always the prospect that at some point they might have to continue elsewhere to the scene of wherever flight 10 had ended up. And for Ana that would most likely mean making an unfamiliar landing.

All around him the mood was subdued. No chitchat. A serious business. Andrew was struggling to push away the grim thought that at some point they might be returning home with more passengers in the hold than in the cabin.

Across the aisle sat three young nurses. Andrew recognised them from the employee medical centre where pilots got their six-monthly physicals and he had his most recent hepatitis and tetanus shots. Their checked bags would contain plenty of that and much more to cover the eventuality of an incident occurring anywhere from equatorial to arctic climes. He was glad his inoculation card was properly up to date. Malaria tablets he could cope with. A needle in the arm was something he preferred not to think about.

Still many hours yet before they would reach Singapore. The wisest thing would be to sleep now as once they landed the opportunity for shut-eye could be a longtime a-coming. Andrew's brain knew this. But his body did not. He knew he should take advantage of having three seats to himself and curl up horizontal. Instead he leaned forward and tapped the screen in front of him. At some point they would lose WIFI connection but right now, still over Europe the signal was strong. Slow, but strong.

Ana was right. *Rogernigel.com* was addictive. Andrew scrolled through the chatroom where a range of plausible fates were being debated in the most arcane detail. He was too tired to focus on terms like *Artex B406-4 Emergency Locator System* and *encoded digital transmission on 406 MHz*. Only one exchange gave him any comfort.

Jim93 12:05

all interesting stuff you guys but if it kept flying that can only have been because of bad motives on the flight deck or else a hijack. I am not convinced about the hijack theory. If it has been taken over then either demands are being kept secret, or there have been no demands. Think about it what are the usual hijack motives? To defect, to ransom the pax? to exchange for political prisoners, to make a 'statement'? But we have not heard any demands or if there are demands someone is keeping them secret for some reason. Is there someone in particular on the plane the hijackers are interested in?

Rotorbladerunner 12:08

how do you hijack a plane these days anyway you cant even get through airport security with a pair of scissors and a bottle of water let alone something properly sharp or something that fires bullets

RadioLuke 12:10

maybe you cant. Maybe we cant but just think about all those who can. There are hundreds if not thousands of poor buggers who get airside every day with minimal checks to clean toilets serve coffee sell fags and booze. Many of them working on zero hours contracts and minimum wage. It wouldn't take a huge sum to persuade one of them to bring through stuff hidden inside a case of shortbread a palette of Evian or a vacuum cleaner. Going through the whole shoes off and no liquids routine is just a nonsense to make our passengers feel safe…they can feel that the stable door is secure without thinking about the Trojan horse that just flogged them an over-priced sandwich

Andrew tapped the off icon and lay down to sleep. A sleep that did not come quickly. Instead he had to endure endless thoughts about Kimberley. Long looping thoughts which with each iteration gathered more fears and worries. This woman he had met so recently had become so central to his being.

Right now he felt sick not knowing what had become of the plane that was carrying her.

Chapter 47

Singapore time: Friday 03:00

The slick arrival formalities at Singapore Changi airport lived up to Andrew's memory and within 20 minutes of landing he had picked up his bags and was already heading for the designated airport hotel, one that was an integral part of the building in one of the other terminals.

He hopped on to the short shuttle train. On any one day such as this up to eight million people across the planet would disembark an aircraft as he had just done. Here, in this tiny capsule was a microcosm of that group, testament to the normality of safe arrivals.

Out of the shuttle train, up a couple of floors in a silent elevator and Andrew was quickly into the lobby of the airport hotel. A temporary sign directed all Blue Yonder employees to one of the ground floor conference rooms. Andrew followed the direction and after showing his ID to two diminutive but armed policewomen on the door, entered into a large space already arranged with a desk at the front facing rows of chairs.

It was the kind of place that could morph from wedding reception, to training session, to concert venue in the flip of a partition and a switch of the stackable furniture. At the back of the room was a growing cluster of luggage alongside a table with three urns of coffee, a stack of pastries and a pile of hot towels.

Andrew grabbed a coffee and pastry even although his stomach was sending him no signals of hunger.

At the front of the room he recognised Bruno Tay, the Blue Yonder local country manager. Singapore Chinese, second generation, he looked serious, unslept, but as always immaculately turned out. Andrew nodded to him as he looked up, but made no move to go over and greet him knowing that now was not the time for back slapping and small talk. Bruno concluded his conversation with the cluster of those around him and then called the room to order.

"I realise not everyone is here yet but let's make a start. I will repeat myself later if needed when others arrive. I know you will all be anxious to go to your rooms to freshen up but that will have to wait."

Along with most of the others Andrew remained standing, emphasising the seriousness of the occasion. He listened intently as Bruno continued. "We have taken over two other spaces. One at the other end of the terminal is for gathering family members. Restricted to parents, adult children and siblings at this time. No friends allowed. And we are not using the term 'next of kin'. At least not yet. That room has staff access only. There are already more than 50 people there. We need to keep that group well away from the media who are in another room similar to this one, directly above us"

"What's the latest news on the plane?" A redundant question from the floor, but Bruno showed no irritation as he continued.

"Tom has been live on-air and online again just a few minutes ago admitting frankly that we have no idea where the plane is, which means that after all this time the only possibility is that it has come down somewhere. We have no evidence to suggest whether that has been done safely or not. The media are beside themselves with excitement, spinning all sorts of nonsense from conspiracy theories to spectacular fireball crash landings."

"And what are our own thoughts?" Andrew this time.

Bruno looked towards the door making sure it was firmly shut before answering him. "For now, we assume it has come down relatively safely somewhere, most probably under the control of hostile forces. The complete and abrupt shutdown of all outbound radio and satellite signals occurred over an area of heavily fished sea, and relatively close in flying terms to the coastline. It is almost impossible that a ditching or an explosion would have gone unnoticed. Therefore, we conclude until proven otherwise that the plane continued to fly for up to five hours more under the control of persons unknown. It would have to be more than one person. Our crew on the flight deck and in the cabin simply would not concede to a single guy no matter how well armed or wired he might be. They have all had the training. At whatever cost, a solitary person would have been despatched long before now."

On the screens in front of him, and in a multitude of languages Andrew could see and hear how the fate of Blue Yonder flight 10 remained the top story across the globe. On one screen, Chinese television, Tom Nichols was delivering an interview in Mandarin with subtitles, making Andrew feel proud of the company he worked for, despite the circumstances.

"Right, that is about as much as we can tell you," concluded Bruno. "Now you know everything that we do. Please come forward and we will assign each of you to a family group. When you meet, tell them anything you can about what they ask but do not under any circumstances be drawn into a spiral of negative speculation."

As Andrew moved forward Bruno beckoned him over. "Please come with me. I have something different for you."

Andrew followed him to a quiet corner at the back of the room where he declined the offer of a seat. He had been sitting long enough already today. Or was it yesterday? It was Friday morning now in Singapore and not quite 36 hours since the last contact from the Blue Yonder aircraft. Now he was literally a world away from having been woken from this sleep on Wednesday afternoon in Ealing. The crisis centre, the call centre shift, the disturbing call from Paul Nickson, the kiss from Joanna, the long flight from London, all crammed into less than two days.

His thoughts were interrupted when he realized Bruno was trying to hand him something. Looking down he saw it was a USB stick.

"Here, you will need this. It contains the passenger list. I am not supposed to give it to anyone else which is why I did not ping it over to you and create an email trail. You are only the fourth person to have it after me, Dave in London and Alex, our manager in Brisbane."

"All very secret squirrel but why?"

"We need to establish who onboard might possibly be part of a hostile take-over. And if this theory is correct then how many of them there are. As far as is feasible we need to eliminate all the genuine passengers and then focus on the remainder."

"Logical. I think I know how I can do that"

Bruno's look begged the question.

"The genuine passengers will all have concerned friends and relatives calling the global help line in London and rushing to one of three places to be on the spot to find out more. What I need to do is to look on the stick at a real-time update for each passenger indicating who is waiting for them either here, in London or in Brisbane. Any passengers who have not had any concerned enquirers by this time will be either people who lead tragically lonely lives or else those who don't want us to know who their friends are."

"I am sure there might be others back in London thinking the same way," said Bruno. "The only thing is that their list is not complete. The London version on the shared drive is already out of date. But the USB file you have here also contains the updated list from here as of ten minutes ago. You will therefore have the full picture."

* * *

Andrew settled in to his hotel room armchair and fired up his laptop, inserting the USB that Bruno had entrusted to him and opened its only file.

The list that popped up on his screen held the 102 names of the Blue Yonder passengers. Against each was a column for the details of all those concerned family and friends who had already been in contact with the airline either remotely or in person. Some names had had dozens of enquiries -popular sociable people with close-knit families- others had just one or two. Similar to Facebook 'likes', only more poignant. Proper connections, ranging from parents who had shared birth, siblings who had niggled and teased, real friends who had celebrated and commiserated over the years. People who had driven them to the airport and bid them a tearful goodbye never imagining that it might be the last one. All of them, united across cultures, and no doubt worried sick and clinging to hope.

But for some names the final column was blank. Andrew re-sorted the list and quickly counted them. Eighteen. Eighteen - either all lonely people with no one who cared about them, or alternatively certain people who were up to no good and did not want anyone enquiring as to whether they were on board. If the plane had indeed been taken over by malign forces, they had so far done an excellent job of covering their tracks. Except that in trying to remain hidden the perpetrators were paradoxically exposing themselves by not at least pretending that others were concerned about them. If the hijack theory ended up being correct then somewhere among the eighteen would be those in control. But how many? Probably not all of them but most likely more than just two or three.

Andrew set to work. He started by pulling up the eighteen archived booking records one by one. Some were couples, some travelling alone. None were overtly travelling as a group. Travelling one way, alone, paying cash and with a short booking lead time before departure were the well-known traits of mischief makers. He saw nothing so blatant. These guys were not that stupid. Every one of the records was for a round trip. All were paid by credit card. If his theory was correct then the cards used by the guilty ones would definitely have been stolen.

He moved on to looking at the booking source codes. Four booked via travel agents could be discarded as that would mean either someone probably would have had sight of the booker or at least a likely valid phone number. That left fourteen booked directly online. Two of these ones were made more than six months previously, therefore highly unlikely. That left twelve suspects. Andrew picked up the phone and called through to Dave.

"Hey, sorry if I woke you. I've lost track of the time here in Singapore, let alone back in London."

"Whatsup, buddy?" An alert reply, so most probably Dave was still in the crisis centre.

"I am going to email you some booking references, a dozen, in fact. All booked online. Can you get hold of the guys in e-commerce and get them to check the IP addresses of whoever made each one. I need to know the location for each, close as they can establish."

"OK, will do. But you realise anything done over a mobile will only give us the network provider address?"

"Yes, but I still need to know."

"OK, send me the details and I'll get back to you as soon as I can. Might take a few hours, but we'll be as quick as we can."

As he hung up, Andrew pinged off the email to Dave, and settled down to wait.

Chapter 48

Singapore time: Friday 11:45

It was almost noon in Singapore. Groggily, Andrew splashed some water on his face. He got dressed and was about to return to the ground floor when his cell rang.

"Andrew, it's Dave. Got some answers for you."

He was about to respond 'Dave who?' when his brain clicked back into gear, remembering where he was and why he was here.

"Shoot."

"OK you sent us twelve booking references. Open the file I just sent you back. Two come from CTrip, the most popular travel site in China, one a direct booking made from a hotel WIFI network in Singapore and one from a Malaysian cell phone network." He paused.

"And?"

"As you will see, all the rest come from a single IP address in Batam City. All eight of these passengers are male. The bookings were made two weeks ago. Tuesday, at 10:30. As far as we can determine, the source location is an internet café in the Mega Mall."

"Never heard of the place."

"Me neither. Ask Bruno. I bet he knows. It's not far from Singapore."

"Sounds like we may have found the source of our trouble." Andrew's tone couched this more of a statement than a question.

"Almost certainly," agreed Dave. "Eight individual bookings made from the same place within the space of two days, is a bit odd. If they are all travelling together then the only reason to make separate bookings is to avoid suspicion.

"Ha. But by doing so they have actually shone a light directly on themselves," said Andrew. "The chances of eight individuals from the same Indonesian city all independently booking the same flight to Brisbane for the same departure date is miniscule.

I reckon it's a fraction of 1% that you would even get two on the same flight."

"There's more."

Andrew tensed.

"None of this group is actually Indonesian. At least not officially."

"Meaning?"

"They are all travelling on Ecuadorian passports"

"Shit. That's one of the places notorious for obtaining false papers. They could be from anywhere."

"Keep it to yourself for now, Andrew. It could mean nothing. The press here are continuing to go ballistic with this story. Almost makes you wish we could have an earthquake or a coup somewhere to get them off our backs."

Andrew clicked off and flicked back to his file containing the passenger list. He quickly located the eight supposed Ecuadorians. Almost impossible that this group were not those responsible for whatever had happened to their missing flight.

He needed to find Bruno.

* * *

"Batam City? Yes of course I know it. Everyone does." Bruno looked perplexed at Andrew's abrupt question. "Batam is the closest Indonesian island to Singapore. Fast ferry takes about an hour. A lot of Indonesians shuttle over from there and then take the metro out to Changi Airport. And we go the other way for cheap shopping.""

"Have you heard of the Mega Mall?"

"Who hasn't? It's right by the ferry terminal to catch the shoppers."

"I need to go there. Now."

"Because?"

"I'll explain later."

Chapter 49

Singapore time: Friday 11:00

Andrew was surprised by how modern the ferry terminal was when he arrived in Batam City Harbor Bay. The short crossing from Singapore had been his first extended time outside since Ealing.

Hurrying across an overpass walkway he looked down at the dual carriageway below. It was choc-a-block with motor bikes, many with a precarious load of people and goods. On one he counted two parents with their three kids clinging to each other like fridge magnets. The walkway led directly into the Mega Mall.

It was not a big mall, and after a quick couple of circuits he determined there was just one Internet Café. At this hour of mid-morning it was almost empty. Other than two men tapping away at the keyboards of adjacent screens in the far corner there were no other customers. Andrew approached what appeared to be the sole employee, a teenager wearing an Arsenal football 'Fly Emirates' shirt. By the looks of it, not the genuine article, but certainly an old favourite.

"Selamat pagi," came the greeting.

"Sorry, I don't speak Indonesian."

"English, then? Can I help you?" returned the youngster.

"A great team, Arsenal. Not doing quite so well at the moment."

The employee looked down forlornly at his shirt. "There is always next season."

"Let's hope so. What's your name?"

"Eko"

"Please to meet you, Eko. I'm Andrew." Do you work here all the time?"

"Only mornings. In the afternoons I study. I am doing computer studies."

"Good, then I am sure you could help me with something."

"Maybe."

"Let me tell you what I need. And let me also tell you what is in for you."

The lad's puzzled look slowly disappeared as Andrew continued.

"Do you keep access logs for these machines?"

"Yes. They archive for a couple of weeks and then just get overwritten. I can access them all from that terminal there." He pointed to a desk by the back wall.

"OK, Eko. How would you like me to send you a brand new Arsenal shirt when I get back to England?"

Eko's eyes widened. He nodded.

"It would be a genuine one, of course. Not a knock-off."

"Why would you do that for me?"

"Because what I would like in return is to take a look at your computer logs from a couple of days two weeks ago. Tuesday and Wednesday."

Eko smiled. "Easy. If they are still there. Come, let's take a look."

As Andrew followed, Eko pulled over a second chair so they could sit together in front of the screen.

"What is it exactly that are you looking for?"

"I need to see if there is any record of access to a specific airline website – Blue Yonder Airways."

"Not difficult."

Andrew marveled at the speed with which the young man began searching, his fingers a blur over the keyboard.

"OK, here's the date range. We still have it, yes. Here, type the URL into this search box for me."

Andrew obliged and then hit enter. Seconds later the screen filled with text, each line beginning with a repetition of the website URL.

"That's it," said Eko. "What do you want to know?"

"How many different times does a new session start on the home page?"

"Give me a minute." Eko ran his finger down the screen. "Eight. Each one at a different time, but always from the same machine."

"I guess people like to take the same seat in here?"

"Yes. These accesses all came from that one over there in the corner. Probably our least favourite position. The light isn't great,

but it's quiet."
Andrew looked over into the gloom and acknowledged the statement with a nod.

"We can also see what else the person looked at during each session. Let me show you how to do that," continued Eko

After brief instruction Eko moved off to help one of the other two men who had stood up and come over to ask something, leaving Andrew free to browse. Most of the sessions were brief, five or six minutes each, never straying beyond the confines of the Blue Yonder website and always ending with a completed booking reference. Andrew compared the reference numbers with the print-out he had brought with him. As expected, an exact match. It was only session number seven that showed the user had browsed beyond Blue Yonder to a couple of different domains, one of which was the Wikipedia page for something called OPM. Slipping a USB stick into the machine he quickly copied and pasted two separate paragraphs from the screen.

We, the people of West Papua, are fighting for our right to determine our own future, a future without foreign domination and oppression. In 1969 the then Indonesian president Suharto used the Act of Free Choice to legalize the incorporation of our country into Indonesia.

The Free Papua Movement (Indonesian: Organisasi Papua Merdeka – OPM) is an umbrella term for the independence movement established during 1965 in the West Papuan or West New Guinea territory which is currently being administrated by Indonesia as the provinces of Papua and West Papua.

The movement consists of three elements: a disparate group of armed units, several groups in the territory that conduct demonstrations and protests; and a small group of leaders based abroad that raise awareness of issues in the territory whilst striving for international support for independence.

Andrew released the USB and quickly slid it into his pocket. He rose from his chair and went over to thank the youngster.

"Did you see what you want?" Eko broke off from chatting to his customer.

"Yes, pretty much. Have you ever heard the initials 'OPM'?"

"No." As Eko replied the customer looked startled and abruptly moved off to rejoin his companion.

"Can you tell me, anything you might remember about the users of that corner computer a couple of weeks ago?"

"Just one guy. It was a pretty quiet couple of days. I noticed him only because he came and went three times on the first morning and then twice on the second. If he returned in the afternoons I would have missed him."

"And?"

"I don't think he was from around here. Different accent."

"Anything else?"

"He had a *gagap*. Sorry, I don't know the English word."

"Never mind. Thanks a lot, you have been very helpful."

As he turned to leave, Andrew flicked his phone to Google translate.

Chapter 50

Local time: Thursday evening/Friday morning

Maarten awoke inside Arief's shack with a feeling of numbness in his hands and feet. All four limbs were bound to his chair, the legs sitting amid shards of glass. His hair was damp. A grainy smell permeated his nostrils.

The uncovered window revealed the night. His head was throbbing. The blow must have been pretty hard to knock him out this long.

He tried painfully twisting and turning his limbs but to no avail. Working free was not going to be easy. An hour went by and he was no further forward. The effort of twisting and turning was rapidly tiring him. He gave up and closed his eyes. Just for a moment.

* * *

It was light now. He was hungry. His head still ached. But more than anything he was desperately thirsty. Whoever had tied him up all those hours ago had done it when his limbs were swollen from the efforts of his return journey in the heat. Now after the night had passed the effect of the comparative coolness had naturally lessened the swelling and his bindings felt just a little looser.

Gradually he jerked his chair over against the wall. That would provide more purchase. Digging his heels into the soft earth floor he tensed his body against the chair back and began to wriggle his wrists. Each movement produced a miniscule slackening. It took a while but eventually he squeezed the fingers of one hand into his palm as tight as he could and twisted free.

After that the rest was comparatively easy. Five minutes later he was able to stand up and rub the numbness out of his limbs. He remembered the girl's phone. It had been in his hand when he was hit. He had a vague memory of dropping it just as he passed out. Quickly he dropped to his knees and began feeling around on the floor. Nothing. If this was a simple robbery his assailant would surely have taken it. Likewise if the intrusion had any connection with the guys holding the airplane. He was about to stand back up when he saw it. A dark shape under the trestle of the makeshift counter top, almost hidden by a large shard of glass attached to a wrinkled black label. Bingo! He must have kicked it under there as he fell.

Grabbing the phone he moved to the window. Only half a bar now, and flashing rapidly a clear indication that the juice was almost gone. But still enough power to bring up the contacts list under 'A' and press to connect.

Chapter 51

Singapore time: Friday 13:30

The ferry from Batam back to Singapore was just about to leave. The boat was extremely full. Andrew squeezed into one of the middle rows of seats on the glassed-in lower deck just as the final few passengers were joining the row behind him. His phone rang. The urgent tone. No caller ID.

"Dave? Did I forget something?"

"This is not Dave. Are you Andrew?"

"Yes. Who is this?"

"You don't know me. My name is Maarten. But before we speak, please tell me who you are."

"You already know my name. I work for Blue Yonder Airways and I am part of the team trying to figure out what has happened to one of our aircraft which has gone missing?"

"That makes sense."

"What do you mean?"

"Because I know where your plane is. I have seen it."

Andrew steeled himself. This was most likely yet another crackpot, one who had somehow got hold of his private number.

"OK, then what do you know?"

"Your plane is on the ground, here where I am. It's covered up so don't expect to see it from the air. Most of the passengers are still inside but some of the women have been taken off. They are under guard but at least for now they look OK. One of them gave me this phone number without being seen."

One of them? Andrew's heart thumped. His mind raced. "That could only have been Kimberley."

"She didn't tell me her name. Frizzy brown hair. Australian accent."

"That is her. So where is 'here'? Where are *you*? Where are *they*?" As he heard his own words Andrew wondered if any of this was making sense. Whoever this was on the other end of the phone his assertions were plausible, yet quite fantastical.

"Listen my battery is about to die. I will need to call you back. It will take me about………."

Silence. No click, no hiss of dead air. Andrew heard nothing as the caller's voice disappeared

He hung on waiting for more. It did not come.

Who could this caller be? Someone who was at least claiming to have seen the plane on the ground and safe. Someone who knew Kimberley had frizzy hair. It had to be someone telling the truth. Therefore, his precious Kimberley was safe. For the first time he allowed himself a pulse of hope. A thought that perhaps they might have a future together.

When the mysterious caller got around to recharging his phone he would find out about the 'where' of the unfolding incident. His investigation of the supposed Ecuadorian passenger group and his trip here to Batam had answered the 'who', and hinted at the 'why?' He had no idea that the only three people who had the answer to the 'what' were 7,000 miles away in an insurance office in London.

The last half hour had provided plenty that his CEO would be interested to hear. Turning his attention to his phone Andrew stabbed 'Contacts'. He pecked a single 'T', enough for predictive text. As he waited for the connection, he looked around for a quieter spot to make the call but clearly no such spot existed on the cramped ferry. The best he could do was lean slightly forward with his head hunched towards his lap.

As he did so, the two men in the row behind him leant forward too. Had he turned around Andrew would have recognized them from the internet café.

Chapter 52

Local time: Thursday 17:00

The Big Guy completed his call and slipped the satellite phone back in his pocket with a half-smile. The onward call to London would be made soon. Let them think a while about how much all this is worth to them. A piece of heavily insured flying real estate plus a hundred warm bodies representing a dozen nations. No one would want that on their conscience, especially someone like Tom Nichols. The man knew his team had done their homework on Tom just as they had done on every other element of the plan. They had established from the start that he was someone who would put his customers first and do everything not to jeopardise their wellbeing.

He had been standing on the ground a short distance from the plane, all the while watching the group toiling up and down the ladder with their armfuls of foliage. He had also noticed the women, especially the one who had disappeared into the cabin for a few minutes and returned with something she had handed to one of his men. For now it was not important. Plenty of time to find out later.

Reviewing the situation in his mind he was more than satisfied that things were going well. Going perfectly to plan. The plane had landed safely in the allotted place and was already virtually invisible. On the ground all the local people had long since been evacuated, most of them to the nearest proper town, several miles away. Here on the ground everything was under control. Splitting the hostages between the plane and the bunker was a smart idea that would keep either group from trying anything foolish for fear of harm coming to the others. However, keeping those onboard in three groups was not ideal. It spread his men too thinly in terms of guard duty. Two groups would be better.

As he ascended the ladder up to the wing the wooden rungs creaked and bent under his weight but they held firm. Entering the over-wing door he lowered his head and then turned left moving through the empty business class cabin towards the flight deck. The cockpit door was ajar. No need for it not to be. The Big Guy stepped through.

* * *

Simon turned as he heard the heavy footsteps of the Big Guy entering the cockpit.

"OK you two, time to move back and join your customers, "said the man. "Better that we keep you all together."

As the captain, the last thing Simon wanted to do was to leave his natural command position. He knew better than to argue. Without comment he obeyed. Nabil followed as they entered the economy cabin, the Big Guy bringing up the rear. Simon surveyed the rows of seats each registering the same details – less than half full, the cross section of age, ethnicity, gender, the whiff of body odour that would no doubt soon get worse, the subdued air quieter than the murmur of an early morning commuter train.

To Simon these were his passengers, the people who he rarely saw as individuals but instead as an assemblage of humanity who unthinkingly entrusted their safety to him. A different group every flight. It did not matter who they were individually. He would not get to know any of them. He never did. All that mattered was that he had the responsibility of flying them through the air and bringing them down safely. He often thought of the difference between himself and his best friend, a surgeon, whose scalpel endangered the life of just one person. The result of pilot error was on an entirely different scale.

Right now his concern was for the welfare of these people. His responsibility. He quickly scanned the faces, virtually all of them angled upwards to look at him. He was used to that. The appearance in the cabin of a patrician figure in a crisp white shirt with its four stripe epaulettes always invited looks of admiration and appreciation. *You will take care of us, won't you?* The return of the reassuring smile. *Of course I will.* He was relieved to see that none appeared to have come to any physical harm. He expected there would have been tears, but for now there were none. No weeping. No yelling. A hush. Simon was relieved. He felt a prod in the back and turned to see the Big Guy motioning for him to sit in the adjacent centre aisle seat. The rest of the row was empty. He sat down. Unrestrained.

* * *

The same scene, the same passengers, but Nabil's take on the situation was entirely different. He was not looking at the mass. He was unconcerned about how they might be feeling or what they were doing. Silently and quickly he was assessing individuals, looking for the strongest in the pack. Apart from the Big Guy who Nabil reckoned he could deal with himself the other hijackers were not that impressive. Fairly slight, not particularly well nourished and possibly not that smart either. Remove their guns and the odds would be heavily on any reasonably fit regular gym goer being able to take one of them down. Nabil reckoned he himself could easily despatch two simultaneously, including disarming them. He was being modest. More likely three.

He scanned a quick flick across the rows of seats discounting anyone whose eyes did not appear above the row in front of them. No visible eyes meant too small. An older man, unlikely strong enough. Two teenage boys, useful but undisciplined. Both wearing headphones. Might not even have noticed yet that they had been hijacked he thought ruefully. That was unkind. His gaze swept past and then instantly returned to exactly what he was looking for. A man, mid to late twenties, with a shirt doing a pretty poor job of hiding impressive upper body strength. That was one to include.

A prod in the back directed him to take the centre aisle seat in the row behind Simon. Feigning misunderstanding, he half stumbled and took the opposite aisle. The one next to Mr Muscle. The guard did not argue with his choice. After all a seat was just a seat. The guard leaned across and clipped a cable tie to Nabil's right wrist. Taking no chances with the one who looked the more dangerous.

As the guard moved away Nabil's neighbor leant over. "You the pilot?"

"Co-pilot actually. Same thing nowadays. I do most of the driving if that's what you mean. I don't expect I will be doing much of that any time soon." Nabil used his head to motion downwards towards his restrained arm.

"Then you might need to use this." Looking down, Nabil saw the knife. "You just need to know the right people," the man said.

"Impressive. Hang on to it for now. I'll use it later when that guy is further away. I'm Nabil by the way."

"Luke"

"Very pleased to meet you, Luke. When the time comes do you reckon you could take one of these guys out?"

He already knew the answer. Which was exactly what his new friend confirmed.

"No worries. With an Aussie rules footy tackle I can ground a 90kg forward like a sack of spuds. Shouldn't be a problem with one of these mites. Apart from that big fella, of course."

"He may be big, but he is probably not that street-smart. Don't worry, I have reserved him for myself. I owe him one. How many of them are there in total?"

"Not entirely sure but no more than 10. Possibly fewer than that. Two left the plane with some of the women. But there are probably some more of them on the ground."

"Very likely. They seem to know exactly what they are doing. Keeping a few passengers on the ground is a very smart move. No point in trying any heroics up here until we know more about the situation down there. Successful action needs communication."

Moments later Nabil got a second surprise as he watched Luke tentatively pulling something from his pocket and proffering it.

"My god, what else have you got hidden away? A rabbit?"

"No, sorry. This is a walkie talkie and that's my lot. Anyway, what do you reckon these guys are after by bringing us down to earth here, wherever precisely 'here' is?"

It was a question that Nabil himself had been pondering ever since the invasion of the cockpit. His previous experiences in Lebanon had trained him to think through such things. The level of planning that had gone in to the plane takeover was considerable. Getting the guns onboard was the least of it. Nabil could think of a dozen ways that could be done easily despite the charade of all the body scans and shoe removal that made passengers feel safer. Dealing with the shutdown of primary and secondary radar, the precise timing of controlling the cabin oxygen, plus knowing the exact waypoints to head for at low altitude were all signs of a planned operation that went well beyond just the bad guys on the plane. A ratio of one guard to ten or so passengers was also spot on, provided the guards were armed, which of course they were. Splitting the group between two locations showed forward thinking designed to frustrate any heroics. Finally, knowing that where they had landed was prepared and ready to handle the Boeing, was a stroke of genius. Wherever exactly it was, they were literally 'off the radar'. No control tower, no terminal building, no people around, and yet a runway long and firm enough to have served them well.

These guys meant business. It was just not yet clear what that business was. The co-pilot had no reply for Luke.

Nabil looked back at Simon who was now seated in the row behind him, the strain of the past few hours clearly telling. He was fast asleep.

The Big Guy returned closer to him again.

"If you think you can escape you are wrong. Stop talking"

"Fuck off." An instinctive verbal response from the younger man.

The Big Guy needed no further encouragement and lifted a hand to strike Luke. Only an entreaty from the other guard stopped him.

"Leave him, Zar."

Chapter 53

Local time: Thursday – Saturday

Kimberley examined the roof and walls of her surroundings. The beams were of concrete and the roof of strong iron. The walls had wooden uprights clad in sheet metal painted goodness knows how long ago and showing definite signs of wear and flaking. But overall the building was sound. Whoever had carved out this place had done it long, long ago and very properly. Robust enough to withstand time. You could drop a bomb on this place, she thought, and it would probably withstand the blast. She had no way of knowing that was exactly the objective of the original architects.

* * *

That night Kimberley slept fitfully inside the sleeping bag that had been doled out to her, laid atop one of the several thin mattresses spread across a concrete bench. Each time she awoke disorientated as her eyes adjusted to the dim artificial light her brain faltered towards recognition of her surroundings. Some times for a moment she thought she was still on the plane and then the absence of any engine noise jolted her into a panic. One time she thought she was back in the flat with Joanna during a power cut. And always, once she had reached a wakeful state she wished she was anywhere at all and snuggled up with Andrew.

Morning was difficult to determine underground, absent from sunlight, but at last Kimberley reckoned the night outside must be past. Exactly how early it was or whether it was already close to noon, she had no idea. As she sat up Julie approached from the gloom and proffered a cup of tea.

"There you go. Rise and shine, we will be landing shortly." Once a flight attendant, always a flight attendant.

"Mmm, thanks. What time is it?"

"I always set my watch at take-off to the destination time so I can tell you it is already 09:30 in Brisbane. As for the time here, well it rather depends on where we are. 08:30 might be a good enough guess."

"Not really sure it matters, other than the fact that I am starving."

"In that case you are in luck. I have been having a nose around and there are some rather decent cooking facilities and provisions in the next chamber but one. Do you fancy omelet?"

"Sounds perfect."

"Powdered eggs, I'm afraid. Let's go through quietly and not wake the others. Just in case it is still the middle of the night."

On the way they passed the two guards, one asleep the other one almost.

* * *

During the next two days the women in the bunker fell into a routine. The main guard, the kindlier one, remained at all times but the other post was rotated every few hours, each time a new face. Once each day, during what Julie's watch determined was after noon, a posse of the women were ordered to gather up boxes of food and containers of water to take over to the plane. Someone had obviously correctly figured that perishables would be better stored in the relative cool and spaciousness underground than on the confines of the aircraft itself. Yet another sign of diligent pre-planning.

On the first day when they were onboard with their food delivery the Big Guy had made them cluster at the back of the main cabin. The males in the cabin had now been released from their shackles after first being reminded of the consequences of attempting any heroics, regarding the women being held elsewhere. Their captor then moved to the front and ordered the rest of the passengers to their feet, standing in their seats and looking forlornly forward.

Then a barked instruction "Give thumbs up."

Unthinkingly most obeyed. A few did not.

Three clicks in quick succession and the satellite phone disappeared back into the Big Guy's pocket before most realised they had been snapped.

As time went on Kimberley noticed that their kindly guard began to look more and more uncomfortable, almost despondent. Looking after female prisoners in a subterranean prison appeared to be way outside his comfort zone. He remained watchful but his gaze also contained a curiosity particularly for his two non-Asian captives. His stare was not one of leering nor did it contain menace. It was as if he wanted to engage in conversation but knew that under the circumstances this was firmly against instructions.

Eventually she could stand it no longer. "I'm going to speak to him," she said to Julie. "Maybe find out what's going on, why we are here."

"Good luck with that."

The chance came soon enough when Kimberley was alone in the kitchen chamber and the kindly one walked in. Realising he was about to be alone with a woman he turned to leave.

"Don't go. I would like to talk to you."

The man looked relieved. In other circumstances he might have smiled.

"What is your name?" A simple conversation opener.

"Zico," the hesitant reply.

"Thank you for treating us well, Zico."

Kimberley realized he may never have heard a Western woman use his name. A half smile showed he liked it.

"But why have you brought us here?" One question at a time.

A longer hesitation this time as if he was thinking how much to tell? Maybe he was just like the others.

"You are here because of the struggle to re-unite my country. Half of our land was taken from us many years ago. We want it back, that is all."

"And how will bringing us here accomplish that?"

"There are those who believe that arming with superior weapons is the answer. Others like me prefer diplomacy. But in the modern world diplomacy is expensive too. Good PR across the world with delegations lobbying vested interests and the U.N. can cost more than a store full of rocket launchers."

"So, it is money?"

"Yes"

"A hundred people up for ransom?"

"No, not if all goes well. Just one airplane. An almost new Boeing 777, an easier bargaining chip than people. A plane has a price. The value of a person can cause too much argument."

"And if all does not go well?"

"That's my brother's department. I have said too much."

Abruptly he turned and left.

***

Apart from the trips taking supplies to the plane there was little else to do to fill the long boring hours underground.

"Let's tell stories," suggested Kimberley. "They can be real or imagined, just so long as they are interesting….and preferably long."

"OK, you start."

"Mine will be real. I will tell you about my childhood and the influence of my grandmother. She is the reason I am taking this trip…" her voice tailed off as Kimberley confronted the reality of the situation and the impact of her imprisonment.

Ever empathetic, Julie caught the mood. "No, go on, tell me about her."

Kimberley began with her earliest memory of childhood visits to her Grandmother's farm. It was really just a smallholding, a few acres. No cows or sheep, but a few chickens, a goat and rows and rows of fruit and vegetables definitely constituted a 'farm' to her childish eyes. Then once she reached her early teenage years, the visits were when Grandmother also doubled as a confidante whose calm advice as a trusted grown-up frequently helped her through the minefield of boy problems.

"I have got a lot more to tell, but let's do it in instalments. Your turn."

"I could tell you about my plans to become a pilot. But that is a bit boring."

"How could it be? Go on."

"When I first joined the airline I just had the usual idea about travelling the world at someone else's expense, but that all changed the first time I entered the flight deck nervously gripping a tray of coffees."

"You didn't drop them, did you?"

"Almost the opposite. The hushed peacefulness combined with the spectacular 180-degree view of an approaching coastline 5 miles below calmed me right down. It was a Zen moment."

"It's beautiful enough just looking out a small side window. I can't imagine what it must be like up front."

"It's stunning, and that is when I said such a stupid thing."

"Like?"

"It's such a lovely sunny day," is what I blurted. "'It's always sunny up here, love' came the smiling reply."

"And that patronizing remark didn't put you off?"

"No. That was it, my mind was made up. One day I would become a pilot. I'm still learning, taking the courses when I'm rostered off. It's taken forever but I should be certified by next year."

"Well done you."

"Right, but if it's a proper story you want, I am going to choose to tell you about two real aviation heroines of mine. Let's start with Sabrina Gonzalez Pasterski."

"You've got me there. Never heard of her."

"Not many people have. Yet. She is a remarkable Cuban American hardly thirty years old. Better known for her scientific endeavors, but let me tell you about her aeronautical achievements. Sabrina's fascination with flight began even as a preschooler and at the age of 9 she started taking flying lessons in Canada where the age eligibility permitted it. But not content with learning to fly at the age of 12 she bought a Zenith plane kit."

"Is that like an 'Airfix' model with all the bits and the smelly glue?"

"No, I'm talking a real airplane kit, for one that flies."

"Wow!"

"The young Sabrina contacted other enthusiasts and along with using the internet she gradually built up to something that was too big to fit her parents' garage. So, the parts were transported to a suburban Chicago Airport, assembled and painted. In early 2008 with her Dad at the controls the plane made its maiden flight."

"Incredible. And where is she now?"

"She is continuing the legacy of her friend Stephen Hawking and setting her mind to various areas of quantum physics that are well beyond the ken of us mere mortals."

"And your other heroine?"

"I will leave that one for later."

* * *

After they had returned from the trip on the second day Julie called Kimberley over into a corner for a whispering session. Considering neither of their captors stayed in close proximity and the other women were quite content to chat amongst themselves in groups of twos and threes without straining to overhear more conversations, keeping a low voice was completely unnecessary. But somehow it still seemed the natural thing to do, especially as the solid walls gave off a strong echo.

"I saw your friend, that Luke guy, when we were over there just now. Sitting restlessly in his seat. He looked fed up."

"Who wouldn't be? At least we are getting a little exercise as we walk back and forth."

"But I also noticed he was in the next row to Nabil, our co-pilot. At the right moment the two of them would make a handy team if we can somehow coordinate a plan of action."

"What are you thinking?"

"It has to be something coordinated between action here and over there on the plane. There is no point in just one group of us independently trying a spot of heroics. Especially if it fails that would just make them mad."

"I guess coordinated success would make them mad too but that wouldn't matter, so long as we had the upper hand."

"And as for the guns, have you ever used one?"

"Sure. But only shooting rabbits in my grandmother's yard."

"Then you are one up on me, Annie Oakley."

"I've been thinking about it this past day or so. After all there's not much else to do. There must be a way that could work to get us out of here."

"I think so too. What we need is some kind of weapon. It does not need to be a gun. Just something that puts these guys out of action."

The answer would come sooner than they thought.

Chapter 54

London time: Thursday evening

Under the circumstances Stephanie had decided not to go home. Despite the caller now having her mobile number Gareth had readily agreed that it would be better if they both stayed in the office. Stephanie was relieved she would not be home alone when the guy might ring back. She was less relieved that Gareth had also agreed with Tom not to call the police. Not yet.

In the late afternoon Gareth's P.A. returned from a nearby outdoor supplies store with two sleeping bags and two camp beds.

During the day Stephanie had tried unsuccessfully to keep her mind on other things. Not an easy task when trying to shut out thoughts of a pending fifty-million-dollar pay-out. Either as a claim or as a ransom payment the outlook was grim. Not to mention that the fate of more than a hundred people would depend on how she and her company responded.

Towards the end of the afternoon she had gone out for a welcome breath of air and an aimless wander through Leadenhall market. On the way back, she stopped into T.K. Maxx to pick up a cheap pair of pajamas, a toothbrush and then to Pret and bought a selection of the day's remaining sandwiches, a salad and a decent coffee.

Around six thirty when the rest of the staff had all left, Gareth knocked and entered Stephanie's office. She offered him a choice of the sandwiches.

He took two. "Thanks, I'll keep these for later. It could be a long night."

"How do you want me to play it, assuming the guy does ring back?"

"The key thing is leave them in no doubt that before we can consider anything we will need some proof that the aircraft is intact and the passengers are all OK. Don't agree to anything for now but give the impression that we will consider everything.

Ask him to be more specific about their demands. Whatever they want we need to let them know we will need time.

"Makes sense."

Gareth nodded. "Alright, I am going back to my office now. The upside is I have plenty to be getting on with now there is some peace and quiet around here. Press my intercom button three times if you get a call otherwise I'll pop back around ten to check in with you for the night."

A wry smile, and he left.

Despite being distracted Stephanie had managed to catch up with her work during the day. Now there was nothing urgent that needed attention. The problem was that there was also nothing else that held her attention. She took out her Kindle and started back into the novel she had been reading in snatches for weeks but that was no use. She read the Evening Standard she had picked up earlier. Not being interested in celeb gossip or football that only took care of another ten minutes. Finally, she logged on to Netflix and plumped to continue the mindless distraction of an episode of 'Scandal'. She had almost given up on the series some time ago due to the increasing ridiculousness of the plot. Now compared to her own situation it did not seem quite so far-fetched.

Before she knew it, she was on the third episode.

* * *

She had nodded off when Gareth entered her office again.

"Sorry to disturb. I assume no contact yet?"

"Correct. I have just been filling the time with mindless TV."

"Alright, I'm going to turn in now. Remember three buzzes on the intercom if they call back."

"Sure."

With a kindly 'goodnight' Gareth left. He did not belong to the world of hugging.

Stephanie prepared for bed. She snuggled into her sleeping bag, laid her phone on the floor beside the low-slung camp bed and propped her laptop open on an adjacent chair. It was two more episodes of Scandal before she finally got to sleep.

* * *

Stephanie was a sound sleeper. She was not used to be woken before morning. Insurance was not the kind of business that lent itself to middle of the night work calls. When the call came it took her a few seconds to remember where she was and why.

"Hello."

"Have you had time to think about it?"

"Yes, but let's start with why we should believe you. Do you think yours is the only call we have had?" The latter remark had just popped into her head. She was glad it had.

"You can ignore any others. We will send you photos. That will show you. Soon"

"We also have hardly any details. Where is the plane? And what exactly do you want?"

"Never mind where it is. For now it is safe. It will stay safe if you give us what we want."

"And what is that?"

"We both know the aircraft is insured for two hundred million dollars. We just want half of that and then you get it back. Also, for that price the passengers will be fine too."

"I am sure you know that we are not the only underwriters. Even if *we* were to agree it could take many days to persuade the others." Stephanie was well aware of wider industry's reputation for moving according to tortoise time. But aviation insurance was the exception. Especially when the insured asset could be seen in flames on YouTube the payouts were usually surprisingly quick.

"You can have three days to sort it out. That is all."

"We need a week at least." Stephanie plucked a timescale from nowhere.

"Five days. That's it." If Stephanie had been more versed in the art of the deal she would have recognised this as a good sign that the give and take of a negotiation had begun.

"After that we will kill two passengers every day until you meet our demands. If it takes longer than five days you will also have passenger claims. I am sure you know that little incident on 9/11 paid out over several million dollars per passenger."

"But...."

"And after seven days it will be five passengers every day until you pay up."

"Who are you people?" A redundant request.

"That is not something you need to know. I will call back tomorrow to check your progress. After that only four more days."

The call went dead.

Belatedly Stephanie pressed the intercom button three times.

* * *

It was still dark when Tom walked back into the boardroom at Richardson Alliance in the City.

Stephanie and Gareth had just had enough time to change out of their sleepwear and appear semi presentable when Tom entered.

"Seems like only yesterday..." Gareth greeted him wryly.

"So what's up?" Tom looked directly at Stephanie.

"Another call. We still don't know who they are but now we have a demand. Five days to come up with a hundred million dollars. That's their price for keeping the passengers alive and us getting the plane back in one piece."

"Shit."

"And as far as we can see from this they are not lying about the situation." Stephanie passed her phone over to Tom. "These came through just a few minutes ago."

Tom stared at the photo showing dozens of nonplussed passengers standing inside the cabin of the missing aircraft, some of them giving a thumbs up. He flicked through three screens and then to another three showing various exterior shots of the intact fuselage draped under what appeared to be a huge green shroud.

"Could be anywhere," he muttered, "and could have been taken anytime, even before they carried out something nasty."

"Agreed," said Gareth, "but for now I think we have no choice but to believe them."

"There is something else you should know," said Tom. "On the way here I got a call from one of our people who is now in the region. What he told me backs up the claim that our plane is on the ground."

"Some good news, at least," muttered Gareth.

"And thanks to some detective work we now know a little more about the guys who are doing this. There were eight of them on the plane and they belong to an organization called OPM."

"And they are?" Stephanie this time.

"A group dedicated to securing the re-unification of Papua New Guinea. The Indonesian's took half their country in the 60s, and now these guys want it back."

"I guess a hundred million dollars would be quite useful to them in that endeavor," said Gareth.

"One more thing from the call," added Stephanie, "If we don't pay up then from day five they are threatening to kill two passengers a day. And also destroy the plane."

The airline CEO jolted upright and turned away, hiding his clenched fist from the other two. If it had been any louder Stephanie would have heard him say 'fuck.'

Chapter 55

Local time: Saturday

Kimberley, along with Julie, was once again undertaking the daily trip from bunker to plane. They had two guards with them. The one she now knew as Zico, plus another, a nameless mean looking man armed with a rifle and a pistol. The two captors seemed keen to prolong their time outside and a short way from the trapdoor they stopped for a smoke and motioned to the women to sit down.

Kimberley moved closer to the area where she had heard the whispering stranger. A low rock. Was it this one? She sat down and glanced over at Julie who remained standing a short distance away, stretching and bending to alleviate the effects of being confined.

At first Kimberley imagined she heard the whispering again. A few seconds passed, then again. Not imagined.

"Hey! How are you doing?"

Turning her head sideways so as not to look directly at the source of the sound behind her she responded quietly, "Very well, thank you." That sounded so British. Maybe she had been too long in London. "Did you manage to pass my message?"

"No, sorry. I had a bit of trouble back in the village. Then your phone died and I can't charge it."

"Shit"

"I know, but if you can give me Andrew's number, I can try again using my own phone," said Maarten.

Kimberley half turned her head back to him. "I don't usually remember peoples' numbers. Except this one is easy. Zero seven nine, double zero, double five, double six, double seven. It's a UK number."

"Got it," said Maarten.

"Good. But how the hell will we ever get out of here? I wish there was a way to overpower these guys. At least they are not very big. With one exception"

"Size hardly matters when they have the guns," said Maarten.

"That's blindingly obvious," said Kimberley. "What weapons can we use against bullets?"

"What did you say?"

"I said 'what weapons....'

"No, no, before that?"

"It's blindingly obvious?"

"Yes, that was it. It's not a phrase I have heard before but it reminds me of something my father taught me the last time we were all here together. Maybe the solution could indeed be 'blindingly obvious' as you say."

"Meaning what?"

"Meaning give me a few hours to figure it out. I will come back tomorrow and explain how there just might be a way for you to get the better of these guys."

"Well good luck with that. I have an urgent need to get to Brisbane which is not helped by being stuck here. You never did tell me your name, by the way?"

"Maarten."

"Kimberley."

It was only then that Kimberley became aware that they were being watched. From the edge of the forest, about twenty meters away stood a small child, staring with eyes wide, and clutching a football under one arm. Maarten saw him at the same instant and urgently began to wave him away as he dropped back to the ground. The boy paid no heed and rather than hide himself he began to bounce the ball in front of him. The rhythmic movement instantly attracted the two guards.

The mean one quickly unholstered his pistol and aimed it in the direction of the boy.

Kimberley gasped. The situation was bad enough, with one death already among the passengers, but were these really the type of men who would shoot a child?

The mean guy took aim, but before he could discharge a shot towards the boy, Zico leapt forward him and tugged at the arm holding the gun. There was a pop as the weapon went off and immediately Zico fell writhing to the ground, clutching at his foot.

It was difficult for Kimberley to make out how badly he had been hurt in his effort to save the child. She turned to see Maarten slithering backwards into the undergrowth.

* * *

On the journey back to the village Maarten's gaze scanned left and right. He knew what he was looking for. A tree with pinkish leaves that could grow anything up to 15 meters tall. *Excoecaria agallocha* was the Latin name. The locals had other words for it. Words that more accurately described the uses to which they put it.

He was almost at the village when he spotted one, at the edge of a small stream. Emptying the remains of his water bottle he stood close to the slender trunk and with his sheath knife began to hack at the soft bark. It was not long before a trickle of milky latex began to ooze forth. Holding the water bottle tight against the gash he began to collect the substance. Patiently he alternately hacked and collected. It took about twenty minutes before his bottle was full and he carefully screwed the top back on.

Back at the village he approached Arief's hut, cautiously at first, making sure that his assailant or assailants had not returned. They had not. Even the dog had departed.

Chapter 56

local time: Saturday afternoon

For the best part of the afternoon the two women explored the options for an escape plan.

"We make a good team," said Julie. "You are not short of creative ideas but they need to pass my sense check."

"OK, there's ten of us down here and only two of them. How about we just beat them up?" suggested Kimberley.

"Female empowerment is all very well until you bring upper body strength and bullets into the mix," replied Julie. "I wouldn't bet on that one. There are three areas we need to attack and despatch them, out in the open ground, on the plane and down here."

"My new whispering friend outside there seems to have the germ of a plan of how we might do that. He is going to share with me tomorrow."

"Well, whatever it is we will need to coordinate with the guys on the plane so we can all act together." Julie again being practical. "If you can get your pal Luke in on it, then he can share with Nabil and Simon."

"And we do that when?"

"Obviously not right now. There is no way the walkie-talkie is going to work from down here. We will have to wait until tomorrow and hope we will be taking more food over to the plane."

"You mean, just talk to them when we are over there?"

"Not that either. If the guards see us speaking together they will assume something is up. We will need to hear back from Maarten first, and then grab the opportunity to use the walkie-talkie when we are out in the open."

"Tomorrow then."

Chapter 57

Local time: Saturday afternoon

Maarten knew it would not happen today, but if things went to plan then tomorrow might see the captives free. Free to do what? To go where? A hundred people and one aircraft in the middle of nowhere. That Andrew guy would have to be the one to solve that bit. Time to give him a call.

Maarten took out his phone. The girl had said it was a UK number. Maarten had had a girlfriend there once. The country dialing code +44 had been etched in his memory long after the relationship had fizzled out. But what was the rest of the number? Double fours, fives, sixes he easily remembered. But something else in front of that. 07-something, zero. He patiently sequenced up from 0710. 0750….0760….0770. Eventually, ninth time lucky. A voice answered.

Chapter 58

Singapore time: Saturday afternoon

Andrew's heart thumped as he answered the call.

"Kimberley?"

"Sorry to disappoint. It's Maarten again."

Andrew quickly recovered after a deflated 'oh'. "Where is she?"

"Not exactly right here, but close by. Don't worry, never mind the long story. What I can tell you is……"

"Where the fuck are they?" The combination of worry and jetlag drove Andrew to interrupt. Swearing was not like him either.

"Papua New Guinea."

"Are all the passengers OK?"

"From what I have seen, yes. But that is only the few who are allowed outside the plane. I have no idea what is going on onboard."

"Thanks. Sorry to snap at you but I've been worried sick. Now if you give me their exact location, we can do something about it."

"Maybe you will not have to. By the end of tomorrow there is chance the passengers may have already done something themselves about their situation."

"Meaning what exactly?"

"Meaning a dose of self-help."

"For fuck's sake, a bunch of our passengers against armed men doesn't sound like a very good idea. Tell me exactly where they are and we can get the authorities involved."

"They are close to a place called Rabaul. If things go well then all you will have to do is come and collect them."

It was typical Dutch bluntness. Andrew took it as confidence.

* * *

Andrew put down his phone and returned to his keyboard. He had heard the word 'Rabaul'. Not a place he had ever heard of.

One click led him immediately to a Wiki entry and his ignorance evaporated.

Rabaul is the former provincial capital of East New Britain in Papua New Guinea. It was evacuated and nearly destroyed in 1994 when the nearby volcano Tavurvur erupted. Because of its war-time history it attracts many Japanese visitors.

Andrew flicked to Google maps and zoomed out. He saw Rabaul was on a direct line east from the last known location of flight 10, above the Java Sea. It was on the same latitude as Brisbane but only much further north. Fuel would not have been a problem, therefore plausible. The distance from the last ATC contact looked to be around 2,500 miles so around five hours flying time. Again, plausible.

A few more clicks and he unearthed more.

Lakunai Airfield was an aerodrome located near Rabaul, East New Britain, Papua New Guinea. The airfield was later known as Rabaul Airport. It is located at the foot of Tavurvur volcano, near Matupit Island. The airport was destroyed by the 1994 eruption that destroyed the town of Rabaul.

But an airport *destroyed?* How badly was it destroyed? Would it ever have been long enough to support the Boeing? He knew the team back in London were already searching for any sea level airfield with at least 5,000 feet of runway. Andrew read on.

The airfield was constructed by the Royal Australian Air Force and consisted of an unpaved 4,700-foot single runway during World War II. The airfield was captured during the battle of Rabaul in 1942 by the Japanese and was extensively modified and expanded.

4,700 foot and then 'expanded'. Even an extra 300 feet would have done it. But, 'destroyed'.

Suddenly the enormity of what he knew dawned on him. If the caller was to be believed, he had become party to the exact location of the missing aircraft.

Thirty seconds later he had Tom on the phone.

Chapter 59

London time: Saturday morning

Stephanie was once again in the boardroom along with Gareth and Tom.

"I have some good news from one of our people out there," the CEO told them. "Thanks to some detective work we now have a pretty good idea of the plane's location. It has landed in Papua New Guinea."

"Has it been spotted?" she asked.

"By someone on the ground, yes."

The three lapsed into silence. They were expecting the next call and had agreed Stephanie would continue to be the initial respondent.

"Could still be hours before they call," Gareth broke the quiet. Then just as Tom was nodding silent agreement the ring tone proved them both wrong.

"Richardson Alliance," answered Stephanie as if this might be any random client calling on a Saturday morning when they were normally closed. As agreed, she pushed the speaker button so all three of them could listen.

"Four days left. Are you making progress with arranging our payment?"

"Yes," Stephanie hesitated, "but it will take the whole time to arrange."

"The 'whole time' has just been changed." came the voice from the other end.

"What do you mean?" Stephanie again.

"You should not have sent your man to Batam. Our people saw him there and followed him back to Singapore."

This last statement meant nothing to Stephanie. She looked over at Tom sensing a mixture of surprise and anger. Not being in full control of the situation was something the CEO was not used to. She realized Tom could stand it no longer as he jumped in.

"Listen here, this is Tom Nichols speaking," he blurted. "You may think you are being so clever, but we know who you are – OPM, the Free Papua Movement."

There was a moments silence from the other end.

"And what good does that do you?"

"By itself, nothing. But it gives us a clue as to where you are holding our plane."

"Papua New Guinea is a big place. Many, many islands. You will never find us….until you pay up."

"Thanks for that. You just confirmed the country."

Another pause.

"But not the place." Stephanie sensed a hesitation in the caller's reply that made it sound more of a question than a statement.

"Don't be too sure about that." Tom again.

"Your actions in Batam give us no choice. Forget four days. You now have just three more days to come up with the full amount. And before that we need an immediate upfront deposit."

"Meaning what?" Tom still controlling the call from the London end.

"Meaning one hundred thousand dollars in cash. We know you have your man in Singapore. He will bring it to Port Moresby airport by this time tomorrow, otherwise you will not get your precious aircraft back. At this time tomorrow, if we get no money, we will blow it up."

"Impossible," said Tom. It will take some time to get the deposit and then it is a long flight from Singapore."

"OK, the money by Monday morning, otherwise it is impossible at our end that you ever get your plane back."

"If you destroy the plane you will certainly never see the $200 million." Gareth's measured tone gave no hint of the tension in the room.

"Exactly," came the reply over the speaker phone. "Then it becomes $300 million. $3 million per live passenger is a fair price, don't you think?"

The call went silent. So did all three people in the room.

Chapter 60

Singapore time: Sunday afternoon

"I've been looking for you," said Bruno, "you need to go and get packed.

Andrew looked blank. "Why? Where am I going?"

"It's Tom's decision. He has been trying to get hold of you. He asked me to tell you to call him back as soon as I found you. I think you are going to want to hear what he has to say."

Andrew fished out his phone and realized it had defaulted to silent. Damn. There were three missed calls from Tom.

A single jab on the 'return call' key, a slight hesitation and then the familiar sound of a UK dial tone.

"This is Tom."

"It's Andrew. You asked me to call?"

There was a slight hesitation before Tom launched into an explanation of the call he had taken yesterday from the hijackers, the reassurance of the photograph, and the demand for an immediate cash deposit. He knew Andrew would do his best without the worry of the additional threat about destroying the aircraft. He left that bit out.

"They want the money delivered to Port Moresby tomorrow," the CEO revealed, "that's where you come in."

The call ended and Andrew handed the phone back to Bruno. As he headed back to the elevator Andrew was overcome with relief.

Kimberley was safe, and tomorrow he would be closer to her.

Chapter 61

Local time: Sunday/Monday

Andrew was surprised at the compact size and weight of one hundred thousand dollars. In hundred dollar bills the cash weighed only one kilo, and fit easily in a hotel laundry bag now nestling at the bottom of his backpack. After instruction from Tom, Bruno had returned from the 24hr bank in the transit area with the required amount, and also a round trip air ticket to Port Moresby.

Andrew made his way down into the Changi terminal and headed for the check-in desk.

"Be careful down there," said the smiling Air Niugini agent as she handed over his boarding pass. "Port Moresby is not the safest place on the planet."

"Thanks for the advice, but I am not planning on staying long." said Andrew, instinctively clutching his hand baggage more tightly than was necessary.

The flight was uneventful. In between intermittent dozing Andrew spent the time musing on what would await him on arrival. He had been given no further instruction other than to arrive alone and carrying a Blue Yonder branded backpack for identification.

Looking around the cabin at the other passengers who were mainly Asian, he realized it would not be difficult to pick himself out in the crowd.

* * *

It was not yet light as they came in to land. The Air Niugini flight was the only early morning arrival. Probably the only arrival for the whole morning Andrew thought as he looked around the smattering of parked light aircraft.

Arrival formalities were virtually non-existent. Andrew had no checked baggage to collect. He was not staying long and was one of the first to pass through into the almost empty terminal building. Almost immediately he was approached by two men who looked to be natives. Squat, squared-faced individuals, each wearing mis-matching and slightly too large suit jackets above what had been at one time quite fashionable trousers.

"Blue Yonder?" questioned one of them.

"That's me," said Andrew as he lowered and unzipped his backpack, reaching inside. "I have something for you."

"Not here," snapped the other. "Keep it safe until you arrive at the next place."

Before Andrew could protest the first man spoke again.

"You need to check in again now. Your next flight leaves soon. You will need this." As he spoke the man alongside him handed over a ticket.

"But I already have my return ticket."

"This is not a return. Our boss wants to see you."

Andrew looked down at the document that had been thrust into his hand. It was a one-way ticket.

Rabaul.

Chapter 62

Local time: Sunday morning

It was hard to gauge when another whole day had passed. Confirmation from the time on Julie's watch was one thing, but the absence of windows took away that most primal indication of a new day. Most of the captives had also quickly regressed to a pattern of more frequent and shorter naps than their routines back at home, like lone sailors released from the strictures of the connected world.

The two of them were dozing fitfully when one of the guards, a new one this time, entered their chamber and indicated via some arm waving that it was time again to gather up some more food supplies for a trip over to the aircraft. Kimberley watched as the guard's pointed arm included her, Julie, and two of the others as the group he wanted for the task.

"Here, put the walkie talkie in your pocket," whispered Julie. "When the time comes you need to be the one to use it. Luke knows you. It will have to be quick. No point in me wasting time on a call having to explain to him who I am."

The guard unlocked and opened the trapdoor with its now familiar thud, and once again the emerging women luxuriated in the warmth of the sunshine and sweetness of the forest air. As they walked across the open ground towards the shrouded aircraft Kimberley permitted herself a momentary indulgence. With arms outstretched she paused and looked up at the sky.

"It's really beautiful isn't it? If we ever get out of here I would be very tempted to come back with just a small tent and a pile of books."

"Of course, we will get out of here," said Julie.

The small party reached the bottom of the bamboo ladder and the guard motioned for them to ascend. Reacting quickly Kimberley feigned a stumble in her last couple of steps and with an exaggerated shriek fell to the ground clutching her ankle. It was a performance that any Premier League soccer player pole-axed in the penalty box would have been proud of.

The guard looked over, at first confused. As Kimberley remained on the ground Julie put down her own box then retrieved her companion's consignment and thrust it towards the guard.

"You. Take this. She cannot."

Even although he did not understand the words, the intent was clear and the authoritative tone of the woman in uniform did the trick. Sheepishly the guard slung his weapon over his shoulder and took hold of the container.

As Kimberley watched Julie mounting the first rung of the ladder, the senior flight attendant turned and nodded her support. Kimberley continued to writhe in mock agony.

As the small party clambered across the aircraft wing and disappeared into the cabin Kimberley realised that for the first time in days she was completely alone. In theory a chance to escape. But where to? And what good would it do to leave the others? The guard must have reckoned it was safe enough to leave her there a few minutes with a badly twisted ankle.

At first she thought she imagined it. But then louder. "Psst." It was coming from just behind where she was now standing.

It came twice more, and then followed by, "It's Maarten. Don't look at me. Take this."

Kimberley heard the almost silent swish of something rolling across the earth towards her and looking down saw a clear plastic drinks bottle at her feet. Not a brand she recognised and containing a milky substance that was definitely not water. Yogurt drink perhaps? She picked it up quickly and thrust it into the ample pocket of her shorts.

"Don't drink it. Here's what you have to do with it."

His instructions were concise and very clear. The missing link! Now the plan was complete.

"Now move away. And good luck," Maarten concluded. He disappeared silently.

Pulling the walkie-talkie out of her pocket Kimberley pressed the transmit call button twice and waited. Nothing. Had the batteries died on Luke's device? Might he be dozing? She tried again. This time, a whispered reply.

"Kimberley? Are you OK? I've just seen that flight attendant come in here with what looks like more tucker."

"Yes, that's Julie. And I'm fine. Listen, we have a plan to get things moving and get us all out of here. Julie and I can handle things outside but we need to coordinate and rely on you and the co-pilot to sort things out onboard."

"Co-pilot? Yes, I have met him, Nabil. He and the skipper are both back here now in the cabin with the rest of us. He seems like a useful sort. I wouldn't like to tangle with him down a back alley."

In the next few minutes Kimberley relayed a combination of what Maarten had just told her and the sequence of how that played into what she and Julie had been scheming. Then looking up she saw the others start to re-emerge from the plane. Time to end quickly.

"I need to go. It will happen next time we come over. Make sure you and Nabil are ready for it."

"Will do. It's a brilliant plan. You are some girl, Kimberley."

Without words the man with the waving gun indicated it was time to return to the bunker.

* * *

On the return journey to the bunker Kimberley had maintained a convincing limp, combined with frequent wincing. But now the two women were back below ground and alone again she instantly dropped the charade.

"Well done, girl, a great performance. I almost thought you really had hurt yourself."

Kimberley grinned. "I'll forgo the Oscar this time. But if you want to reward my efforts how about another story?"

"It would be my pleasure. But this one will be much longer. Coffee first?"

"Definitely."

* * *

Back below ground, swaddled in a blanket and clutching her mug Kimberley was momentarily less tense. And ready for her story.

"So which paragon of female endeavour do you have for me this time? Kylie Minogue?"

"Amelia Earhart."

"Ah, you mean that woman who almost flew around the world?"

"That's the one. AE, as she liked to be known, was an aviation pioneer and is the woman referred to by the senior curator of the US National Air & Space Museum as 'our most famous missing person'. It is true to say that for a certain older generation she holds the same fascination as Lord Lucan, but being Australian that name probably means nothing to you either."

Kimberley's blank look confirmed the assertion.

"People love an unsolved missing mystery. It fascinates them. How can it be in this modern, connected, media saturated world that unknowable things can still happen? How can a simple question like 'where are they?' not have an answer?"

"You know there will be plenty of people we have left behind thinking that very same thing about us right now?"

"Indeed, and for them the 'not knowing' is worse than the knowing. It's only when the 'not knowing' concerns other people outside of our own friends and family that we relish it. In that case, so long as it is someone else at the centre of the missing, the 'not knowing' can become something quite delicious. Something to be picked at, savoured, put away and then brought out and worried at again whenever we feel like it."

The combination of a hot drink, a blanket and the prospect of a good story was having its universal effect. Kimberley felt herself relaxing.

"And what did this Amelia woman do that was so remarkable"

"She was what the Americans like to refer to as an 'a-vee-iat-or'." Julie spat out the word in four elongated syllables with a poor imitation of an American accent. "In many ways her character reminds me of you. Spirited and adventurous. Not quite as precocious as Sabrina Pasterski, Amelia was 24 before she had her first flying lesson. Ten years later she became the first woman to fly solo across the Atlantic."

Julie continued the story becoming more and more animated as she recounted the tales of Amelia's exploits. Kimberley learned that not only was AE a great proponent of aviation she also toured the country giving lectures and endorsing a wide range of products from luggage to fashion and even at one stage, cigarettes. A female role model and super-star long before the celebrity days of television and social media.

"How come you know so much about her?"

"Despite me being a bubble-head trolley dolly I'm not one for celebrity fandom. I couldn't give a shit about actresses, singers and reality TV celebs. I prefer to understand more about women of real substance who have actually done something positive for the world. People like Sabrina and Amelia are the ones we should have on the front covers of magazines."

"I am right with you there."

As the story continued all of the adventures were leading up to the one thing for which Amelia Earhart was most famous – her disappearance in murky circumstances in the summer of 1937 as she attempted to fly the longest circumnavigation of the globe along an equatorial route. She was 39 years old.

Julie spun the tale with a mixture of relish and sadness.

"And where exactly did she disappear?"

"She was three quarters of the way done, flying west to east. The people who were waiting for her on that leg of the trip were on tiny Howland Island in the Pacific Ocean. By some accounts of the last known radio transmission she was almost there, within just a few miles. But communications were not that sophisticated in those days and there are plenty of alternative theories about where she might actually have crashed…or landed. Some even suggest she might have turned back and be nearer to her starting point than her destination."

As Julie continued, Kimberley heard that the resultant search operation had revealed exactly nothing. And then the conspiracy theories had started, everything from her being a spy captured and executed by the Japanese to the suggestion that she faked her own death to escape the relentless celebrity and an unhappy marriage. Some had postulated that she was having an affair with her onboard navigator, Fred Noonan, and that the pair hatched an elaborate plan to land somewhere secretly and literally disappear.

"How romantic," interrupted Kimberley.

"Maybe, but I am not so sure about that theory. The man was a bit of a drinker. Inevitably, of course, abduction by aliens had to get in on the act too. That one even made it into an episode of Star Trek!"

The echoes of both their laughter bounced off the hard walls. Kimberley was the first one to regain her posture.

"Oh god, I hope we don't end up like a plane-load of Amelia Earharts. However this ends I hope the outside world knows what has happened to us."

"They will, just as soon as we carry out 'the plan'."

Chapter 63

Local time: Monday morning

Now, despite the odds it was time to put the plan into action. Earlier at breakfast Kimberley had decanted the substance that Maarten had given her into two squeezable plastic ketchup containers, one each. Not difficult to do as the guards left them alone at meal times. As instructed, she had taken great care to thoroughly wash her hands afterwards in case any of the substance might have leaked onto her fingers.

Out in the open she was walking yet again towards the shrouded aircraft, the group in single file, as always with one guard leading the way and the other taking up the rear. The trapdoor had banged shut moments before, leaving the other two guards below ground. As previously planned Julie was at the front of the posse of captives with Kimberley the last in line. They had agreed to act sooner rather than later. Any disturbance short of an explosion would not be heard by those shuttered below ground while there was always the danger the closer they got to the plane that a guard onboard might be looking out of a window.

Besides, these past few hours their guards had somehow seemed more on edge. Kimberley could not figure out why, but something was up. Even Zico was keeping his distance. Since the incident with the pistol he had been sporting a heavily bandaged foot.

It was time to act. Dropping the box she had been carrying with both hands Kimberley waited one beat before spinning round to face the guard behind her. With the extra step he was virtually in her face, his questioning eyes wide with surprise. Exactly what she needed. Before he had any time to back away Kimberley deftly removed the ketchup bottle from the right-hand pocket of her shorts, flipped the cap with her thumb, pointed the container at the man's face and gave two quick squeezes.

Two bolts of milky latex substance shot forward, one landing almost perfectly in each eye. With a startled yelp the man's hands instinctively jerked upwards to rub his face. Too late. Already his world had gone dark.

The liquid had done exactly what Maarten had explained it would, the sap coming from a particular mangrove tree that his father had taken great pains to teach him to avoid. The complex Latin name for the plant she had instantly forgotten but the more common one had stuck, 'Blind-your-eye Mangrove'. *Does exactly what it says on the tin*, thought Kimberley as she recalled Maarten telling them that even slight contact with the eye causes temporary blindness.

As the guard stumbled forward Kimberley stepped aside and stretched her leg upwards to kick him in the groin. The poor man was in a quandary with only two hands and three places in sore need of being clutched. Holding onto his gun was no longer a priority.

Hearing the commotion, the lead guard turned to see what was going on. Within seconds Julie had made sure he met the same fate as his compatriot. The other women in the party looked on in astonishment as Kimberley and Julie kicked their respective captors to the ground.

"That was almost fun," said Kimberley. "I could get used to this."

"No time to enjoy. These two won't be giving us any trouble for the next few hours. Blind as bats, both of them."

"Grab their rifles and let's get to the plane. Quick."

Without bothering to explain to their fellow captors the two women picked up a weapon each and sped toward the plane. They were quickly up the ladder, over the wing and at the door. Four short knocks was the signal. They had seen it often enough to know.

The door was opened incautiously by the guard beyond. After several days of routine operation he had no reason to be alert to anything other than his compatriot leading in the food detail. The man was unarmed. His welcoming smile lasted less than a second as Kimberley repeated the disabling dose of two quick squirts from the ketchup bottle to his eyes. The man crumpled backwards as she kicked him to the floor. Over his prostrate body she caught sight of both Nabil and Luke three rows back already standing alert and ready. Judging the distance, she turned her rifle parallel to the ground and flung it towards the co-pilot. With outstretched hands Nabil caught it as safely as a fireman might catch a plummeting infant.

* * *

To Kimberley it was just a gun but Nabil instantly recognised it as a semi-automatic. In a trice he spun round and aimed quickly at the next nearest guard. The man was standing by the closed doorway opposite to the one that had just opened. Nabil had a clear shot. He discharged two in quick succession. Always two. Instinctive. The way he had been trained. One to the right shoulder and the other to the left leg. At such close range both bullets went straight through the man's flesh and then penetrated the aircraft door before exiting out into the jungle beyond. The guard dropped to the floor.

As had been the routine for the past few days the guards had been rotating duties, allowing two at any one time to retreat to the business cabin for rest and meals. Two down, one of them writhing on the floor nursing his gunshot wounds. The other not even able to see the end of his nose, a situation that would persist for at least several hours according to Maarten's assessment of the efficacy of the contents of the ketchup bottles.

Now there were two left in the main cabin with the hostages and two resting. Thankfully the Big Guy was one of the latter. Nabil knew in theory it would be easier to tackle him in there, but the sound of the gunshot would already have taken away any element of surprise. He also knew that the fewer holes in the aircraft the better. A door would be relatively easy to replace. All going well, which it was so far, one day the plane might fly out of here. Reckoning that dispensing with his own weapon would make the remaining guards less likely to fire, first he dropped the rifle to the ground and yelled to Julie to do likewise.

The two remaining guards in the cabin were not the brightest sparks but they were savvy enough to realise that Nabil and Luke posed the greatest threat, each now standing in opposite aisles three rows back from the bulkhead. The split second they each wasted pondering exactly how to react was enough to seal their fate. Although from very different backgrounds, one from the military the other from amateur sport, the two captives were thinking along identical lines. Two brains nurtured thousands of miles apart were both instinctively in sync. They rushed forward in unison, separated only by the central aisle where uncomprehending eyes watched their lightening progress. It was only as they simultaneously reached their respective captives that their actions diverged.

Luke crouched and went in low with a flying tackle clasping his hands around the back of the man's calves while using the momentum in his shoulders against the thighs. The same simple principle embodied in the humble see-saw. Input force, output force, with the knees as the fulcrum. The way a small person destroys a much larger one. Luke knew it. Archimedes knew it too when he supposedly declared 'give me a place to stand and I shall move the earth'. The guard obeyed the rules of physics and his earth moved. He hit the floor. Luke was on top of him in an instant with a swift punch to the face knocking the man into unconsciousness.

Meanwhile Nabil eschewed the sporting approach and had settled for the universally effective swift kick to the groin followed by a head butt. Different method, same result.

Looking up as he hovered over the comatose body of his foe Nabil felt his sense of victory evaporate. Bursting through the curtained divide from the business cabin was the Big Guy, the satellite phone hanging limply in one hand, his gun in the other pointing firmly at the Lebanese man's chest. Nabil dropped his arms in despair and was just about to mumble a subdued surrender when the advantage reverted. The Big Guy's eyes bulged in surprise as he flailed to the floor dropping the phone and his weapon as he fell. Behind him and at almost the same height Nabil saw flight attendant Emma, triumphantly clutching her weapon of choice. The fire extinguisher from the adjacent galley had been as effective as a baseball bat when applied to the back of the Big Guy's head.

"One advantage of being tall," she murmured, "That'll teach him to under-estimate women. Not tying us up is almost an insult."

The numbers were quickly improving. Two blinded outside, one inside. Another nursing his flesh wounds, then three knocked unconscious including the Big Guy. Seven in total. That left one still in the forward business cabin, and two in the bunker.

Knowing the remaining onboard enemy was now reduced to a single guy Nabil retrieved the weapon Kimberley had thrown him and in less than a second parted the curtains by the bulkhead and charged through to the front cabin. He need not have bothered with the gun. The final guy was fast asleep, spread across three seats with the arm rests up.

Nabil pulled up sharply and quietly and then crept past him through the open door into the cock-pit. It was days since he had been in here. It felt like coming home, this place where he had spent so much of his working life. He knew exactly where to look for the hand-cuffs. The prerogative of all captains was to maintain the safety of their aircraft and that included restraining unruly passengers. The co-pilot remembered Simon telling him once that the last time he had used them was to curtail a famous tough guy movie star who was insisting on his right to light up a cigarette. This time they were to be put to more serious use. When guy number seven eventually awoke he would be not be going anywhere other than his seat.

Nabil gathered up the Big Guy's gun and returned to the other cabin. More importantly he also took the satellite phone and stuffed it into his trouser pocket.

* * *

Simon and Nabil were back on the flight deck, their captives now secured to the seats in business class with cable ties. The Big Guy had two on each wrist. Just in case.

Like two little boys returning to their bedroom after a holiday, the pilots moved around the cockpit reacquainting themselves with their surroundings, instinctively running fingers lightly over various switches checking their positions, their eyes scanning screens and dials all of which were either blank or reading zero.

A pointless activity. This aircraft was not going anywhere soon, especially with two bullet holes in one of the doors. But it made them both feel good to be back in their natural habitat and adopting routine.

With the auxiliary power supply still whirring away at the rear of the aircraft, Nabil watched as Simon activated a couple of panels in front of his seat. It was only a few seconds before one of them registered their position.

Nabil knew exactly what his captain was doing. "So where are we then?"

"Same place as we landed." A poor attempt at pilot humour. "The numbers say S419.3 E15207.5 but in plain English we are a few miles south east of Rabaul, Papua New Guinea. Also, awfully near that volcano that we saw as we came down."

"And where is the nearest decent runway for help to reach us?

"You could easily get a chopper in here, but if you mean a proper airfield then it's Tokua Airport. By road it looks to be around 20 miles from here."

Nabil reached for the VHF switch on the panel in front of him, his finger poised.

"No, not that one," commanded Simon, "We don't want anyone listening in. I will do it, using Satcom."

Simon punched the directory on one of the screens in front of him and scrolled down. Tom Nichols had insisted that his personal number be programmed into every aircraft in the Blue Yonder fleet. The connection took less than twenty seconds.

Chapter 64

Local time: Monday morning

Kimberley had easily persuaded Nabil that it was not necessary for him to accompany her back to the bunker to sort out the other two guys. As Zico was one of the remaining two, she did not relish the possibility of him taking a bullet from the action man. She also agreed when Julie announced she would stay onboard to settle the passengers.

"There's only two of them back there. I'll go with Luke. I think you have seen how handy he can be in these situations and besides, I have my 'magic potion,'" she grinned as she brandished the ketchup bottle. "There is still plenty left so don't argue with me or you might lose."

As they crossed the ground walking towards the bunker Kimberley heard a muted cheer. Turning in the direction of the sound she saw Maarten, no longer prone in the undergrowth, standing erect with a huge grin across his broad face,

"Great work. I saw what you did to those poor guys. Amazing what two women can do with a combination of chemistry and kick-boxing."

Kimberley noticed the puzzled look coming from Luke. *The poor guy has no idea who this stranger is*, she thought, but now was not the time for introductions.

As they approached the bunker entrance she enlightened him as to the final step in the plan. "Now we give four knocks on the trapdoor. Then leave it to me. All you need to do is stand around and look pretty."

"So I don't get another footie tackle?"

"As we discussed you can have one more kick. Besides, I think what you did back there would qualify as an illegal play."

They reached the trapdoor and Kimberley gave four clear knocks.

One of the guys on the steps below slowly opened the trapdoor using the flattened palm of his right hand. His left hand clutching the rim of the door frame to steady himself against the considerable weight. As the light began to reveal the captor Kimberley was relieved to see it was not Zico. The guard took a single step upwards. That was as far as he got.

Kimberley waited until the rise of the solid platform approached a 45-degree angle. Then she leapt on the door with both feet and let gravity do the rest. As the heavy contraption slammed downwards the only hindrance to its firm closure was the guard's fingers. The poor man yelled in agony. *That's his violin playing days over.*

The presence of the man's mangled hand had left just sufficient space for Luke to crouch down, quickly slide his fingers into the gap and with a single heave throw the door wide open. Kimberley saw him then swiftly stand up, bend over the opening and kick the guard in the face. As the man rolled back down the steps she quickly clambered after him. Standing at the bottom of the steps Zico was uncomprehending, stunned into inactivity, his gun held limply at his side. This was not what was supposed to happen.

Pointing the container inches from the man's face Kimberley hesitated a moment as she caught the look of despair in those brown eyes. She remembered Maarten's assurance that the blinding effect of the potion would wear off within a few hours but even so there was something in that look that held her back. This one was not like the others, certainly not like the Big Guy. Here was an intelligence and a kindness that the others lacked even although he obviously shared their obsession with working to reunite his country. Unknowingly her subconscious was telling her that in terms of a freedom fighter this man was more Mandela than Bin Laden. Someone who under the right circumstances might be able to use his brain to achieve his political ends.

In the micro second of her pondering the man could have shot her. Zar would have. Instead Zico dropped his gun and raised his arms.

"Well done, girl," said Luke admiringly, "what now?"

"There is some rope in the next room with all the tools. More than enough to truss this turkey." She pointed at the man still writhing on the ground. Then motioning towards Zico, "Leave this one. He won't be giving us any trouble. I'll get the rope. You and Maarten can do the wrapping."

Then she remembered that Luke did not actually know the name of the stranger.

"Him," she said, pointing up at the Dutchman who was now peering down through the open trapdoor.

The remaining captive women, abandoned by their guard, had heard the muffled commotion from several rooms away. Timidly they had headed in the direction of the noise. Kimberley met them in the tool room. There was no time to figure out how to convey in sign language all that had just happened during the last ten minutes both here and back on the plane. She settled for a smile and a thumbs up as she grabbed the rope and returned to the entry room.

* * *

For the first time in almost a week, with the tables turned, Kimberley was now free to move between the bunker and plane as she chose. The first thing was to lead the remaining women out into the late afternoon sunshine. There was no need to leave anyone below ground. The restrained guard was not going anywhere.

Kimberley was mindful that Zico too had been stuck below ground. She had easily persuaded Luke it would be safe for him to join them in the fresh air.

As the other women sat thankfully perched on the low wall luxuriating in the fresh air Kimberley introduced Luke to Maarten. "This is the guy who supplied us with the magic potion. I have no idea how he knew about it but it certainly did the trick."

Kimberley stood with the others while Maarten succinctly filled them in on where they were, the wartime history of the site, briefly mentioning the reason for his return to this place at this time. Maarten seemed pleased to be at last standing upright after hours lying prostrate in the undergrowth.

* * *

Zico was standing close by and looking over towards the shrouded aircraft he watched as some of the passengers descended the ladder from the wing, led by a uniformed flight attendant. Once on the ground many of them offered their outstretched arms skywards to acknowledge their freedom. None of his compatriots were in the group. It was clear that things had changed there too. *What would happen next in their fight for freedom?* This attempt to secure funds by ransom had failed. If he was to have any part in the continuation of the struggle it would be best if he were not around here when help inevitably arrived to rescue the passengers. He could run now, but that would mean abandoning the others. Also, it would betray the trust that the girl with the frizzy hair had placed in him. That should not have been a consideration but for Zico somehow it was.

* * *

Julie spotted the trio over by the low wall and came over to join them.

"Hi! I was going to ask if everything went to plan in the bunker but looking around I guess it did?" The hesitant inflection at the end almost denying this was a question.

"Yep, one down and one behaving himself." Kimberley motioned over to Zico. "And this is Maarten," she continued, introducing the Dutchman. "Maarten has been regaling us with tales of his boyhood in these parts."

Maarten acknowledged. "There is one more thing I also found. It is something very close to here and quite special. Would you like to see it?"

The release from the tension of the past few days was evident on the three faces whose nods gave him the answer.

"Why not?" said Kimberley. "Nothing else to do."

"I need to take care of our passengers," chimed Julie, "but a few minutes will not hurt. Simon has already been on the sat phone to London. It will be hours yet before anything gets organized."

"We should take him with us." Kimberley motioned towards Zico. "Not that I don't trust you, Maarten, but if you get us lost he does know his way around this place."

"Great, then first one of you go and fetch a shovel from the bunker. I know there always used to be plenty of tools down there." Kimberley obliged and five minutes later Maarten shepherded the four of them towards the edge of the forest.

As Kimberley walked with Luke she began to ponder the difference between him and Andrew. Physically one was stronger, the other smarter. Luke was the more attractive one, the one you would give a second glance in the street and a third and fourth glance in the bar. A really nice guy. She was sure he would make a great 'friend-boy'. With or without benefits? But the spark was with Andrew. She cast her mind back to their first meeting at the party and then fast forwarded to the last time they had been together. Yes, Andrew was the one.

For the umpteenth time since their landing she felt a pang of desperation about the plight of her grandmother. Family first. And then Andrew.

Chapter 65

London time: Monday 02:00

Tom Nichols was becoming very familiar with the offices of Richardson Alliance. This was the fourth time he had been here since the crisis began. Or maybe it was the fifth. He had lost count.

It was 2:00 am in London, but Tom knew that despite the hour they would not complain about being called together when they heard what he had to say.

Tom was smiling as he turned to Stephanie and her boss. "I got a call a couple of hours ago from Simon, our captain. He confirms our passengers are all safe, and our plane is on the ground in one piece."

There was a long pause as he watched their incomprehension melt into incredulity.

"Where?" the obvious question came simultaneously from two relieved faces.

"Now we know exactly. It's near a place called Rabaul. He gave me the co-ordinates. It seems that after the hi-jack the plane was landed safely on a grass airstrip. The best news is that a short while ago those responsible were overpowered. Blue Yonder flight 10 is back under the control of our crew thanks mainly to the actions of two of our passengers and our senior flight attendant."

"That's fantastic! So, what now?" Stephanie asked, turning to Tom. "How will you reach the passengers and get them back to wherever they were going?"

"And get your plane back?" added Gareth.

Tom was already well ahead of them.

"We have a relief aircraft ready in Singapore. Right now it is refueled, crewed and ready to fly to Papua New Guinea. From what Simon told me that will take around seven hours flying time so it will get there tomorrow morning, their time."

"What about getting people already on the ground there to reach them more quickly?" asked Stephanie.

"No. Involving the locals at this stage would be a diplomatic nightmare. Not only would they want to crawl all over things the red tape could tie us up for days. Also, they would want all the glory. A story like this will put their country on the map."

"I must confess even I have no idea where it is," said Gareth.

"I do," blurted Stephanie, "It's half of the second largest island in the world, split with Indonesia. Directly north of Queensland, Australia. Mainly rain forest. The people are desperately poor."

"It is better that we get to the site ourselves before we alert the world that we know where the aircraft is," said Tom. "Otherwise the press will beat us to it. We need to get our passengers out of there before the wolf pack arrives. I'll get on to Jill, our PR person, to drum up a diversionary story. Once our relief plane takes off again from Singapore we need to keep the media thinking it is heading elsewhere, somewhere that Flight 10 might feasibly have landed. Then once we are overflying the actual area where it is, we can arrange an emergency diversion."

"Tell her it would be plausible to pretend it has come down in Fiji," said Stephanie.

Tom looked at her, puzzled.

"Sorry, ever since my Geography A-level revision I have kept maps in my head," said Stephanie looking somewhat embarrassed. "Fiji is more or less on the same latitude as Brisbane."

"Oh well, I guess that is the excitement over from our end?" remarked Gareth. "Back to the humdrum world of insurance."

Tom stepped out of the office with a curt 'excuse me'. He was already listening as his phone connected and began buzzing Andrew's number. If the hundred thousand dollars had not yet been handed over then saving it would be a bonus. He let the phone ring a full two minutes.

No reply. No voicemail.

Chapter 66

Local time: Monday 11:00

Andrew's feet had barely touched the ground in Port Moresby. Now he was airborne again and coming in to land. The flight had taken less than 2 hours, with most of the journey over a long thin island, which looking down appeared to be sparsely populated with a single coastal road and nothing beyond except densely forested mountains. All of which explained why despite numerous attempts he had been unable to get a phone signal to call Tom. In a few minutes he would be on the ground and hopefully be able to re-establish a connection.

Landing was surprisingly smooth and the aircraft reached the low-slung terminal building less than a minute later.

Port Moresby had struck him as being sleepy, but this place was comatose, thought Andrew as he walked across the tarmac looking around. Wherever this place was, he hoped he was now closer to the grounded Blue Yonder plane. Closer to Kimberley.

The flight had not been busy, and inside the terminal only a smattering of greeters hovered around the single baggage belt.

Two men stepped forward from the small crowd and made towards Andrew. Similarly attired to the ones he had encountered in Port Moresby, but somehow even less friendly looking.

"Come with us, we have a car outside." A command without even a perfunctory greeting.

"I don't need to go anywhere. I have what you want. You can take it and then I will leave you."

"That won't be possible."

Before Andrew could protest further the two men flanked him, and taking an arm each began to propel him towards the front exit. For a moment he thought of untangling himself, dropping the backpack and making a dash for it. But where to? Outside was unknown territory, and the simple building itself was hardly a labyrinth of hiding places.

"Look, you can have the money as soon as we are outside," he protested, "but I need to be on a plane back to Singapore."

"That is not going to happen," came the response. "Right now, it is you we want. Do you think we care about only a hundred thousand dollars? That was just the excuse to get you here."

"What do you want with me?"

"Our boss wants to stop you running around poking your nose into our organization," said the same man. "You will meet him shortly. You will give him the money in person."

"You should not have gone to Batam," emphasized the other. "That was a mistake. You will not make any more mistakes."

Outside, parked right by the door was a dust covered Japanese sedan that might have been the latest model two decades ago. A right-hand drive model, just as he had seen in Singapore. It was empty. And unlocked. From what little he knew about Papua New Guinea as one of the most lawless countries on the planet, leaving your car unlocked was either a sign of extreme foolishness or supreme confidence. The men did not look stupid.

One of the men opened the offside rear seat and bundled Andrew into the back seat then slid in alongside him. The door on Andrew's side appeared to be wedged shut. A crude metal plate that looked like it had been there forever welded the door to the frame of the vehicle. No escape from that side.

In contrast the door on the side of his captor was ill fitting and would not stay closed of its own accord. As he slammed it shut the guy grabbed the end of a thin piece of rope that was attached to the interior door handle and lashed it to the headrest in front of him in order to secure it shut. The rope was way longer than it needed to be and the extraneous end lay loosely coiled in the footwell.

"Where are we going?" The obvious question.

"Not far. But first give me your phone," said the man beside him.

"And if I don't?" responded Andrew.

The answer was a sharp smack on the face from a clenched fist. It did not hurt immediately. It would soon. Andrew handed over his phone cursing himself that he had not already called Tom from the tarmac. His assailant handed the device forward to the driver who dropped it into the side door pocket.

The car started at the third attempt and moved off driving on the left, just like home. As they drove through the airport exit Andrew heard a muffled ringing sound coming from his phone. Most likely either Bruno or Tom checking on his progress and wondering why they had not heard from him hours ago in Port Moresby. The driver ignored it. Eventually it stopped.

Fifteen minutes later they arrived at a town announcing itself on a sign as Kokopo. For such a small place it was thronged with people. Must be market day thought Andrew. But then again, he could not see any roadside stalls. Also, many people in the crowd appeared to be struggling with bundles of belongings, some contained in bulging cloths wrapped on their backs and shoulders. Others pushed bicycles laden with caged chickens and assorted household items.

It did not take long to pass through. Shortly beyond the town the car was forced to a halt by a makeshift barrier of wood and oil drums stretching across the road. A sign with words he did not understand was accompanied by a crude sketch of what appeared to be a pyramid with bubbles coming out of the apex. Four armed men loitered nearby. One started to approach, but then appearing to recognize the driver of the battered vehicle he lifted the central plank of wood and waved them through. The man beside Andrew gave a nod through the window.

As they continued along the coast road, the sea on the right, they rounded a clifftop headland and Andrew looked out across the spectacular dark blue ocean towards the sight of two cloud topped volcanos.

"Tavurvur and Vulcan," murmured the driver.

Ealing it 'aint, thought Andrew. It now occurred to him that these men in the car most likely knew exactly where the plane and the passengers were being held, and if the boss man was hands on and close to the action, then very probably that it was somewhere nearby.

The bad news was that any attempt at escape would be one against two. Two who had already demonstrated their readiness to resort to violence with a smack in the face, whereas Andrew's experience of physical aggression was limited to his love of reading tough guy action thrillers. Working in a London airline office was hardly an environment that embraced frequent fisticuffs.

Being in a confined space would give him an advantage. So would the fact that the two men were small and light, and that one of them had his back to him. In a rackety old car.

Andrew had never been in the Boy Scouts, but he did always carry a penknife. A useful little multi-purpose tool, mainly because of the cork screw and bottle opener. Waiting until his captor was looking out of the window, he quickly removed the implement from his right-hand trouser pocket. As he flicked open the blade, he could not remember the last time he had used it. The days of having to sharpen a pencil had long since passed. Hopefully it was not too blunt.

The guy in the back seat was still looking out the window. His mistake. Up ahead the car was approaching a sharp left-hand bend in the road, hugging close to the land side. Andrew waited until the driver started to tug the steering wheel anti-clockwise and in the same instant he flicked his knife upwards until it met the rope holding the offside door shut. There was a moment of resistance and then the blade cut cleanly through. Released from its restraint the door flew open. Just as the man beside him let out a cry, Andrew gave him a hefty push and the momentum of the vehicle turn did the rest.

The man's body hurtled out onto the blacktop and rolled over several times before disappearing off the roadside and down a sharp drop into the sea.

Without a pause Andrew picked up his backpack and flung it at the back of the driver's head. As the man slumped forward his grip on the wheel pulled the car to the right. Andrew braced himself in horror as the vehicle slewed across the oncoming carriageway heading straight for the cliff edge. Luckily the driver was alert enough to realise what was happening and quickly corrected his action. Unfortunately for him his self-preservation instinct over-corrected and instead of regaining the direction of travel the car now swung too far leftwards and slammed into some roadside bushes coming to an abrupt rest against a large boulder.

Andrew was flung tight against the seat back in front of him and then bounced back upright. Despite the lack of a seatbelt he was winded but unhurt.

In front of him the driver lay unconscious, his bloodied head resting on the steering wheel which he still gripped with both hands. Andrew jumped out and opening the driver's door pulled the inert body onto the undergrowth. Quickly back into the car he cut the extra length of rope free from the headrest. Useless before, but not now.

In a matter of minutes, the driver was trussed up and concealed in the undergrowth, covered from the road and from the rapidly warming sun. *He'll live*, thought Andrew, noting the position of the damaged bushes and the large boulder. At some point he would let someone know. But not yet.

Miraculously the car engine was still turning. Andrew jumped into the driving seat and put the vehicle into reverse. For a moment nothing happened. Then with a sudden jerk the car shot backwards onto the road. Quickly braking, Andrew straightened the wheel and then accelerated forward in a continuation of the direction they had been following.

The only trouble was he had no idea where he was heading.

Chapter 67

Local time: Monday 12:00

The road was empty of traffic. As he rounded another headland the checkpoint with its crude conical sketch and the vista in front of him suddenly made sense. The two volcanoes in the distance certainly looked serene but Andrew vaguely recalled newspaper stories of surprise eruptions across various parts of south east Asia.

A moment later he pulled the car over onto the rough verge. Keeping the engine running for fear it might never restart he retrieved his phone from the door pocket and stabbed a thumb on his contacts list. Seconds later he was connected to Tom.

"Are you OK? How did it go in Port Moresby? What took so long?"

"Long story. I'm somewhere else now."

"Are you on your own?"

"I am now. I met some guys but I decided not to give them the money."

"That might have caused a big problem. But not anymore. Where exactly are you?"

"I had to take another plane. The ticket said Rabaul. We landed at Tokua airport. I'm driving now. Last place we passed through was called Koko-something."

"We?"

"Yeh, that was the two other guys. One's gone now. The other is resting by the roadside. He is not going anywhere."

"OK, I have some great news from this end too. The passengers are safe. The hijackers have been 'taken care of' shall we say."

"ALL safe?"

"I'm afraid one of the older males has died, but the rest are all fine."

Andrew held back a yell of relief. Inappropriate. Selfish.

"I'll explain later how it happened. For now, I need you to go back to the airport. You will have to wait a while but Ana will be landing there late afternoon your time."

Chapter 68

Local time: Monday 12:15

The small group had been walking for less than five minutes yet all were drenched in sweat. Pushing back the undergrowth was no easy task. Just as he had conjectured all those years ago Maarten found it hard to believe they were only a short distance from the expanse of cleared ground that surrounded the old runway.

"Whatever this surprise is I hope it is worth it," said Luke. "My whole body's dripping like a sailor's armpit."

"Don't worry, we are here already." Maarten's remark was met by four puzzled faces as the others looked on at a small hillock, a wide mound of earth covered with vegetation and rising about four meters high.

"Come up here." Maarten was already clambering towards the low summit clutching the shovel and torch that Kimberley had retrieved from the bunker. In a line behind him the others obeyed, Zico bringing up the rear.

Maarten reached the top and quickly began to flick away a few spadesful of earth. "This is the other place I used to play."

It was not long before he had uncovered the circular antenna, the one that had first alerted him to this treasured find all those years ago. Moments later he was brushing away the final clods from the rectangular roof hatch of his secret aircraft. The others looked on. Maarten could see they were still not yet comprehending what they were standing on top of.

Maarten pulled back the hatch and shone the torch. Kimberley and Julie peered downwards at the two battered seats in the cramped quarters of the aircraft cockpit below. A cockpit that was way smaller than the one on the plane they had arrived on.

Kimberley looked at the two large steering wheel-shaped joy sticks. "Are those things not usually just crescent shaped?" She turned to Julie for the answer. "You know all about this stuff, don't you?"

* * *

There was no immediate reply from the older woman. Already on all fours she first furiously brushed away the remaining earth from the loop of metal on the aircraft roof. Then she stuck her head through the open hatch to get a closer look in the dim torchlight. It was difficult to make out the contents apart from a rusty unopened can with a peeling label picturing what appeared to be tomatoes, laying alongside a very faded National Geographic map titled 'Pacific Ocean'. After a long silence she withdrew and stood up to address the others. Julie had spent more than enough time looking at old black and white Getty images to know exactly what she was looking at. The location was a puzzle but for her there was no mistaking the aircraft.

Her lips were moving but no sound was coming out as she trembled with excitement. Finally, she managed to speak. "Oh my god, you know what kind of plane this is?"

Blank looks and silence. A bird of paradise shrilled in the distance.

"It's a Lockheed Electra 10-E. Back in the 1930s they only ever made 15 of these. And only one of them had this thing." She pointed down at the metallic circle, slightly larger than the circumference of a soccer ball. "It's a loop antenna for a Bendix radio direction finder. You know whose plane that makes this?"

The blank looks continued. It was a full half minute before Julie was calm enough to fill the silence with the name that was reverberating in her head.

"Amelia fucking Earhart."

To Maarten the name meant nothing.

"This is all very interesting but I have no idea what you are talking about. Who is this Amelia person?" he asked.

"Not who she 'is', it is who she 'was'," replied Julie, still shaking. "Depending on what version you believe she has been dead for anything up to seventy years."

"But when you told me the story the other night in the bunker you said she was supposed to have been heading for some island in the Pacific. Howland?" said Kimberley. "Oh my god, is that where *we* are?"

Maarten enlightened her. "Where we are is Rabaul, Papua New Guinea."

Zico had not so far uttered a word during the short excursion. Now he interjected. "I know of this woman you are speaking about. Some years ago, an Australian group came to look for her plane and paid some of us to guide them around. But where they were looking was many miles from here, up by the Yarras river. After two weeks they found nothing and went home."

"Yes, I read a lot about them, too" said Julie, "a very tenacious group. After part of an engine cowling and other wreckage was uncovered at the end of the war by an Australian army patrol, they have spent years chasing the theory."

"I remember when these Australians came looking," said Zico, "they told me that most of the world thought them a bit crazy and that they were looking in the wrong place."

"What did the locals, your friends and neighbors think about that?" asked Maarten.

"Well, once we had it explained to us many of the elders realized that if the story of this lady was so famous then it would be a great thing for our country if we did find her plane. Such a discovery would bring many tourists to the region."

"You have no idea how true that is," said Julie. "Although it has ebbed considerably in recent times, seeking the truth about the fate of Amelia Earhart remains an obsession for millions of people, especially Americans. There have been thousands of articles, books written, television documentaries and two movies about her. As for theories about what actually happened, they are endless."

"Including that she might have ended up here, providing my playroom?" Maarten was wide eyed, once again a 12-year-old little Dutch boy.

"Yes. I always thought it was far from the most likely explanation but then again I have no doubt that this is Amelia's plane," said Julie.

"If there is such great interest how come no one has found this plane here...until I did?" Maarten turned to Julie for answers.

"Simply put the world has been looking in the wrong place. On her last flight she took off from Lae Airfield, Papua New Guinea which must be just a few hundred miles from here. She had enough fuel in her extra tanks to stay airborne for around 22 hours. Her target, over 2,000 miles away was a place called Howland Island, which is where her last radio transmission was received. At least that where she thought she was and that is where the search area was concentrated."

Luke, who had so far been silent, interrupted. "Well we know from that Malaysian flight that they spent weeks fossicking around in the wrong place. Instead of continuing forwards from where it disappeared the bloody thing had apparently turned around."

"Yes," continued Julie, "and that is exactly the same theory that must have led the Australian team here looking for Amelia. One of them wrote extensively about the rationale and feasibility of a turn back from the original destination. His workings were predicated on a deep knowledge of aircraft dynamics and fuel capabilities. In a nutshell he reckoned that Amelia, and her navigator Fred Noonan, badly miscalculated where they were, got lost and in the face of stronger than expected headwinds they turn around and sped back westwards buoyed by tailwinds. Between their take-off from Lae and the Howland Islands, Rabaul had always been the only existing contingency airfield. Anywhere else would have meant a sea ditching or an attempted beach landing on a coral reef. Amelia had already crashed her beloved Electra once before and high on her list was to ensure that never happened again."

The group remained in silence as each pondered the implications of what he had stumbled upon all these years ago. It was Maarten who voiced the obvious questions. "You are saying she did manage to land here safely just as your plane did? What then? How come the plane was hidden? How come no one saw her and her navigator?"

"I doubt no one saw her," replied Julie, "but I can immediately think of a number of reasons why things ended up as it appears. Amelia was a super star of her age and there was plenty of speculation that she was eager to disappear to a quieter life.

Money could have bought silence from the few Australians who would have been here at the time. And as for any locals who helped with dragging her aircraft off the landing strip and covering it up, they could have been frightened into keeping quiet."

"Life expectancy in this remote community is very low." added Zico. "Anyone who saw anything would be at least three generations back by now. And anyway, reciting a story about a white woman descending from the sky as a pilot could easily get you marked as a sorcerer. The consequences of that are not pleasant."

"So what?" Maarten continued to probe. "She and this Noonan guy just stepped out and ended their days here farming coconuts?"

"Who knows?" said Julie. "Some think her navigator was already incapacitated or even dead which is why she got lost in the first place. Whether or not that was the case we will never know. We will also probably never know what became of Amelia. Claimed sightings of her probably peaked just before Elvis took over the top spot."

"Exciting as this is, we had better head back to our own plane." It was Kimberley's turn to be the practical one.

"Alright, but for now not a word to anyone about this." Julie was still struggling to keep the tremble out of her voice.

* * *

But it was Zico who was already thinking the furthest ahead. He was remembering his tourism studies at University and the phrase 'unique marketing proposition' jumped to the forefront. From Julie's enthusiasm over the past few minutes he reckoned that was exactly what they had found. Here was a reason that the world would now want to visit his homeland. And with visitors, perhaps millions of them, would come investment, infrastructure and jobs. Jobs that would not be in the logging camps. If ransoming the plane was no longer an option then surely this presented a new opportunity to bring massive amounts of tourist dollars into the region. Rescuing the economy would surely be a cleverer way of building up the resources and political will to press for reunification. He could already think of a multitude of ways in which the Amelia Earhart discovery could be used to leverage the cause.

Chapter 69

Local time: Monday 18:00

There had been not much excitement at Rabaul Tokua Airport since a minor volcanic eruption caused a one-day closure in 2006. A busy day was one that saw the arrival and departure of four domestic flights from the national carrier with their 100 seat Fokker aircraft. Two had already come and gone that day and of the two-man team in the control tower one was drinking coffee and reading his newspaper. The front-page headline 'Found in Fiji' covered the fate of a missing foreign aircraft that had missed its target of Brisbane and been forced to land, 1,600 miles off course on a Pacific island. A rescue aircraft was on its way there.

The other man was asleep. Had either been watching their screens they would have noticed a solitary aircraft entering their controlled airspace.

Suddenly one of the radio speakers cackled into life. "Rabaul Tokua, Mayday, Mayday. This is Blue Yonder special flight seventeen oh nine. Requesting urgent permission for precautionary landing."

One man groggily opened his eyes. The sound of a female voice surprised him. The other put down his newspaper. Both looked out the vast window. At first, they saw nothing.

Newspaper man was slightly quicker off the mark and donned his headset. "Blue Yonder, what is the nature of your emergency?"

"Elderly man with suspected heart attack."

"We have no medical facilities here at the airport. The nearest hospital is in the town."

"That will do. Do I have your permission to land?"

"What is your aircraft type and how many passengers onboard please?"

"Boeing 777. Light load, 12 plus crew."

The two men looked at each other in bewilderment. The runway length could take it, but there was no ground handling set-up to accept an incoming international flight the size of a triple seven. On the other hand, it would provide a welcome diversion from the daily monotony. Something to tell the family about. Maybe even get a story in the local newspaper.

"Roger, permission granted," said the one with the headset. The other nodded.

Ten minutes later the giant Boeing came to a halt in front of the single storey terminal building. In the absence of a jetway it sat there a further twenty minutes until one of the more enterprising ground handling staff recalled the shed where they had stored the service stairs last used months ago to accommodate a charter arrival. The rusty contraption was not mechanized and it took three of them to drag it outside and across the tarmac to the side of the plane. The first guy bounded up the steps and gave three rapid knocks on the aircraft door. Behind him a second man held a rather inadequate looking first aid box.

Chapter 70

Local time: Monday 18:15

It had been a long wait. Andrew was thankful for the lack of security at Tokua airport which made it easy for him to cross the tarmac to the bottom of the rickety steps. Several feet above him at the top of the stairs he watched as Ana explained something to a man who had bounded up clutching a box displaying a rudimentary red cross. The man turned and came back down the stairs. He looked disappointed.

After a brief chat with Ana, Andrew turned to notice a man walking towards the plane. A tall man who bounded easily up the steps, his hand outstretched.

"Welcome, I am Arief. You must be Andrew?"

"Pleased to meet you."

"Your man Bruno got in touch with my office several hours ago and explained the situation. He found us online. I have three buses already waiting near the site. Come with me, we can drive to your plane ahead of them."

"Will our people need to go through some sort of passport control?" Andrew motioned back towards the plane.

The tall man smiled. "In theory yes. But we only have three officers in these parts. They mainly check the cruise passengers who arrive at the port down in the town. That gives them a headache a couple of times a month. Other than that, they only come here for the occasional special charter. Can't remember when we had the last one."

"So, I guess they can pass without let or hindrance then?" For the first time in days Andrew allowed himself a small laugh.

As they headed back into the terminal building Andrew took out his phone.

"Tom, It's Andrew. The plane has arrived."

He listened for several minutes as Tom outlined the arrangements that had been made.

"The main thing is to get all the passengers out of there as quickly as you can. Bruno has filled me in regarding the guy with the buses. Seems he owns a small inbound tours operation."

"Yes, that's Arief. We should be back at the site in less than an hour."

"Good. Get everyone back to the airport as quickly as you can. Hand baggage only. Simon and Nabil will stay with the plane but all the rest need to leave. Ana's got enough fuel to take off again and make it to Brisbane with as many as want to head directly there."

"And those that don't want to do that?"

"We have arranged for the local carrier to send a Fokker 100 to take them to Port Moresby. From there we will fly them back to Singapore, or frankly, anywhere else on the planet that they want to go." Andrew detected a note of relief in Tom's voice. "I want you to go with that group."

As he clicked off the call Andrew realized that in a few minutes he would see Kimberley.

Chapter 71

Local time: Monday 18:00

Julie entered the cockpit where Simon sat alone.

"I see you are back in charge of the ship, captain," she smiled.

"Not that I can just take off again as I would like to" he replied. "What's Nabil up to back there?"

"He and that Australian bloke, the one with the muscles, are looking after our captors back in the bunker where I was held with the others."

"And our passengers?"

"Most of them are outside enjoying a good old stretch."

"OK, get the rest of them out there too. I need to talk to them all."

"But it'll be dark in a few minutes."

"I'll switch on the landing lights"

* * *

As Simon descended the makeshift ladder the ground area was lit up like a sports field. He paused and turned to address his passengers, three rungs from the bottom. He sensed a mixture of agitation and relief from the waiting crowd.

"Ladies and Gentlemen our ordeal is almost at an end. For those of you who might not know already the place where we are is the island of New Britain, Papua New Guinea. With the help of some of our passengers the people who forced us to land here have now been overpowered and are safely in captivity in a facility close by. I want to thank those people and also all of you who have kept calm and resilient under these difficult circumstances. I have been in touch with Blue Yonder head office by satellite phone and can now tell you that help will arrive shortly."

"Where will we go?" the inevitable heckle from one of the men in the crowd

"Rabaul has an airport very close to here and we already have a plane there that will leave first thing tomorrow, directly to

Brisbane for all those who now want to continue to that destination."

Without asking for it there was an immediate Pavlovian show of hands from the majority of passengers.

"For anyone else there will be a local flight later in the day which will take you to Port Moresby, the capital. From there we will organize for you to return to Singapore or indeed anywhere else you wish to go."

"And how much will that cost?" The same guy.

"All flights and other expenses will be taken care of by Blue Yonder." Simon knew that Tom had also already agreed that each passenger would receive a compensation payment for inconvenience to the amount of twenty thousand dollars. No need to mention that at this point. Getting out of here was more important than financial matters.

"Those of you who wish to spend a last night on the plane may do so. However, there are slightly more spacious quarters available for anyone who does not mind going below ground. Julie here will show you the way now if you want to see the place before making any decisions." Only a handful came forward, human nature determining the preference for known surroundings.

It was now fully dark and the plane headlights were attracting insects by the swarm. The crowd quickly dispersed, most of them up the ladder, over the wing and back into the aircraft.

Chapter 72

Local time: Monday evening

"What time are we expecting the cavalry?"

Simon smiled at the questioner, pleased in one way that she and his passengers would soon be heading back to normality.

"Soon. I'll miss you, Julie, but someone's got to stay and look after the bus until we can get some engineers out here to fix those bullet holes."

"I know. I hope it won't be too long."

Simon patted the small box in his trouser pocket and decided that now was not quite the right time. "It won't be. And I promise by then that things will be different for us."

"Good, I'd like that."

As Nabil entered the cockpit Simon quickly switched the conversation.

"Have you let everyone know they can only take cabin bags with them?"

"Yes," replied Julie as she looked pointedly at Nabil, "I think they get the message that there is no way we can get their checked bags out of the hold without the proper equipment."

Nabil smiled at both of them. "Don't worry, you two, your secret is safe with me. Doesn't take a genius to see what was going on back in the Fairmont."

Chapter 73

Local time: A few days later

Outside, Kimberley sat waiting quietly with Luke and Maarten. They concluded a discussion on something that had occurred to all of three of them, and now her thoughts were bouncing between the imminent arrival of rescue and the prospect of reaching her grandmother. Maybe it was already too late?

* * *

Zico sat a short distance apart from the trio turning over a thought that had been growing ever since the discovery of Amelia Earhart's plane yesterday. He could make a run for it. But that would betray the trust of those who let him remain unshackled. He could forget it. But that would be to let slip an opportunity that could quite literally put Papua New Guinea on the map. Not just on the map for scuba divers, bird watchers and WW2 nuts, but for a far wider catchment comprising those with minds that relished seeking the truth behind conspiracy theories.

Zico knew from his tourism studies just how important it is for a country to be on the mind map, to be in the consideration set of those who in the dark winter months of the northern hemisphere plan their holiday escapes to far-off places. But more important to him than being 'on the map' was the potential to change the map that would bring his country a far healthier economy than it had at present. The removal of that line arbitrarily drawn down the middle of his country was the end goal. That is what all this had been about This failed attempt to realise one hundred million dollars for the cause was a pin prick compared to what could be done using the magnet of Amelia's story. He remembered the statistic he had read regarding the value of inbound tourism to the GDP of neighbouring Indonesia. $30 billion dollars was the amount. Okay, they had Bali and Lombok, but even a fraction of that figure would be amazing.

* * *

"I'll go and get him," said Luke, moving off in the direction of the bunker.

"Are you sure about this?" Maarten asked when they were left alone.

"Yes. We know that when the authorities arrive Zico will be treated the same way as the rest of them. He has not harmed us. We need to let him go"

"I guess you are right."

"I am. It is only fair that we say nothing about the Amelia Earhart discovery. This is his country and her plane is his story to tell as he chooses."

"I will forget I ever found it." The Dutchman's eyes were smiling.

* * *

Luke returned to the group bringing Zico. Zico's culture was not one of hugging. As Luke's news sunk in he gave a quick wave, and within seconds he was invisible within the forest. He was leaving his compatriots and his brother behind. But he was taking his story to the world.

Chapter 74

Local time: Monday evening

Kimberley glanced over at the spot where Zico had entered the forest, a solid wall of foliage. No movement, no sound. He was gone.

"Good luck to him," muttered Maarten.

In the distance an unaccustomed sound grew slowly. The rumble of several vehicle engines became increasingly discordant, until the noise obliterated the wall of birdsong. Looking in the direction of the sound Kimberley counted three empty buses as they drew into view and stopped just behind the plane. The drivers remained in their cabs and switched off the engines.

Moments later a small car containing a driver and one passenger arrived and came to a halt in front of the parked buses. As the two occupants stepped out of the car all heads on the ground swiveled in their direction.

Kimberley strained her eyes but Maarten beat her to recognition. "Hey, I know that guy. Arief, over here," he yelled.

As Arief accelerated his gait towards the trio Kimberley's gaze switched to the figure who had been shielded behind him. Her eyes immediately knew who it was but her brain took a moment to catch up.

The figure at the back broke into a run and quickly overtook the other. Kimberley stood up but made no attempt to move, still not quite sure what was happening or why this person running towards her should be who he was. She was still standing motionless, but smiling now as Andrew reached her with outstretched arms. As they locked into the tightest of embrace the words came gushing out of her mouth, staccato bursts of banality punctuated with wild kisses.

"Are you alright?"

"Yes."

Kiss.

"How did you get here?"

Kiss. Kiss.

"Are you really alright?"

"I thought you were in London."

Kiss.

"You look great."

"I am fine."

"So do you."

Another kiss.

"Hate to be a gooseberry, but you two obviously know each. Quite well it seems."

"Sorry, Luke. Yes, this is Andrew. He works for Blue Yonder," explained Kimberley.

Andrew took a step back to address all three of them. He definitely looked happy.

"I am sorry the cavalry seems to have arrived too late. But looks like you did fine by yourselves. I am so relieved you are all alright. Where are the guys who took over the plane?"

"Don't worry about them," said Kimberley. "They are all taken care of. They are all here, safely restrained." She did not mention the one who had already gone.

Andrew quickly switched back into official mode. "It looks like all our passengers are more than ready to get out of here. I assume they have already been told about our plans to do that."

Kimberley nodded. "Good. We need to muster them onto these three buses. The ones for Brisbane in the front two and those for Port Moresby in the third one."

"If you don't mind, I would like be on the one for Port Moresby. From there I need to get back to Amsterdam."

Kimberley replied to the one person who had not been on the passenger list. "If it was not for you, Maarten, we would never have been able to break free. I am sure Blue Yonder can take care of that." She pre-empted Andrew's puzzled look. "Don't worry, I will tell you all about it later."

As the passengers eagerly began to board the buses, supervised by Julie and her crew, Andrew intercepted Kimberley. "I need to have a quick word with our flight deck crew first. I will meet you back at Rabaul airport. It will be a short while yet before our plane there is ready to leave."

"And will you be staying behind?"

"I need to travel back to Singapore to escort those of our passengers who are returning. There will still be work to be done there to re-unite them with their families and shield everyone from the media."

"And I really need to get to Brisbane."

"Yes I know you do. I hope your grandmother is…" Andrew hesitated

"Still alive?"

"I hope she is more than that."

"Me too."

A parting hug.

"I Love you."

"Love you too."

It had been said.

* * *

It was time for another airport goodbye. Naturally the setting of Rabaul's tiny Tokua airport made it seem more intimate and romantic than the expanse of Heathrow.

"Before you leave me again," Andrew said, "I just have two more questions."

"Fire away."

"Can I trust you to board another flight with that Luke guy? Even I have to admit he is quite good looking."

"You noticed? Just as well he is not my type because if the two of you were fighting over me, I am pretty sure who would win."

They both laughed.

That was just the warm up question. Now for the serious one. No point in preamble.

"Who is Paul Nickson?"

Kimberley made a face. Andrew's heart missed a beat.

"Why?"

"He contacted me. Actually, he rang the airline emergency call center. He did not know he was talking to someone who knew you. He seemed very worried about you." Andrew deliberately went no further.

Kimberley paused before answering. "Paul is someone I used to be very close to. It ended months ago. The problem is that he has never accepted it. I think the correct phrase is 'he finds it hard to move on.' He was not always the nicest of people so I didn't tell any of my friends we were an item. Not even Joanna."

No need for a third question. Andrew was relieved. Until one came from Kimberley.

"Speaking of Joanna, did she look after you? She can be a bit of a flirt."

"Yes, she did. And yes, she is."

Andrew reddened.

They both laughed again. Easily.

Chapter 75

Brisbane was fast coming out of winter. For the first day in months the thermometer had hit 30C. Kimberley was sitting in her Grandmother's garden under the shade and sipping lemonade. Happy because her grandmother was doing likewise. It was a week now since she had been released from hospital with no more frightening advice than a caution to 'take it easy'.

"I think I will be around for a while yet," the old woman twinkled. "I have heard enough about the adventures you had on your travels. Now tell me more about this boy."

Kimberley felt she was fifteen again.

Epilogue

At 12 years old Maarten had been picked. The lucky one.

His parents had also been picked, not so lucky and no chance to avoid their fate.

He had not planned to be a survivor that first time. It had just happened and the guilt had followed him.

This time, over one hundred people survived. Because he had helped them to make it so.

He felt better now.

End Note

Amelia Mary Earhart, born July 24th1897, disappeared over the Pacific Ocean on July 2nd 1937 while flying her Lockheed Electra Model 10-E, en route between Lae, New Guinea and Howland Island. She and her navigator, Fred Noonan were never found. Amelia was pronounced dead *in absentia*, on January 5th 1939

At the time of her disappearance she was considered to be one of the four most famous people in the world after President and Eleanor Roosevelt, and Charles Lindberg.

At a time when most women were confined to domestic roles, Amelia was a passionate ambassador for women's rights and undertook hundreds of speaking engagements to support the cause.

"I believe that a girl should not do what she thinks she should do, but should find out through experience what she wants to do"

Malaysia Airlines Flight 370 was a scheduled international passenger flight that disappeared with 227 passengers and 12 crew, on 8 March 2014 while flying from Kuala Lumpur International Airport, Malaysia en route to Beijing, China. A huge international media circus fed on the incident for many months afterwards.

At the time of writing neither aircraft has been found. The whereabouts of each remain a mystery that fascinates millions and haunts the memories of loved ones.

A vast number of theories circulate concerning the possible fate of these and many other missing aircraft. This fiction has no desire or intent to add to any of them.

Authors End Note

Human flight is amazing. It allows us to see things differently, to explore places we might otherwise never reach, and to spend precious time suspended above the everyday cares down below.

In the real world the true marvel of an aircraft is its fantastic ability to help us conquer distance. In researching this novel, I did the same thing, much of it by merely Googling. Without ever leaving home I was taken to different places and discovered people and experiences that originally had no part in the initial idea of a simple tale about a missing plane. As a result, to the best of my ability, I have tried to accurately portray the factual situation of the politics, geology and WW2 history of one of the least known parts of our planet.

Being previously involved in airline Emergency Response planning and operation across a string of serious incidents has given me unbridled admiration for those who dedicate their talents to creating contingencies for a thousand things they hope will never happen. It has also, at times, brought me too close to the unbearable anguish of those on the ground during the first hours when little is known, and for some, worse still when fate becomes clear.

Only towards the latter part of writing did Amelia Earhart's story pop up in the course of my research. The resonance was stunning. Here was a truly feisty woman, not unlike Kimberley, whose exploits and fame in the field of aviation long preceded our age of female empowerment and celebrity overload. Not only that, once I learned that her last flight originated in Papua New Guinea where I had already settled the fictitious Blue Yonder plane, she just had to be a part of the story.

I am not a pilot and make every apology to those who are, if my attempts to describe the technical workings of an aircraft are not 100% accurate. In flying a plane I am thankful that you guys are perfectionists. As a writer I hope you will grant me some latitude.

www.iaincharles.com

Visit website for contact, news and more.

Now also available as an audiobook through all major distributors

Thanks

First and foremost to my lovely wife, Linda, who, as well as her love, gave me the kind of support I needed – the space and time to indulge in months of research and writing without ever once asking 'is it finished yet?'

Thanks to those whose names, in whole or in part, I have shamelessly borrowed to pepper across the characters in my story. These people are not you, but you have lent them a sprinkle of colour.

You know who you are. In no particular order other than alphabetic, my thanks go to – Ana, Arief, Bruno, Emma, Juliana, Judi, Nabil, Paul, Stephen (sorry about the transgender thing!), Richard, Tom and Zar.

Thanks also to Graeme whose calmness at a real airline took me and the team there through a number of false alarm call-outs and insisted on continuous contingency and refresher training.

A debt of gratitude to the handful of pilots and engineers at www.pprune.org who agreed to read and improve the authenticity of my flight deck chapters. I took onboard most of what you advised, but in some parts you will find narrative pace and tension still trumps authenticity.

Thanks to Linda Gillatt, Jean Doidge, Maureen Miller and Peter Gerstle for their diligence in preview reading and helping to correct my finger and brain trouble. Also Hakan Unlu for his eagle eye over this 2nd edition.

And,finally, thanks to Jericho Writers (www.jerichowriters.com), to Harry whose weekly emails continue to provide invaluable guidance, to my fellow aspiring authors there, and the editorial support of E.V. Seymour who put me straight when I foolishly thought my novel was already finished. I blame her for what I originally thought were all the good bits that now languish in my Recycle bin.

Research Acknowledgements

Many websites greatly assisted my armchair research. For those who want more background, the following are among them.

Real-time Flight Monitoring
wewv.flightradar24.com

The Airfield at Rabaul
https://www.pacificwrecks.com/airfields/png/vunakanau/index.html

Papua New Guinea Politics
https://www.culturalsurvival.org/publications/cultural-survival-quarterly/west-papua-forgotten-war-unwanted-people

Rabaul Volcanic Eruptions
1937
https://sites.google.com/site/simpsonhafen/1937
1994
http://volcano.si.edu/showreport.cfm?doi=10.5479/si.GVP.BGVN199409-252140

Poisonous Plants
http://www.wildsingapore.com/wildfacts/plants/mangrove/excoecaria/excoecaria.htm

WW2 Museum Kokopo
https://www.pacificwrecks.com/provinces/png_kokopo.html

Amelia Earhart
Debating the claim that she might have landed near Rabaul

https://pacificwrecks.com/aircraft/electra/earhart/#nb

Last footage
https://www.awesomestories.com/asset/view/Amelia-Earhart-Last-Footage-Leaving-Lae-New-Guinea

Her plane - details
https://www.thisdayinaviation.com/amelia-earharts-lockheed-electra-10e-special-nr16020/

Article with maps showing theories of final fight
https://www.dailymail.co.uk/sciencetech/article-5992271/The-final-days-Amelia-Earhart-Researchers-analyze-haunting-distress-calls-pilot.html

Printed in Great Britain
by Amazon